Stuart Littlemore QC is an Australian barrister and former journalist and television presenter. He was the writer and host of the ABC's *Media Watch* program from its inception in 1989 until 1997.

Stuart Littlemore

HARRY CURRY
Counsel of Choice

HarperCollins*Publishers*

HarperCollins*Publishers*

First published in Australia in 2011
by HarperCollins*Publishers* Australia Pty Limited
ABN 36 009 913 517
harpercollins.com.au

Copyright © Stuart Meredith Littlemore 2011

The right of Stuart Littlemore to be identified as the
author of this work has been asserted by him under
the *Copyright Amendment (Moral Rights) Act 2000*.

This work is copyright. Apart from any use as permitted under the
Copyright Act 1968, no part may be reproduced, copied, scanned, stored
in a retrieval system, recorded, or transmitted, in any form or by any
means, without the prior written permission of the publisher.

HarperCollins*Publishers*
Level 13, 201 Elizabeth Street, Sydney NSW 2000, Australia
31 View Road, Glenfield, Auckland 0627, New Zealand
A 53, Sector 57, Noida, UP, India
77–85 Fulham Palace Road, London, W6 8JB, United Kingdom
2 Bloor Street East, 20th floor, Toronto, Ontario M4W 1A8, Canada
10 East 53rd Street, New York NY 10022, USA

National Library of Australia Cataloguing-in-Publication data:

Littlemore, Stuart.
    Harry Curry : counsel of choice / Stuart Littlemore.
    ISBN: 978 0 7322 9342 0 (pbk.)
    Short stories, Australian.
A823.01

Cover design by Priscilla Nielsen
Cover images: Barrister at courthouse by Rob Homer/Fairfaxphotos; all other images by
    shutterstock.com
Author photograph by Kezia Littlemore
Typeset in Stempel Garamond LT Std 11/18pt by Letter Spaced
Printed and bound in Australia by Griffin Press
60gsm Hi Bulk Book Cream used by HarperCollins*Publishers* is a natural, recyclable product
made from wood grown in sustainable forests. The manufacturing processes conform to the
environmental regulations in the country of origin, Finland.

5 4   11 12 13 14

*Our modern hero! Our Odysseus
Sailing sidewalks towards the turd of
Truth and touching it at last ... in triumph!
The honest, disillusioned — child!
You sicken me!*

                                  J.B., Archibald MacLeish

Contents

How It All Started	1
Not Much of a Terrorist	63
The Live Dead Man	108
Travelling South	151
The Set-up	234

How It All Started

It begins in the manner of so many movies: a jet descending in bright sunshine over a calm sea to land at a coastal airport. The heavy plane's tyres chirp as they hit the tarmac, and there's a sudden burst of smoke that immediately blows away. Cutaway shot to the small terminal, where friends and family in holiday clothes move forward to watch the disembarking passengers.

The difference from the usual crowd of holidaymakers arriving and spent holidaymakers leaving is the men in dark blue uniforms, baseball caps and aviator sunglasses, trousers tucked into the tops of their combat boots, holding leashed sniffer dogs. Some of the more feral spectators under the 'Ballina Airport' sign look at each other, then back at the dogs.

Two girls — young women in their twenties — are among the first to descend the aircraft steps, one shielding her eyes as she scans the waiting crowd. She fixes on the ferals. Before she and her companion reach the terminal gate, the little tractor is pulling away from the plane with the first load of luggage. The dogs strain at their leashes and, when the tractor stops, they are let loose to climb over the bags, tails wagging. As the dogs move across the trolleys, passengers pull their bags clear and walk away.

Finally, there is only one bag left — a large suitcase — and a dog perched on it, very excited. The two girls stand off to one side, indecisive. The ferals are further in the background.

A policeman takes hold of the dog, clipping its leash back on. He looks across at the girls. 'This your bag?'

The taller girl looks at him. 'We don't have to tell you, do we?'

'Can I see your tickets and the luggage stubs, please?'

The second girl puts her hand on her companion's arm. 'I think we want to speak to a solicitor first.'

The policeman signals to another to join him and walks over to the girls, the dog beside him. 'You're both under arrest on suspicion of possession of prohibited drugs. You are not obliged to say anything, but anything you do say will be taken down …'

As the girls are taken into custody at Ballina Airport, a near-vintage Jaguar, light in colour, slightly low on its suspension and blowing smoke, is gliding south along Macquarie Street, Sydney, driven by a tall man in a chalk-striped suit, shirt and tie. On the passenger seat is a blue barrister's bag with the initials HMC embroidered on it. The car turns into Art Gallery Road, then left into Hospital Road and slowly through iron gates, held open by a uniformed man, and into a parking lot. The driver climbs out, taking the blue bag. He crosses the gravel courtyard of the Barracks and enters a small room, using a key. The room is practically empty — furnished only with what look like a government-issue desk, chair, bookcase and industrial locker. Last year's calendar is on the wall behind the desk. The tall man starts taking law books from the small bookcase, and putting them into the bag.

The man with the Jag is Henry Mould Curry, a member of the New South Wales Bar.

A barrister, an advocate, a trial lawyer. One of those who wear the wigs and gowns. His friends, who are not numerous, know him as Harry Curry.

He looks very much the genuine article: may it please the Court, with great respect, *res ipsa loquitur*. That sort of thing. Son of an eminent — why do they always say that? — QC specialising in the legal problems of the rich, whose practice funded Harry's GPS school, good university and an easy transition straight from law school into expensive chambers in Phillip Street: $350,000 just to put his bum on a chair. That suit was made in Sackville Street, Mayfair; and Harry may well be the last man in Australia to wear suede shoes.

A professional man, a man of substance.

Well, yes and no. The Jag isn't Harry's. It belongs to one of his clients, who's doing ten years for a major drug importation. Harry's minding it for him, but the client doesn't exactly know that. Harry parks it in a judge's spot behind Macquarie Street while the judge is on sick leave — heart condition. He won't be coming back, Harry has been heard to say, and it would be a shame to waste the space.

Finishing his removal of the modest law library, Harry sits in the hard chair. He's squatting in the little room because his expensive chambers in Phillip Street asked him to move out after he failed to pay his rent for eighteen months. The invoices were left in a stack of unpaid accounts — well beneath the summer lease on a villa just outside Florence, the demands for unpaid income tax and three uncompleted Business Activity Statements. Very embarrassing for all concerned — the Head of Chambers had been Curry QC's pupil, all those years ago. Still … So now Harry is camping in a prison officer's room, surplus to requirements, under the parole board's old courtroom. The parole board has moved away, and Harry abhors a vacuum. He slips a few dollars to the right man, drinks the odd glass of Chivas with the officers, and the phone stays connected, the parking lot gates open. Always the opportunist.

But it's come to this: Harry's packing up the tools of his trade. It's what others might call a watershed in his career. He's just come from a hearing of the Bar Association's disciplinary committee, where he defended himself on a charge of professional misconduct. 'Defended himself' may not be quite the way to put it: 'committed professional suicide' was what the committee was saying later, in the common room.

Let's look at him for a moment: Harry Curry is a big man, reasonably mature in years, hard-looking, like an old rugby player, and strikingly ugly. A heavy (the unkind might say 'Neanderthal') ridge at eyebrow level, eyes too close together, crowding against a much-broken nose. Thin lips and a mouth that has difficulty breaking into a smile. A shock of black, unmanageable hair that fails to hide big ears of the half-cauliflower variety. The whole result is intimidating.

Whether Harry's physical presence at the disciplinary hearing was enough to intimidate the committee would be moot. This was the scene in the committee room, just an hour earlier: two men and one woman sit in their suits at a long table in a panelled room; microphones, cables and papers lie in front of them, an obscure coat of arms, with the motto 'Servants of all, yet of none', on the wall behind them. Barristers, wanting it both ways. Harry sits at a small, bare table facing them across a stretch of deep blue carpet. At a side table sits the registrar, with a TV/video and an audio recorder. The proceedings are being taped, and a transcript will be produced for legal posterity (and, perhaps, the Court of Appeal).

The chairman clears his throat, drinks from a glass of water, and lifts a single page of type. He reads. 'The complaint is as follows: Henry Mould Curry, member of the outer Bar since 1995, is charged that he is guilty of professional misconduct in that on 15 March 2010 he gratuitously insulted a judge of the Supreme Court by the unwarranted use of an obscenity in the course of argument.'

The chairman raises his eyes to look at Harry. 'Respondent, is the allegation admitted?'

Harry's eyes slide across the faces of the committee and come to rest on the woman. She looks down. 'No, Chairman, it's rejected.'

The chairman looks uncomfortable. 'What's the basis of the denial? Do you deny speaking the obscene words?'

Harry's response is fast. 'That's an improper question, isn't it?'

'It's going to be like that, is it?' The chairman unscrews the cap of a Montblanc pen and reaches for a yellow pad. 'What's your objection to my question, then?'

Harry smooths both hands across the empty surface in front of him. His hands look very big. 'You haven't established that the words — there's only one word, anyway — that it was obscene. In its context. So your question — which was, do I deny speaking the obscenity — is improper. It presumes there was an obscenity. I object to the question. That is in issue.'

His voice is deep, confident.

The man beside the chairman speaks. 'It *is* going to be like that.' His voice is high-pitched, whining. Not cultured or confident. He is a barrister specialising in equity matters in a court where, Harry is wont to say, the loudest noise is the rustling of affidavits.

Harry looks at him. 'And, Chairman, members of this committee would do well to remember that the rules of natural justice apply. Any apprehension of bias on the part of any member of the committee will undoubtedly result in your decision being set aside as procedurally unfair.'

The whining man jumps in. 'By whom, Respondent? By the Supreme Court? You might not find too many friends there after what you said to Justice Moses.'

Harry looks at the woman, who drops her eyes again. 'So this committee is of the belief, is it, that the Supreme Court makes its rulings on the basis of cronyism, not judicial principle?'

'That was quite uncalled—'

Harry cuts in: 'Of course, you're probably right.'

The chairman keeps going. '—uncalled for. Respondent, we don't intend to allow you to turn this hearing into a circus, so I shall thank you—'

'Then why bring the clown?' Harry has some history with the whining man.

'—to be silent. I am not going to run this matter as some sort of debate, or opportunity for you to take free kicks at the committee. None of us want to be here, or to sit in judgment on a learned colleague, but it has to be done. The Chief Justice has complained, and the matter has to be the subject of a ruling.'

The transcript of the hearing, duly prepared, checked and vetted, continues thus:

Curry: With unfeigned respect, Chairman, one wonders about the value of a ruling in this case from a committee of three counsel who have never appeared in a criminal court, never addressed a jury, never negotiated a plea bargain, and never made submissions on sentence. Equity practitioners, rustling their affidavits in a hard-fought three-week contest where their fees exceed the claim by a factor of ten … One is not entirely convinced that the committee is equipped for its task.

Chairman: We shall bear that slight with all the fortitude we can muster. Let me get back to your plea: do you admit speaking the words?

Curry: What words?

Chairman: Respondent, don't make this any more distasteful than it has to be. You were served with the complete brief of the complaint against you, including the court's security tape showing you speaking the words.

Curry: Well, if it makes it any easier for you, I concede that the videotape is a fair and accurate record of what I said. What I do *not* admit is that the words — or word — was obscene, or insulting.

Chairman: Thank you. What I intend to do now, unless you have any objection, is to play the videotape. After that, we shall hear whatever submissions you wish to make.

Curry: There is some background that the committee should be made aware of before you see the tape.

Member: Must we? I mean, isn't it a matter of *res ipsa loquitur*? Doesn't the tape speak for itself?

Curry: Members of the committee, context is everything. And, because none of you has any knowledge or experience — none whatever — of defending a man on a charge of murder, it is essential that I be permitted to attempt to give

you some sort of contextual background. If you want another Latin tag, the maxim is *audi alteram partem*, meaning ...
Chairman: We know what it means.
Curry: ... 'hear both sides of the story'. Are you willing to listen to me?

At this point, the vetted transcript excises the following exchange, included in the original version:

Member: (*whispers to Chairman*) Before we hang the bastard?
Chairman: Go on, Respondent.
Curry: I am indebted to you, Chairman.

Reverting to the authorised version ...

Curry: The context is that my client was indicted for murder — the murder of his former wife. He shot her at the kitchen table after a weekend of bitter arguments over access to his daughter. He came to the matrimonial home from the caravan where he was now forced to live, and had retrieved his .22 rifle from his old shed.

He told police in the interview he only intended to scare his wife with it — to scare her into agreeing to let him see his daughter at weekends. But it went off, and a bullet struck her in the head, killing her instantly. Although the charge was murder, the Crown Prosecutor and I did a plea bargain: my client agreed to plead guilty to manslaughter, and the murder charge was dropped.

The trouble was that Mo — Justice Moses, I'm sorry — was determined to force my client into the witness box so that he could cross-examine him about how the gun came to be loaded. And I wasn't going to let that happen.

Member: Why not?

Curry: Because that would give him some basis for a much tougher sentence. The whole purpose of the plea bargain was to limit the evidence to the facts agreed upon with the prosecution, that it was an accident. I wasn't going to let that judge — or any judge, but particularly Moses — rip my client apart, get some basis for finding premeditation, and then give him the murder sentence he wanted to impose anyway. So my bloke wasn't getting into the witness box.

Chairman: Anything else?

Curry: Not before you look at the tape, no. That's probably all you need to know.

Chairman: All right. I'll ask the registrar to play the tape. I think everyone has a copy of the transcript?

The committee and Harry push their chairs back and watch the registrar as he inserts a DVD into the player and, after some false starts, plays it. They turn the pages of their transcripts.

The picture reveals a courtroom, with judge and two counsel in wigs and gowns. A man sits in the dock, guarded by a policeman. The figures are all small on the screen, and facial expressions impossible to judge. The sound is clear enough, but shuffling of papers and throat-clearings are prominent. The committee read from their papers, occasionally looking up at the screen. Harry looks at the screen.

The transcript from the court reads as follows:

Judge: That's all the evidence for the prosecution, is it, Mr Crown?

I have the agreed statement of facts, the record of interview between the prisoner and Detective Sergeant Madden, the postmortem report on the cause of death, and the prisoner's criminal record. I've read all that material, such as it is.

Crown: Yes, your Honour. We close our case.

Judge: Do you wish to tender any evidence, Mr Curry?

Defence: Just the psychiatrist's report, your Honour.

Judge: I've read that. Mr Crown, I am a little troubled about your accepting a plea to the lesser charge of manslaughter.

Crown: Mr Curry's very persuasive, your Honour. It would have been a long trial, and we took the view that it was not without its difficulties. The Crown accepts the plea of guilty to manslaughter in full satisfaction of the indictment.

Judge: Hmm. I remain somewhat disquieted.

Crown: As your Honour pleases.

Judge: Mr Curry, one question — perhaps the most important question in this entire matter — remains unanswered.

Defence: Yes, your Honour?

Judge: And there's one man in this court who can answer it. I would be greatly assisted if your client were to give evidence and answer my question.

Defence: I shall do my best to assist your Honour. My

client will not be giving evidence. We are content for your Honour to impose the sentence on the basis of the statement of agreed facts tendered by the prosecution.

Judge: Why will you not put him in the box, Mr Curry? I need his help.

Defence: With what, if I may ask?

Judge: With telling me how the gun came to be loaded.

Defence: Your Honour has all the material there is, dealing with that issue.

Judge: And it doesn't answer my question. The prisoner is the only person who can do so — and it's but a short walk from the dock to the witness box.

Defence: (*to solicitor sitting beside him*) Not so long as your arse points to the ground, Mo.

Judge: I didn't catch that, Mr Curry.

Defence: It wasn't thrown in your direction, your Honour. I can only repeat that we are content with the material tendered.

Judge: I want to know what the prisoner says, Mr Curry. I want a straight answer from him. How did the gun come to be loaded, if all he intended to do was scare his ex-wife? No bullet was necessary if that was really what he was doing, let alone a full magazine. What does he say?

Defence: To what?

Judge: To my question, Mr Curry. Don't be obtuse.

Defence: Your Honour has no right, and certainly no power, to force my client to give evidence.

Judge: Don't you presume to give me lectures on my rights as a judge.

Defence: No, your Honour. May I say this: I speak for the prisoner. Your Honour, if he has any further questions, should put them to me.

Judge: Very well, Mr Curry. Here's a question for you: what is your client's explanation for presenting a loaded gun at his wife, if all he intended to do was scare her into letting him see his daughter?

Defence: What does he say, do you mean?

Judge: Precisely. What does he say was his reason for loading the gun?

Defence: I'm fucked if I know, may it please your Honour.

Judge: (*After very long pause*) What did you say, Mr Curry?

Defence: I said: I'm fucked if I know. May it please your Honour.

Judge: No, Mr Curry. It does not please me. How long have you been at the Bar?

Defence: This is my sixteenth year, your Honour.

Judge: Do you imagine that your father, whom I knew well and who was universally respected as an advocate, would tolerate your addressing a court in such terms?

Defence: Without doubt.

Judge: Are you serious?

Defence: Every remark I address to this court is serious.

Judge: Why should I not cite you for contempt of court?

Defence: On what grounds?

Judge: On the grounds of your obscene insult to me.

Defence: I did no such thing.

Judge: Did you not say to me that you were fucked if you knew?

Defence: I certainly did not.
Judge: You did. I shall ask the court reporter to play the tape back, Mr Curry.

(*Reporter plays extract*)

(TAPE)
Judge: *Precisely. What does he say was his reason for loading the gun?*
Defence: *I'm fucked if I know, may it please your Honour.*
Judge: (After very long pause) *What did you say, Mr Curry?*
Defence: *I said: I'm fucked if I know. May it please your Honour.*

(*Hearing resumes*)

Judge: There you have it, Mr Curry. Despite your denial, you *did* say to me that you were fucked if you knew why he loaded the gun.
Defence: Not at all. I said *my client* was fucked if *he* knew why he had loaded the gun. Quite another thing, your Honour.
Judge: What are you saying?
Defence: Your Honour has been demanding to know what my client says about why he loaded the gun, am I correct?
Judge: As you well know.
Defence: Thank you. Would you be so kind as to look at the record of interview?
Judge: What page?

Defence: Page 32. Question 151. Sergeant Madden asks him: Why did you load the gun, Kevin? And he answers: I'm fucked if I know. I trust I have now reminded your Honour of my client's answer to your Honour's question.

The TV screen goes blank, the registrar switches it off, and the committee members put down their transcripts. Harry looks at one of the portraits on the committee room's walls — a particularly severe-looking judge in a red gown and a full-bottomed wig. Harry recognises him as a friend of his father's. There is the suggestion of a smile on his face for a moment.

The chairman screws the cap back on his fat fountain pen. He keeps his eyes on it as the man to his right speaks.

'A sentence hearing in the Supreme Court is no place for you to humiliate a judge.'

Harry looks at the woman. 'So I should have applied for a change of venue?'

The chairman looks up. 'Do you have any submission to make as to the ruling of this committee, respondent?'

'Would there be any point?'

The chairman gathers his papers into a pile and puts the pen in his inside jacket pocket as he rises. 'We shall reserve our decision. The hearing is adjourned.'

Harry doesn't wait for them to clear the room, but leaves the building and walks out into Phillip Street where the Jaguar is parked in a loading zone. He stands beside it and lights a cigarette.

On a floor in the building immediately above the Jaguar's illegal parking space, Arabella Engineer is seated behind her desk, in her

Bar jacket and jabot but without her wig and gown. She is speaking to a client and his solicitor. Both are short, fat men of swarthy appearance. Arabella is tall, elegant and obviously of Indian heritage. Her accent is middle-class London. She speaks to the solicitor, who is looking distinctly uncomfortable. 'Mr Gibson, who Mr Waldron originally briefed to appear for you, has asked me to look after your case tomorrow, because he's still in Canberra. You don't have a problem with a woman as your barrister, do you, Mr Tomas?'

The client looks at his solicitor. 'Is it possible to have the case later, when Mr Gibson can come?'

The solicitor shakes his head. 'No, Mr Tomas. The court's given us a judge for tomorrow, and we have to go on then.'

Mr Tomas deflates. 'If we have to, we have to.'

Arabella flicks through some papers in a white folder. 'I haven't read the brief yet, so you'll have to bear with me. Can I run through your statement? Just tell me what happened, Mr Tomas, as if you're in court.'

The client leans forward in his chair. 'Well, I come to work at seven o'clock and I get changed in the locker room upstairs. I put on the boots they give me, and I'm walking downstairs to the floor where we make the tyres.'

Arabella makes a note and looks up. 'Did anyone see you going down the stairs?'

'No. I was a bit late, so everyone else was already changed.'

'Do you remember the date? The day of the week?'

'It was Monday. I don't know exactly what date.'

The solicitor says, 'Doesn't matter — the insurance company's got all the ambulance and hospital records, so they know it was the first of March. Tell the barrister what happened.'

'Well, I didn't see it, but there was little bits of rubber all over the stairs. They didn't clean it on the weekend. And my foot slipped, and I fell down the rest of the stairs.'

Arabella makes another note. 'How many stairs?'

'I don't know exactly, but maybe ten, twelve. And then I couldn't stand up. My ankle was broken, and I fell down.'

The solicitor asks: 'How long were you lying at the bottom of the stairs before someone found you?'

'About five, ten minutes, then the union rep came. Then they got the ambulance. It's nearly two years now and I still can't work. This is terrible for my family.'

Arabella is still writing. 'Ever injure that ankle before, Mr Tomas?'

'No, nothing. Oh, maybe hurt a bit playing football in Uruguay when I am young. That's all.'

'Did you break it?'

'No, not break. Just … you know …'

The solicitor looks at Arabella, then at his client. 'Sprain?'

'Yes, sprain. Only sprain.'

Arabella stands and holds her hand out for the client to shake. 'Mr Tomas, I'll have to see you again in the morning, I have another appointment now, and I have to go. Can you be here at 8.30, please? May I assume that that will be all right with you, Mr Waldron?'

'It's a bit inconvenient, Ms Engineer.'

Arabella stands. 'I'm sorry — I have to go to a disciplinary committee.'

The solicitor risks a joke: 'You're not in the gun, are you?'

Arabella laughs. 'No, a colleague. Look, I'll take the brief home tonight and I'll be on top of it all by the morning. This is what happens when someone throws you a flick pass.' She closes the cover on her brief and puts her pen on top of it. 'Don't worry, Mr Tomas, we'll get you some money. We don't have the most generous judge on the Supreme Court, but even he's got to do the right thing for you. Now I really must go. Can you find your own way out?'

In Phillip Street, Harry is standing beside the car, lighting another cigarette. Arabella emerges from the building, almost at a run.

Arabella comes to a halt in front of Harry, speaking quietly. 'It was over before I got there, I gather.'

Harry pauses before he responds. He certainly knows Arabella by sight, but no more than that. Why should she care? 'They wouldn't have let you in, anyway. It's always that way in the Star Chamber.' He drags on the cigarette and blows the smoke away from her. 'What's your interest in this, anyway?'

'Just showing you a little moral support. A concerned learned friend, albeit a very junior one, and not very learned.'

'I still don't understand your interest. Have we even met?'

Arabella smiles. 'You watched me getting dressed for court in the robing room at Darlinghurst once.'

Anyone in his right mind would want to watch Arabella Engineer putting on her robes. In the unisex squalor of the barristers' changing/lunch/witness interview room at the Taylor Square court complex, the wastepaper baskets flowing over with discarded coffee cups and the metal lockers stuffed with long-forgotten trial transcripts and documentary exhibits, most learned friends had the good manners to avert their gaze when counsel of the opposite sex were getting dressed, but not Harry. Not in Arabella's case.

'True. Then I should thank you for coming.'

Arabella smiles in acknowledgment. 'The registrar told me it was a bit of a self-inflicted bloodbath.'

'You probably wouldn't have approved of my strategy.'

'Is it absolutely essential to pour petrol all over your bridges before you burn them?'

Harry drops the cigarette on the wet pavement — it has been raining — and grinds it under a suede shoe. 'Only if you're quite sure you never want to set foot on those bridges again. And, if nothing else, looking at the faces of those complacent, self-satisfied, self-congratulating offspring of country publicans has persuaded me that I need the Bar somewhat less than the Bar Association needs me.'

'I trust those won't be Harry Curry's famous last words.'

The registrar appears in the door of the building, looking for Harry. He approaches them. 'Ah, Ms Engineer. Mr Curry, the committee is ready for you now.'

Arabella touches his sleeve as he turns. She is nearly as tall as he is. 'Good luck.'

Harry turns to the building. 'Better save your good wishes for when they might possibly work. This one's lost.'

'Best wishes anyway. And when it's over, I expect my care and compassion to be duly acknowledged.'

Harry stops for a moment and looks at her, puzzled. 'I doubt that you'd enjoy dinner at the Eastern Suburbs Rugby Club.'

'Try me.'

He re-enters the building as if cheerfully joining a violent ruck, catching up to the registrar.

And that was it. A fortnight later, the committee issued its formal decision. Not that it was news by then around the chambers of Phillip Street — indeed, some were later to say that the street knew before the decision had been typed up — but no learned friends were to be seen making the short walk across to Harry's squat to offer any comfort.

The room remains Harry's refuge for two weeks, pretty well emptied out. A copy of the committee's decision is hand delivered, but he leaves the envelope unopened.

As night starts to soften the surfaces around the parole court building, Harry picks up the last of his books, turns off the light and locks the door, humming quietly and none too musically. His foot strikes an empty bottle standing by the door, knocking it spinning onto the gravel. The prison officers also heard about the committee's decision, and came to share with Harry the last remaining bottle of Scotch given to him by a grateful criminal. That done, they help him stack his books and court gear in the Jag, and one holds open the gates for him as he heads home to Erskineville. Erskineville! Harry's mother would have died of shame. She was one of the Cheltenham McGuffickes.

At least Harry has always been lucky with parking spaces. There's a Jag-sized gap right outside his house, the middle of the ten-house terrace across from the Erskineville railway station. As he climbs out of the car, a train speeds through, its windows lit yellow and empty. The noise fades, and Harry locks the car and crosses the footpath, ducking under the drooping branches of the mulberry tree that grows wildly behind his cast-iron fence. Most of the terrace has been gentrified, but not Harry's house. The few steps to the front door are littered with fallen mulberries, and Harry's large shoes flatten many of them. He selects the front-door key from the bunch in his hand and turns it in the lock, putting his shoulder to the door and pushing. The carpenter hasn't been returning Harry's calls, because Harry hasn't paid him for last year's work in the kitchen.

'Honey, I'm home.' Into an empty house. Wiping his feet on the threadbare mat. He walks on the bare boards of the hall floor, which feel gritty under his shoes, through the living room, where he turns on the TV with the remote, and into the kitchen. He takes a beer from the almost-empty fridge and walks back to the sparsely furnished living room to watch the TV news, drinking beer from the bottle and removing his tie with the other hand. He sits on the couch and thumbs up the sound on the ABC. A reporter is standing outside a country courthouse.

> … two members of the Isle of Lesbos Band were granted bail in the Byron Bay court today after being committed for trial on charges of supplying five kilograms of marijuana. The women — Lesley Manning and Justine Lahood, both twenty-three — were arrested at Ballina Airport earlier this year when a sniffer dog allegedly located the drug in their suitcase. The police prosecutor, opposing bail, told the court they had brought the marijuana from Queensland. The trial will begin in Mullumbimby next week.

The telephone starts to ring and Harry lowers the sound as he walks out to the hall to answer it.

'The Sydney Swans will be without …'

The phone is on an unstable table, which sways as he lifts the receiver. 'Curry.'

'I heard what they did. Are you okay?'

'Mizz Engineer, is it?'

'It's Arabella.'

'I don't want to sound rude, but how did you get my number?'

'I threatened your clerk. I rang her at home.'

'I don't have a clerk.'

'Your old clerk, then.'

A long pause. Harry listens to see if he can hear her breathing, but there is no sound.

'Are you still there?'

'Listen — I don't want you to misinterpret this, but can I come in?'

'What do you mean, *come in*?'

'I'm actually parked outside, in the street.' Arabella sounds reluctant to say it.

'Good God. And how, exactly, could I misinterpret that?'

He hears Arabella laugh. 'Be hard to, wouldn't it?'

Another long pause. 'I'll open the door.'

He hangs up, crosses to the front door and pulls it open, then stands there taking off his suit jacket and watching Arabella leave her car, lock it, and walk to the house, ducking under the same branches. She stops two paces back from the open door. 'Awkward moment. Were you watching the news?'

'I just got in. But I had it on, yes. Come in.'

He steps aside and she enters, brushing against his sleeve. Closing the door with an effort, he leads her into the living room and waves at the couch. He hangs his jacket on the door's top corner. She sits and looks at the television, which he extinguishes with the remote.

She speaks quickly. 'Did you see the story about the girls charged with a planeload of drugs at Byron Bay or wherever?'

'I wasn't taking a lot of notice.'

'That's my next case — well, after my work accident thing. I have to defend those girls. Well, maybe. I can't see much alternative to pleading guilty.'

'Who's briefing you?'

'David Surrey. He called on the mobile.'

Harry grimaces. 'How nice ... the body's not even cold, and my best solicitor has transferred his affections to some woman.'

'I didn't think you'd take it like that, Harry.'

'Sorry. Ungracious of me. It hasn't been a day of triumph. How did you find out where I live?'

'Same source as the phone number, I'm afraid.'

Harry, who has been standing next to the TV set, sits on a kitchen chair against the wall, which boasts the now-fashionable distressed look, his desultory paint-scraping efforts having been suspended months ago.

'You're lucky, if you can call it that, to find me here. I was going to go and see my father. To tell him I've been rubbed out. I couldn't do it — got across the Harbour Bridge and turned back at Crows Nest.'

'You don't mention your mother.'

'She's dead, which is probably a good thing. She wouldn't have accepted it. It wouldn't have been possible for her boy to be guilty of professional misconduct. He came from such a good family. His father was president of the Bar. No, it'd be the Bar that was wrong.'

Arabella pushes her hair out of her eyes. 'I'm with your mother.'

Harry nods. 'Actually, I think they *did* stuff it up. One of the miserable bastards added some comment when they delivered the ruling, about what I said to that idiot Judge O'Kelly last year …'

'So?'

'So they've fallen into error. They can't take into account some offence — or imagined offence of rudeness to a judge — that I haven't been charged with. They've suspended me for two years.'

'You will appeal, then?'

'No appeal — an application for judicial review.'

'When can you do it? Can you expedite the hearing?'

'Maybe. I've got twenty-eight days, and I want to do some thinking first. Maybe I don't want to be a member of that club any more. Maybe I'll let it go.'

'You can't do that!'

'The last time I checked, I made those decisions for myself.'

Arabella colours. 'Sorry.'

Yet another awkward silence. Arabella looks around the room. There are a couple of paintings leaning in their frames against the wall. Landscapes, they look European to her.

Harry looks closely at her. To him, she's rehearsing her next remark. Then she speaks, not looking up.

'Of course, if you don't challenge them, you'll have plenty of time to help me with the girls in the band and their green vegetable matter.'

'The ones on the news?'

Arabella nods and goes to the fridge. Looking back over her shoulder, she asks, 'May I?' and Harry nods absently. She helps herself to a beer and holds a second out to him. He shakes his head.

'Those are the ones. You might not be able to practise for a while — not before you can get the decision set aside, anyway — even if you want to. So you'd better make yourself useful.'

Harry shakes his head again. 'I don't think so. I was thinking about going down to Bombala to terrify some trout. Get out of town.'

'I'll come.' And before he has a chance to respond, she says, 'I've fished with a fly before — the River Wye in Herefordshire. My father was appalled that I would do it, despite the fact that he always set out to be more English than the English. But we can't go before you come up with a defence for those girls.'

Harry is still taking in her offer to go away with him. It's been a long time. A very long time. Arabella continues, speaking very quickly to cover her embarrassment. 'Surrey says the airport police forced them to identify their bag, even though they said they wanted to speak to a solicitor first. And the cops just went right on interrogating them, taking no notice whenever they said they didn't want to answer questions without getting legal advice. That's their best chance, I think — to get the confessions thrown out for police misconduct.'

'Where's the trial going to be?'

'Mullumbimby. I've never been there. What's it like?'

'Beautiful little courthouse. Do you know who the judge'll be?'

'It's always Fairfax up there. He's been the resident North Coast judge since the beginning of term.'

'UnFairfax, you mean. I didn't know he'd grabbed that circuit. Wonder how he worked that? Still, you've got no hope of knocking out the confessions, not with him on top. Better think of something else, or they'll have to nod their heads.'

Arabella shakes her head, hard. Her hair swings in front of her face. 'And spend the rest of their lives inside? Hardly.'

This is going too hard and fast for Harry. Why is this girl — woman, he corrects himself — bouncing him? Does he have a stalker pushing in here, announcing that she'll come fishing with him, enlisting him to help her when all he wants to do is come to terms with what the Bar has done to him? But she isn't slackening the pace for a moment.

He doesn't really know what to say. 'You'll have to choose your clients more carefully.' It sounds pathetic to him as he says it.

It doesn't register with Arabella. 'I was thinking, sitting out there in the car. You can always come up with a strategy …'

'Even if it's pleading guilty?'

'You know you can. That's your real gift. Certainly seducing judges is not your strong point. What I was thinking …'

Harry is even more puzzled. How does she know all these things? 'Making plans for me, are you?'

'… was that you could spend the next two years as a kind of consultant for solicitors defending criminal clients. If you can't be a criminal defender, you could set up as a criminal defence strategist. Tell them whether there's a defence that they could use, and how to do it. How their barrister could run the cases and win.'

Harry didn't see it coming. 'Barristers would love that — being dictated to by a struck-off loser.' He thinks to himself: now I'm coming off as self-pitying.

Arabella will have none of that. 'Not struck off, suspended. And not a loser. I wouldn't be attracted to a loser.'

Christ! Harry looks closely at her, then goes and gets himself a second beer. Arabella keeps talking. Attracted? It's been a very long time since Harry believed any woman was attracted to him. The last woman who cared about him was his university girlfriend, he believes. Wrongly, as it happens.

'And you wouldn't be dictating to other barristers, either. Just me. All the solicitors who brief you are your friends, anyway, so if you explain that you'll really be running the case, with me as the mouthpiece, they'll still brief you. Or me. Or us.'

'Oh, I see. Mizz Engineer's full-time consultant strategist. I make the bullets, and you fire them.'

'You have a better suggestion?'

'You don't really know me. That isn't me.'

Arabella smiles. 'Not yet.'

At 11 o'clock, in the Supreme Court of New South Wales, Arabella Engineer, for the plaintiff, is watching her client undergo cross-examination in his personal injury cause. He's being taken through his work accident by the insurance company's counsel.

'When you were found in a heap at the bottom of the factory stairs, they put you on a stretcher, did they?'

Mr Tomas smiles and nods enthusiastically. 'Yes. My ankle is very swollen. Like a football.'

The insurance company's barrister looks at his notes. 'And you told Ms Engineer when you gave your evidence, didn't you, that you'd never had any injury to that ankle before?'

'Yes.'

'No injury at all?'

'Oh, you know — maybe a sprain playing soccer in Uruguay once or twice.'

I covered all this, Arabella is thinking. Couldn't they just make us a reasonable offer?

The X-rays are clear enough. Nobody says there wasn't a fracture.

But her opponent isn't going to let it go. 'Nothing since you came to Australia? No fractures?'

'No, nothing.' Looking a little nervous now.

'Sure of that?'

'Sure.' He doesn't look it.

'Ever been treated at the Lewisham Hospital?'

'Petersham. The ambulance took me to Petersham Hospital. They did the X-ray and put it in plaster.'

'Yes, I know about the Petersham Hospital. You finished up there. I was asking whether you'd had the ankle treated at Lewisham. Ever had an X-ray there?'

'Can't remember.' Looking very worried.

The defendant's counsel turns to the judge, looking across the jury as he does so. 'Your Honour, might I have access to the documents produced on subpoena by Lewisham Hospital?'

The court officer collects a large white envelope from the court officer and carries it to the barrister, who starts sliding out X-rays. He holds one up to the courtroom lights and squints at the bottom left corner where something is typed.

'You are Enrique Tomas?'

'Yes.'

'And as at the first of March two years ago, you lived at 5 Kirkham Street at Lakemba?'

Again, Mr Tomas agrees.

'Was there anyone living there at that time who had the same name as you?'

'No.' The plaintiff is starting to squirm in his seat.

The barrister turns back to the judge, and indicates to the court officer to take the envelope. 'Might the X-rays from Lewisham Hospital be marked for identification, your Honour?' The judge's associate is handed the envelope and staples an identifier to it.

'Number 3, your Honour.'

Arabella looks to her right at her opponent. He's taking his time, lining up the edges of the papers on the table in front of him. He tugs his gown up on his shoulders and looks at the deeply troubled plaintiff.

'Mr Tomas, will you listen carefully to me? You went fishing off the rocks at Botany Bay on the day before this accident at my client's factory, didn't you? On the Sunday?'

Tomas speaks quickly. 'No, I never go fishing.'

Counsel sits down. 'That's my cross-examination, your Honour.'

The judge's face changes, almost imperceptibly. It couldn't be called a smile, but he is plainly enjoying himself. Makes a change from tiresome calculation of medical expenses.

'Re-examination, Ms Engineer?'

Arabella is out of her depth, but determined not to show it. 'One moment, please, your Honour.' She turns away from the bench and bends over to whisper to her solicitor, sitting behind her.

'We're in trouble here. Did you know about this?'

'Of course not. Can you keep going?'

Arabella, still whispering: 'Plan B, I think.' She straightens up and faces the bench.

'Your Honour, may I have a brief adjournment before I re-examine?'

The judge frowns. He wants the jury to see blood on the walls. 'I don't see why, Ms Engineer. That isn't how it's done.'

Arabella suppresses her anger at the slight — telling the jury she's wet behind the ears.

She puts a compliant expression on her face. 'I think it might be in both parties' best interests if I were to have an opportunity to take instructions from my client at this point, your Honour.'

The judge, after a long pause in which it might have appeared that he smiled at the defendant's counsel, relents. 'Very well. We'll take the morning tea adjournment a little early. Twenty minutes be enough for you, Ms Engineer?'

'I'm most grateful, your Honour.'

'All rise!' The court officer stands to attention, looking at the high ceiling of the courtroom, where a fluorescent tube has started winking.

The judge heads for his chambers. Tea and a chocolate biscuit, Arabella assumes, and to see if an early finish might give him time for nine holes at Royal Sydney. As the jury files out, Arabella gestures to her client to leave the witness box and approaches her opponent, who has sunk back into his chair and removed his wig. She takes the seat next to him. 'You'd better tell me what you've got, Dusty.'

'It's what you've got, sweetheart. A Monday morning accident.'

'So?'

He looks levelly at her, saying no more.

'All right, you've got me — I don't normally do this work. What's so special about Monday morning accidents?'

His look is almost pitying. 'Look, the dogs were barking it at the factory. Old Enrique broke his ankle on the rocks at Botany Bay on the Sunday. Maybe he wasn't fishing, but he was there, and he had a fall. The private detective took statements from his friends.

'Your punter had already been to the Lewisham Hospital and got it X-rayed on the Monday morning before he went to work. You can have a look ... actually I can't see a break when I look at it, but our orthopod can — he says it was undisplaced at that stage. But your client limped in to work and lay at the bottom of the stairs until he was found, and now he wants my client's insurer to pay him a fortune for something that happened in his own time. Which we are reluctant to do.'

Arabella blows out her cheeks. 'Sounds like I'd better move for a verdict for the defendant. You win.'

He spins his wig in his hands. 'I couldn't be heard to oppose it. You'll be up for the costs, of course. Not that I think Enrique could pay them.'

'Thanks, Dusty. I'd better straighten this out.'

Rising, Arabella signals to her solicitor and client; they follow her outside and into an interview room. They all remain standing.

'Mr Tomas, you'd better come clean with us.'

For a while, he tries to bluff it out. 'Must be a mistake. Must be the wrong X-ray.'

'Mr Tomas, you don't understand. This case is no longer about how much money you'll get for your broken ankle — it's about whether this judge, who is a bit of a bastard, to be frank, is going to refer the papers from this trial to the Attorney-General.'

Mr Tomas blinks. 'I don't know what that means.'

The solicitor steps in. 'It means you might be charged with perjury. Telling lies on oath.'

'Jail?'

'Usually.'

Arabella sits down and puts a yellow pad and pen on the table. 'Now. This time, the truth.'

Arabella's flat in Elizabeth Bay looks like something out of a magazine. Modernised art deco. Leather sofa, media wall, the whole *Vogue Living* thing. Harry is sitting in an Eames chair (probably the real thing, he thinks) across from the occupant, drinking red wine from a very big glass. His hand seems to threaten the very survival of the glass's fine stem. There is the bright green of cricket at Lord's on the TV, and the remains of a pizza on the Jacobsen coffee table.

It may be Harry's first visit to the flat, and there may be a certain frisson in the air, but he's not without social skills and a high level of self-confidence. A bystander would judge Harry to be playing the part of the urbane guest.

Harry empties his glass and moves to refill it from the bottle. 'I thought everyone knew about Monday morning accidents.'

'I do now. They don't figure much in armed robbery trials.'

'What did Ray the Rat do in the end?'

'Ray the Rat?'

'Your judge. Did he refer the papers to the AG?'

'In the end, no. I batted my eyelashes at him, and he insisted that my client explain himself. Not in the witness box. He let him give his explanation from the well of the court.'

'How did that go? God, look at Hussey …'

'Pretty well, really. He told the judge that he had been at Botany Bay, but not fishing, and he admitted that he did fall on the rocks. On the Monday morning, his ankle was hurting so he did go to hospital and had it X-rayed, but they couldn't see a fracture. So he went to work. But it was very swollen, and the union rep told him to lie down at the bottom of the stairs. He was crying when he said all this to the judge. Said he had two little girls, and his wife wasn't working, and no money. He said the union rep told him everyone did it — it's only an insurance company.'

'Poor bugger. So you won't be briefed to defend him on a charge of perjury?'

'No, thank God. In the end, I think even the judge felt sorry for him.'

Harry thinks about it, watching the match. 'Not much risk of that. Still, there's a lesson in it for us all. Go on, hit the bloody thing …'

'Never believe your client?'

'Of course not, but what I meant was make sure he has his accident on Tuesday. And not first thing in the morning.'

A wicket falls. 'I hate this Twenty20 circus. Dunno why I watch.' He takes another sip. 'Anyway. I'd better be going — I have to see my father.'

Arabella doesn't attempt to hide her feelings. 'I thought you might want to stay longer.'

'Thank you, no. I'll pick you up downstairs at eight … it's going to take all day to drive to Mullumbimby.'

'Is the solicitor coming with us?'

'David? We'll collect him on the way.'

'Pity.' But Harry doesn't hear her.

The South Turramurra aged-care complex, later that night. Harry's Jaguar sits alone in the parking lot, Harry in the driver's seat. He has come to see his father, a resident there, but has been immobile for ten minutes.

Not all nursing homes smell of boiled cabbage. Wallace Curry QC, retired, widowed, lives in a care facility (not a nursing home, not a retirement home) on the upper North Shore that offers WiFi, yoga, manicured gardens and an impressive cellar. The nursing staff call him Mr Curry. Never Wally.

Harry leaves the car and walks into the building. He enters an otherwise empty room where his father sits, looking straight ahead at a switched-off television set. Harry kisses him. An awkward conversation follows, in which Harry eventually comes to the point.

'Dad, I haven't been able to devise an easy way to tell you this. So I'll just tell you.

'There was a misconduct complaint, we had the hearing, and the Bar Council has rubbed me out for two years. Suspended. Guilty of professional misconduct.'

Curry QC thinks about it. 'I was president of the Bar, twice.'

'I know. Maybe I can get it set aside. I've filed a motion in the Supreme Court. There are strong grounds. But that's not the point. Right or wrong, it's happened. Everybody knows about it by now.'

He looks around the room, hating the pastel colours in the wallpaper. 'I came to apologise to you. I know you never wanted me to get into criminal defence. You always said that involved sailing far too close to the wind. Which is perfectly true, as we both know. But your practice, Dad — tax and customs duty and equity were never going to suit me. No juries. No persuasion. No flesh-and-blood client to thank you afterwards. Nobody to save — just entries on a balance sheet, and all very well mannered.'

Harry looks at his father, whose expression concedes nothing.

'There *is* a point to what I do: I'm the only thing standing between those poor bastards and the might of the state. I know I don't have to tell you this, even if you never did a criminal case in your life. And there's nothing ... I'm sorry, Dad, but it's true ... there's nothing like that feeling when the jury comes back, and the foreman stands, and the judge asks for their verdict. I'm always so scared, but so alive.

'So, I'm sorry. I did go too far — even if the thing is reversed, I was far too self-indulgent. It's like that joke — I wasn't trying to show my contempt for the court, I was actually trying to hide it.'

Harry has been speaking while looking at a faded McCubbin reproduction high on the wall. Now finished, he looks at his father, who is impassive, unresponsive to the catastrophe.

'No, not funny. Sorry. Anyway, I'm sorry about the whole thing. Forgive me, will you?'

His father replies in an instant. 'Of course.'

Harry's face softens. He feels his skin relax.

'You'd be amused. There's a woman barrister. Putting aside your views about women advocates and dogs walking on their hind legs, she's not what you'd expect. The timing could have been better — as her career gets going, mine's arrested. I'm going to give her a hand with a trial up on the North Coast tomorrow.'

Still no reaction from the old man, who picks up his teacup and looks inside to find it empty.

Harry puts his hands on his knees and leans forward. 'Well, I'd better get going. I'll see you next weekend, Dad.'

As Harry stands, his father looks up at him, steeply, through milky eyes. Harry is standing close, and he is tall. 'Thank you for the visit.'

Harry reaches down and touches his father's hand. The old man says, 'Now, I'm sorry — who are you again? I'm not on the Bar Council any more, I'm afraid.'

Harry squeezes the hand he was touching. 'Look after yourself, Dad.'

As Harry told Arabella, the Mullumbimby courthouse is a charming little building.

Edwardian, Harry thinks. At least it's not that wedding-cake Victorian self-regard that sits next to the police station in every country town in the state.

On the courthouse verandah, Harry, David Surrey and Arabella are drinking coffee from plastic cups. The men are in rumpled suits, and Arabella is in her Bar jacket, white jabot and gown, holding her wig and her brief in her free hand. The two girls arrested at Ballina Airport are drinking water from bottles, nervously, on a bench further along the verandah. Police and others are coming and going. It feels like some sort of market day.

David Surrey is a man of about fifty, who affects the look of a country solicitor. Tweed, wool tie, elastic-sided boots. In fact, he was a schoolteacher who studied law at night sporadically over fifteen years before changing careers. Twenty years in high schools has given him a deep understanding of the criminal mind. He puts the lid back on his cup and looks for a bin to put it in. 'It's just as well I trust you, Harry. I must be mad.'

'Relax, Dave. Arabella'll be fine. She really doesn't have to do anything.'

Arabella pretends to feel slighted. 'Thank you for that vote of confidence. Couldn't I just cross-examine the federal police for half an hour? They're obviously verballing the girls. They deserve a bit of a touch-up.'

Harry takes Surrey's cup and heads off around the corner in search of a bin.

'Not necessary.'

Arabella turns one palm up. 'Killjoy.'

'He doesn't care if I get a heart attack, does he?'

'Harry would only ask if there was anyone else at your firm who could send us briefs.'

'Well, there isn't.'

Harry has returned. 'In which case, I do care. Let's go in. Come on, girls.'

As the team of five push through the heavy front door, Surrey reminds Harry that he won't be able to sit at the Bar table with the lawyers.

Arabella looks anxious. 'You can pass me notes. If you have to.'

'I shouldn't bloody well have to.'

Inside, Arabella installs herself at the Bar table with a nod to the equally bewigged and begowned Crown prosecutor, and Surrey directs his two clients to sit in the dock — a wooden enclosure with a hard bench inside and a policeman guarding the exit. Harry sits behind the rail separating the public from the body of the court, off to one side. The prosecutor tries to attract Harry's attention — they have fought trials before — but can't catch his eye.

The shorthand reporter and the court officer take their seats, and the judge's associate enters. It's the same old ritual, Harry thinks. Now we bow and scrape. There are three knocks on a wooden panel, and Judge Fairfax appears in his wig and purple gown, and sits. The others bow, and Harry moves his head forward by a centimetre for a second.

The judge notices.

The judge's associate, a failed law student whose father plays golf with Fairfax J, reads out the charges in a halting voice, several times having to go back and repair mistakes she has made. The gist of it is that both young women are charged with possession for the purpose of supply of something more than five kilograms of cannabis.

With the help of Arabella, they enter pleas of not guilty, so faintly that the reporter has to ask them to speak up.

It's at this point, the pleas having been entered, that Harry is conditioned to stand up and announce that he has the honour to represent the defendants. With some effort, he remains seated while Arabella claims them as her clients.

The judge takes ten minutes to explain to the jury panel the process of selection, and the jury box is filled with the first twelve people whose numbers (names are never given) are pulled out of a receptacle by the associate. Arabella is itching to challenge some of the jurors, but Harry has already forbidden it. If the case gets to the jury to decide, we'll lose, he has told her. The strategy is to exclude inadmissible evidence of guilt on legal grounds, not to try to persuade the jury of something they won't have a bar of.

Same old, same old, thinks Harry, as he mouths the words that will come next from the judge: 'Yes, Mr Crown?'

The prosecutor stands, makes a shallow bow towards the bench, and turns to the jury. He opens the Crown case against Arabella's clients. 'Members of the jury, the Crown anticipates that the evidence will show as follows: on the 25th of May, the accused flew from Brisbane to Ballina. At Brisbane Airport, Ms Lahood checked in a suitcase and Ms Manning kept the stub of the tag attached by the airline's staff to the suitcase.'

His solicitor hands him an airline ticket. 'I tender the ticket of Ms Manning, with the tag attached.'

Arabella looks back and across at Harry, who shakes his head, but minimally.

'No objection, your Honour.'

The judge makes a note. 'Exhibit 1. Show it to the jury, please.'

The court officer takes the ticket from the prosecutor, and hands it to the jury foreman. One by one, the jury members look at the ticket and pass it along. Finally, the court officer retrieves it and hands it to the associate, and the prosecutor resumes.

'The airline staff at Brisbane airport noticed a strong smell coming from the suitcase, and alerted airport police. The airport police decided to allow the suitcase to be loaded on the plane, after confirming by telephone that officers of the Joint Drug Task Force were able to attend at Ballina Airport when the plane landed, and maintain the security of the suitcase.

'At Ballina airport, the accused both refused to collect the suitcase after it had been the subject of detection by a trained dog.

They were spoken to by drug squad officers and admitted the bag was theirs.

'The suitcase was opened in the presence of the accused, and was found to contain green vegetable matter. A sample was taken out for analysis, and the suitcase and contents were sealed in a plastic bag.'

A uniformed policeman sitting at the back of the court is signalled to, and brings up a large wheeled suitcase, handing it to the prosecution solicitor. The Crown points to it, and the court officer takes hold of its handle.

'I tender the suitcase and its contents.'

This time, Arabella doesn't look at Harry. She knows what to do. 'No objection.'

The judge numbers it Exhibit 2 and the court officer places the suitcase on a table in front of the jury. The judge tells them it will be taken to the jury room much later in the trial, when they will have a chance to look at, but not touch, it. The jurors register their disappointment.

The Crown continues his opening speech. 'The sample of green vegetable matter taken from the suitcase was submitted to Mr Murray, the Commonwealth Analyst, and he produced a certificate stating his expert opinion that the substance is Indian hemp.

'I tender the certificate of the Commonwealth Analyst.'

And this is the point at which Harry's strategy is to be executed. He tenses, but Arabella appears unfazed, in control.

The judge satisfies himself that the defence has a copy of the analysis and has no objection to its admission into evidence. Harry can see that Arabella's insouciance at this critical point is beginning to worry him. UnFairfax wants to know who's running this. He's trying to guess what we're doing.

Ms Engineer wants to add something: 'I don't object to the tender, your Honour, but I wish to make it quite clear that the defence does not concede that the certificate is probative of the nature of the substance contained in Exhibit 2.'

'That's all a bit cryptic, Ms Engineer. Do you want to say anything about that, Mr Crown?'

'No, your Honour. I rang Ms Engineer last week to say that Mr Murray would not be available to give evidence — he's at a conference in Perth this week. Ms Engineer told me that she did not wish to cross-examine him in any event, and I asked that she agree to my tendering his certificate. Ms Engineer told me on that occasion that she wouldn't object, but that she would argue that the certificate is not determinative of the issue.'

Fairfax J looks at Harry, who avoids his gaze, looking instead at the pressed-metal ceiling.

'I shall be fascinated to hear what she means by that.'

The prosecutor nods. 'In due course, no doubt.'

The judge looks at the jury. 'No doubt. Ladies and gentlemen, the analyst's certificate will be Exhibit 3.'

Arabella stands, causing the Crown to resume his seat. 'Would your Honour be so kind as to call it "the certificate of Mr Murray" rather than "the analyst's certificate"?'

'If you wish. Am I getting a hint here, Ms Engineer?'

'No doubt your Honour is.'

Everyone takes a moment. Arabella sits, and the prosecutor returns to his lectern.

'If the offences are proved against the accused, we shall be asking the court to impose the maximum penalty permitted by law.'

'Which is?'

'Twenty years' imprisonment, your Honour, for a large commercial quantity of cannabis leaf.'

Fairfax wants Harry where he can see him. He has smelt but not identified the rat, and Harry's notorious sandbagging stunts are obvious in the business about the drug analysis.

'Ms Engineer, I see that Mr Curry is in court. Would you like him to sit closer to the Bar table?'

'I would, your Honour.'

'Mr Crown, I'm sure you have no problem with Mr Curry sitting alongside Mr Surrey?'

'Oh … it may be a little irregular, your Honour.'

'Nonsense, Mr Crown. I'm sure Mr Curry has a role to play in assisting the court, even if his status is somewhat changed. Please come forward, Mr Curry.'

Harry never doubted that Fairfax had heard the news of his suspension. Who hasn't? But he might as well play the game.

'You're very kind, your Honour.'

'Mr Curry, as far as I'm concerned, you can only be of assistance in this process. I regret I won't be able to hear you. Or see you, I suppose.'

He's referring to the convention that the court can only 'see' a barrister who is fully robed, and can only 'hear' a duly qualified lawyer.

Harry smiles — the first time he has ever smiled at this judge.

'No, your Honour. I've become not only inaudible, I believe, but also invisible.'

Enough of the niceness. Fairfax J wants to see this played out. There has to be something coming.

'Call your first witness, Mr Crown.'

Harry, now seated with Surrey, whispers to him: 'Jesus, Dave, I'd always thought he hated me.'

'Didn't you know? He hates Justice Moses more.'

The Mullumbimby District Court isn't the only judicial factory with its doors open today. Down in Sydney at the Supreme Court registry, where all the new cases are filed and sorted, the clerks are hard at work. Phones are ringing, computer screens are consulted, the court's seal is stamped onto statements of claim and notices of motion, and the queues of solicitors and legal clerks move slowly forward.

Having waited for twenty minutes, a solicitor approaches a clerk with a folded paper in his hand. 'Morning, Jacko. Here's a little job for one of your judicial stars in the administrative law division.'

Jacko opens the document and reads the first few paragraphs. 'Henry Mould Curry versus the Bar Association! Harry's taking them on, is he?'

'That's what it says.'

'The Chief will want this.'

'Hates Harry, does he?'

'We all love Mr Curry up here.'

'Yes, but you don't speak for the judges, do you? Certainly not Justice Moses.'

'A point in Harry's favour, I reckon. Got a cheque for me to cover the filing fee?'

Meanwhile, back in the Mullumbimby courthouse, the trial is taking shape. The jurors are thinking about morning tea at 11.30, but the lawyers are deeply engaged. A detective in a baggy suit is giving his evidence, reading from a typed statement: '... and there was at that time only one suitcase left on the trolley. The accused were standing alongside the trolley, and I approached them and identified myself as a member of the Joint Drug Task Force before issuing the usual caution. I said: "I have reason to suspect that your suitcase contains a prohibited drug, and I intend to ask you questions about that matter. You are not obliged to answer any of my questions, and any answers you give will be taken down and used in evidence. Do you understand that?" Both accused replied that they were prepared to answer my questions.'

The accused, in the dock, whisper loudly at Arabella. 'He didn't caution us! We said we wanted a solicitor!'

The judge and jury hear them perfectly clearly. 'Any objection, Ms Engineer?'

Arabella can't help herself. 'There certainly is, your Honour. I submit that the witness ...'

But Harry clears his throat, loudly.

'... and the High Court made this clear in *Driscoll's case* ...'

Harry leans forward and tugs her gown and Arabella stops speaking. She turns and bends to hear his whisper, which neither judge nor jury will be able to hear.

'No, Bella, don't object. This evidence doesn't make any difference! Now, either you stick to the strategy, or I'll tear that gown off your back and do it myself.'

'God, Harry — who's running this case? You or me?'

'You want me to answer that?'

Arabella straightens up, takes a last resentful look at Harry, and turns to the bench. 'I withdraw the objection.'

The judge nods to the detective to continue reading his statement.

'I said: "Is this your suitcase?" They both said yes. I said: "Did you pack it yourselves?" Ms Manning said: "Look, you've got us. We're not saying anything else."'

Manning can't restrain herself. 'Bloody liar! He's verballing me!'

The judge puts on a stern look, but seems to be enjoying it. 'We'll leave the legal submissions to the elegant Ms Engineer, will we?'

The Crown asks his witness to proceed.

'The other accused said: "What will we get for this?" I said: "That depends — it's a lot of dope. Maybe life." She said: "Well, we're not saying anything else until we get legal advice." I then told them they were under arrest. Shortly after that, they were placed in the caged truck and taken to Ballina police station where they were charged and later admitted to bail.'

That's the signal that he's finished, and it's the defence's turn. Cross-examination time. Arabella stays seated, looking at her papers. The judge waits for thirty seconds.

'Do you wish to cross-examine, Ms Engineer?'

Arabella turns and looks at Harry. He simply looks back at her.

'I gather not, your Honour.'

'Very well. You can step down, detective, thank you. Now, Mr Crown, what other evidence do you have?'

'May it please your Honour, we have evidence of the search of the property of the accused. A certain amount of money was found in the handbag of Ms Manning, and in the carry-on bag in Ms Lahood's possession we located a number of plastic sandwich bags. We don't rely on those items as proving supply of a prohibited drug. That will be our case.'

The prosecutor sits, which means Arabella stands.

'Anything else in issue, Ms Engineer? I notice you haven't cross-examined any witness, or challenged any of the other evidence. All you've indicated is that the defence doesn't concede the validity of the evidence that the material in the suitcase is marijuana, isn't that right?'

'Indeed, your Honour.'

'You heard Ms Engineer, Mr Crown. Can I take it that you close your case?'

He does, which puts the ball in the defence court: this is the point at which Arabella would (had she been running the case) have put her clients in the witness box. That isn't going to happen — not with Harry Curry in the role of strategist. No court can compel an accused person to give evidence, and what can the girls say — if they are to tell the truth — that won't ensure a finding of guilty? Harry's rule has always been that you win cases by keeping evidence of guilt away from the jury, not by attempting to call alibis, or some other assertion of innocence.

So the judge calls on Arabella to start her case, and she shows her hand: now it will all become clear. 'I have an application to make, your Honour, that you should direct the jury to return a verdict of not guilty.'

Fairfax J is, at last, enjoying what would otherwise have been a humdrum case: overwhelming evidence of guilt, some unconvincing lies from the accused, a doomed appeal to the jury's compassion, and a quick finding of guilt, followed by a delayed and difficult sentencing, in which the higher courts will expect him to lock them up until they're way past childbearing age.

'That sounds interesting, Ms Engineer. On what basis?'

'That there's no case to answer.'

Promising to listen to her argument — or will it be Curry's? — after lunch, the judge leaves the bench in a good mood. At last — some law to decide, not just the meaningless ritual of lip service to justice, a mere cog in the revolving door of social work.

Out in the sunshine at the nearest coffee shop, the accused, Harry, Surrey and Arabella — without her wig and gown — are giving their lunch orders to a startlingly tattooed waitress.

Laborious writing, then she checks the orders: 'That's three toasted ham, cheese and tomato sandwiches, and two tofu burgers. Anything to drink?'

Arabella jumps in. 'Two short blacks. David — you'll have a flat white? And what about you, girls?'

Lesley Manning speaks for them both — mineral water — and the waitress leaves.

Justine says that she thought the judge would keep them in the cells over lunch, but Harry explains that he was trying to save the government the cost of their tofu burgers.

Arabella takes pity on her clients. 'Take no notice of him, Justine. The judge obviously doesn't want you to do any more time behind bars than you have to.'

Lesley's face clouds. 'Look, I'm sorry … I know we're just ignorant defendants, but I don't follow this. Aren't we going to give evidence?'

Harry beats Arabella to the punch. 'That depends on what happens next. If you haven't got a case to answer, that's the end of it. Then there'd be no evidence to give — it's all over. If he decides you do have to run a defence, that's when you jump into the box.'

Surrey says, 'Let's hope you don't have to. No disrespect,

Lesley, but I don't think you can match it with this prosecutor. He's on a mission from God to stamp out dope-smoking, lesbian tree-huggers. His wife votes for Fred Nile.'

Lesley hasn't forgotten the Crown's chilling reference to a sentence of twenty years.

Arabella attempts to soothe. 'That's the maximum, Lesley. You wouldn't get the maximum. You couldn't … that's for the worst possible case.'

Justine is almost in tears. 'I don't want to get anything. It's only dope. Everyone smokes it, even judges.'

Surrey shakes his head. 'Not this judge, believe me.'

Harry says quickly, 'But we have to be honest with you. If this application of Bella's fails, we haven't really got a defence.'

'Why not?' In unison.

'Because you did it, for God's sake.'

Lesley is angry. 'But that detective was lying. He didn't caution us, and we didn't admit it was ours.'

Arabella hasn't the same experience as Harry or Surrey in the mounting paranoia of clients at this point in their cases, and she tries logic. 'Even so. That wouldn't win the case for us, even if the judge thought the policeman was the biggest verballer unhung.'

Harry watches their faces. In the manner of every criminal client, they think they can balance their wrongdoing with any unimportant transgression on the part of the authorities. Arabella shouldn't waste her breath. There is silence for quite a long time, and their food is delivered. They look at it.

Surrey is the first to speak. 'Here we go again. Harry Curry's eggs are all in one basket. It'd be nice to be let in on the secret. My heart can't stand much more of this.'

Harry picks up his sandwich and gestures with it. 'Eat up, ladies. It's traditional.'

'What is?' Lesley asks.

'The condemned lesbian always eats a hearty meal. Tofu burgers and a bottle of mineral water seems about right.'

Arabella groans as the tears start flowing. 'Oh God, Harry …'

At five to two, they return to the courtroom. The accused look dreadful. Arabella busies herself with her brief, and Harry studies the Edwardian detail in the roof trusses, admiringly. On the dot of two, the judge returns.

'Now, Ms Engineer, I have asked the jury to wait outside until I've heard your legal argument. I don't want to hurry you, but would it be better if I sent them home for the day?'

Arabella stands and shakes her head. 'No, your Honour, I think not. I can deal with this point — which we respectfully submit entitles us to a verdict of acquittal — rather quickly. Half an hour at the maximum.'

'Very well. Your time starts now.' Impress me, he's saying. Persuade me to accept a proposition that, right now, hasn't a snowball's chance in Marble Bar.

Arabella's voice betrays her nervousness. Harry is looking at the sky through a high window, off to the side.

'The offence with which my clients are charged is possession of what amounts to 5.5 kilograms of Indian hemp, as defined in the *Poisons Act*. That is, of course, well in excess of the large commercial quantity and carries a maximum sentence of twenty years' imprisonment. Given the seriousness of the consequences, the prosecution must dot every *i* and cross every *t* in adducing evidence of guilt. That goes without saying. Guilt must be strictly proved.'

Fairfax indicates that, so far, he's with her. 'Indeed it does.'

'In an attempt to prove that the substance in that suitcase — Exhibit 2 — is Indian hemp, the Crown tendered the certificate of Mr Murray.'

The judge notes the conclusiveness of Exhibit 3 — the certificate of analysis. Arabella begs to differ.

'Well, no. The law provides that proof that the green vegetable matter — that not very green, and extremely smelly matter over there — is in fact a prohibited drug is to be facilitated by the production of an analyst's certificate.'

Again, a judicial intervention. 'I'm sure you'd agree that's a sensible provision, Ms Engineer — given the popularity of marijuana with a very significant number of citizens, and the efficiency of the drug squad, we would otherwise need a team of several hundred analysts, running around all over this state, to give evidence in trials concerned with dealings in the stuff.'

'Quite so, your Honour. The *Poisons Act* requires, then, two things: (a) that a person who is an analyst as defined by the Act should (b) certify that the sample she or he analysed is, in fact, Indian hemp as defined by the Act.'

Fairfax decides to wait and see. 'And your killer point is?'

Taking them from her folder, Arabella holds up a sheaf of papers. 'I've reduced my submissions to a written outline, your Honour. There's one for my learned friend.'

The court officer collects the papers from Arabella, hands one set to the prosecutor and passes the other to the associate. She stands and passes it back to the judge.

Fairfax reads the two pages, quickly flicking back from the second to the first. He smiles. 'Perhaps you'd better develop this argument.'

'Certainly. As your Honour and my friend can see, my point is double-edged: first, that Exhibit 3, Mr Murray's certificate of analysis, is not an analyst's certificate at all; and second that even if Exhibit 3 were admissible (which it is not, we say), Mr Murray has failed to certify that the substance over there, Exhibit 2, is Indian hemp from which the resins have not been removed.'

The judge is not sure about that. 'What's the significance of your second point?'

Arabella tells herself to be patient. Hasn't this man kept up with the Court of Criminal Appeal decisions at all?

She looks at Harry, who sighs and then nods. Speaking slowly, she addresses the judge, with the occasional sidelong look at the prosecutor, who has his head in his hands.

'The law is quite clear on this: Indian hemp with the resins removed is old rope, not a prohibited drug. I dare say that every fishing boat moored at Brunswick Heads is tied up with rope made of Indian hemp. But nobody's smoking it, and there's no law against it.'

'Because the resins have been removed.' The eminent jurist has got the point.

Arabella smiles benignly at him. 'Your Honour is ahead of me. The resins are the active part — the THC. Tetrahydrocannabinol. The part that gives you the high.'

Fairfax frowns. 'Not me, it doesn't.' He turns to look at the other end of the Bar table, where the prosecutor and his solicitor are whispering together.

'What do you say, Mr Crown? She's got you there, hasn't she?'

The prosecutor has a last word with his solicitor, and stands. 'Touché. The authority is what the Court of Criminal Appeal had to say in the matter of Ringstad versus Butler.'

Displeasure is evident on the face of the judge, and for several reasons — the first being that he is a stickler for court etiquette. 'Ringstad *and* Butler, Mr Crown. We never say "versus", even if it's written there. That's one of the traditions of our British judicial heritage that seems to be slipping away. I don't expect that from a Crown, to say the least.'

Mr Crown is chastened. 'As your Honour pleases.'

Fairfax hasn't finished. 'A prosecutor even referred the other day in my court to the witness *stand*. It's the witness *box*, for God's sake. We're not the fifty-first state of America yet.'

'No, your Honour.'

Slipping a finger under the judicial wig and lifting it slightly — it's getting sweaty and unpleasant under there — the judge makes it plain that he hasn't finished with the prosecutor yet. Not by a long chalk. 'And what am I to conclude from your acknowledgment of the Court of Criminal Appeal decision putting the kybosh on your crucial evidence — that you knew the certificate was defective? What were you doing, Mr Crown — hoping that the defence wouldn't pick it up, and I would proceed to let the accused be convicted on the basis of inadmissible evidence?'

Still standing, the prosecutor looks down at his copy of Arabella's written argument and says nothing.

Arabella looks at Harry and smiles. He gestures with his right hand, palm down. Stay down, say nothing.

'Ms Engineer, I don't think the prosecutor is going to persuade me not to enter a verdict of not guilty, and I don't think he's even going to try. But I will be interested to know why the Director of Public Prosecutions brought this case to court if he already knew he couldn't prove it was a prohibited drug, and I shall be writing to him about that. Still, that's for another day and another place. But what about your first point, Ms Engineer? Do you still want to argue that the analyst's certificate is not an analyst's certificate?'

Arabella turns to Harry and leans over to listen to him. 'Of course, Bella. We want a judgment on that — it's just as good a point as the no-resins stuff-up.'

Arabella straightens up. 'For the sake of completeness, yes, I do.'

'Go ahead.'

'The point there is that for the purposes of the New South Wales *Poisons Act*, which is the statute under which my clients have been charged, the definition of an analyst is "an analyst employed by the state government". Given that Mr Murray is the Commonwealth Analyst, he is not an analyst at all.'

The groan from the Crown's end of the table is audible. The prosecutor glares at his solicitor, sitting in the row behind the Bar table.

An even bigger smile from the judge. 'Let me take a look at that.'

He says 'Poisons Act' to his associate, and she hands him a small tome with a crest on its plastic cover. 'What section?'

Arabella turns to the relevant page in her own copy. 'Section 4, the definitions.'

There is silence while the judge reads, closes the statute, and hands it back to his associate. Arabella looks down so that he can't see her grin.

'Caught and bowled, Mr Crown.'

The prosecutor's misery is complete. 'As your Honour pleases.'

Harry has been scribbling on a yellow pad. He tears off the page and hands it to Arabella, who starts to read it. The judge notices, and draws the obvious inference. 'I see Mr Curry has passed you a note, Ms Engineer, and I can make an educated guess as to what he wants you to do. But don't ask me for an order that the Crown pay your clients' costs, because I would be most reluctant to do that. The accused are not going to be that lucky. You know that suitcase is full of dope, I know that suitcase is full of dope, the jury knows that suitcase is full of dope — but, even with all the forensic resources of the mighty New South Wales Government at its disposal, the Crown can't prove that suitcase is full of dope.'

Arabella puts a look of astonished innocence on her face: 'My clients have a grant of legal aid, your Honour.'

'You mean it's not costing them anything, anyway?'

Arabella decides to try something that should have been left to Harry, and then only on a good day. 'I suppose an application for an order that the police return to my clients their suitcase and its contents is out of the question?'

Fairfax, fortunately, is amused. 'You should be careful, Ms Engineer, lest Mr Curry becomes a bad influence.'

The prosecution solicitor laughs, but Fairfax frowns at him. 'Officer, bring the jury back. I'm going to direct them to acquit the accused.'

The court officer disappears through the door to the jury room, and the accused lean out of the dock past their police guard and embrace Harry. Fairfax J pretends not to notice.

He's had a good day, and they're rare enough.

Two hours later, on the verandah of the pub, Harry and Arabella are watching a lone sculler skimming along the estuary in the distance. The late afternoon is calm, and the slim boat is inscribing a long V on the top of the water. Harry finishes his beer.

'I used to do that.'

'An expensive education, I take it?'

'Well, it wasn't exactly the Henley Royal Regatta and, so far as my parents explained it, rowing was supposed to teach us to fill a role in a team. Not to stand out. Pull together, that sort of thing. I didn't discover this until years afterwards, but most people — the nouveau riche anyway — send their sons to those schools so they can have a network afterwards.'

A somewhat pitying look in response. 'Contacts. I'm pretty sure it's the same thing at Eton and Harrow.'

Harry reaches into his pocket and leaves a tip on the wet tabletop as he stands. 'It's not a decision I'll ever have to make.'

'No children?'

'No network either.'

Arabella also rises and they walk down to the water's edge. The sun is getting low, and black cockatoos fly overhead towards the trees on the other side of the river, squalling as they go.

Arabella returns to the private-school theme. 'The Bar's like a boys' boarding school, isn't it? Calling people by their surnames, wearing a silly uniform, espousing redundant values, accepting the arbitrary discipline, tolerating girls but never accepting them as equals …'

'And competing, just like the under-15Ds on Saturdays.'

Arabella nods her agreement. 'Eternally competing. God, Harry, you might be a loner, but you're nothing if not a competitor.'

'Something my clients seem to appreciate. Sorry, got the tense wrong. My clients *used* to seem to appreciate my competitive nature.'

They stop at the shore and Harry looks at his watch. 'How long's Surrey going to be? We have to get on the road.'

'I think he's gone to the bank with the girls to cash their cheque. They have to top up the legal aid grant. Can we make it back to Sydney tonight, do you think?'

Harry shakes his head. 'Not a chance — it's a long way. Maybe we could make Port Macquarie. Is that all right with you?'

'Only if you're going to sleep with me.'

Harry doesn't look at her. He keeps his eyes fixed on the cockatoos, which are settling in the branches of a dead tree.

Arabella speaks again. 'I've been celibate for six months, waiting for you.'

'What am I supposed to say to that?'

'Yes would be good.'

Harry looks slightly angry, disappointed, sad. All at once. 'It doesn't work like that. Not with me, anyway. Maybe we're a generation apart in these things, Bella.'

Arabella hasn't taken her eyes off his face, still looking across the water. 'Harry, in my family I'm way past marriageable age. You're not the only one who wants to row his own race … If you'd seen the parade of candidates that I've had to endure …'

'Candidates for husband?'

'No, candidates for the general election. Of course candidates for husband, Harry! Listen, I know you don't like this — I know it makes you uncomfortable. Women aren't supposed to make the first move in the Harry Curry culture.'

'It isn't that. It's just that I have no illusions about my situation. I mean personal and professional.'

'As in?'

'As in I am deemed to be unfit to work as a lawyer — the only thing I'm qualified or able or willing to do — and the only thing I'm interested in doing. As for personally, I'm a confirmed irascible. I'm awkward with women unless I treat them as honorary men. Or as solicitors, which is even worse. I would rather not deal with the matter of sexual competence …'

Arabella looks shocked. 'Can't I be the judge of that? Ten per cent of Harry Curry would be enough for me.'

'You don't strike me as a ten per cent sort of woman.'

Arabella's eyes light up. 'Harry, you can't ask me to feel sorry for you. I don't. I admire you. I've been watching you for as long as I've been in this country. You may not have noticed, but I've sat in the back of the court and listened to you cast a spell over juries and I've watched you intimidate judges. It's all I could do not to cheer out loud. I can't do that stuff. Everything I do is a cliché — my court work sounds like a pastiche of everyone who ever made a stumbling, bumbling plea in a magistrate's court. I'm like everyone else, and you're your own man.'

A rueful response: 'You can see where that gets you.'

On the hill between the couple and the pub, David Surrey has appeared and is walking down the path towards them. Arabella sees him coming. 'I don't want to say this in front of David, but I doubt that I can make it at the Bar. Five years of struggling and pleading guilty in hopeless cases is not much of a career. Maybe I'll take the job as a solicitor at Woolgoolga.'

'Woolgoolga?'

'Yes, Harry. We came through it on the way up here, and we'll drive through it again on the way south.'

'I know where it is, Bella. Is that where your family is?'

'Not really — they're all Sikhs there. Although there's a tenuous connection to one family by marriage. My family's still in London, anyway. But there's a committee looking for an Indian lawyer to handle all their business affairs — banana growing, property developing. There's only one thing that's stopping me.'

Harry lets that one go through to the keeper. 'You just got a directed verdict, for God's sake. Two directed verdicts. You're winning serious cases.'

She shakes her head. Surrey has almost reached them. 'Well, that's the point, isn't it? Look, I know I didn't win that case — you did. But I'm not such an egotist that I can't accept the job of shooting your bullets for you.'

Harry starts walking to meet up with Surrey. 'You won't always feel like that, of course.'

Arabella nods her head. 'Probably not, but I'm learning. And only because I'm inside your thinking. I couldn't have done that for myself, and I don't know any other defender in Sydney who could.'

They reach Surrey, and all three fall into step, heading for the Jag. Harry starts taking off his tie, rolling it and putting it in the side pocket of his jacket. 'Maybe not, but that tells you more about them than it does me. Still, the point is that I don't want you to get out of the car at Woolbloodygoolga.'

Surrey looks baffled. 'Where?'

They ignore him. Harry is pulling off his jacket as he walks. 'The way we did this — it can work.'

Surrey brightens. 'Well, it did, didn't it? Quite a result.'

At the northern end of Phillip Street, Sydney, is Mammon: the Deutsche Bank. To the south is God: St James's Anglican Church. In between, barristers' chambers, the Law Society, the Bar Association, Rugby League headquarters, and the Supreme and Federal courts. Harry's mother used to say that all inhuman life is there. She refused to set foot in Curry QC's chambers, and never attended a floor social function.

Barristers, solicitors and clients stand on the steps of the Supreme Court building. Some are praising themselves, and the rest are advising their clients to appeal.

As the Jaguar resumes its journey south after stopping overnight at a Port Macquarie motel (three separate rooms were taken and paid for), blowing blue smoke from both tailpipes, the phone line between the Supreme Court and Counsels' Chambers is running hot. Harry's challenge to his suspension made it in record time to the desk of the Chief Judge of the Administrative Law Division, who within twenty minutes was on the blower to the president of the Bar Association, known to his learned friends as Frosty.

Harry's client had a phone installed in the Jaguar (so convenient for his trading activities in illicit substances), and now it rings as they pass west of Foster. Harry takes one hand off the wheel to answer it as the Pacific Highway unwinds beneath the car. There's no handset, so Arabella and Surrey listen in.

'Harry? It's Frank O'Farrell here.'

'Morning, Frosty.'

The president would rather it were kept more formal.

'Harry, could you find time to come and see me before lunch today?'

Harry smiles at Surrey. 'Why would that be, Frosty? I hardly come under your jurisdiction any more.'

An uncomfortable pause from the other end. The engine is audible, and the tyres smack across expansion joints in the road surface.

The president clears his throat. 'Yes, well … let's try not to make this any harder than it has to be.'

Harry feels he has the upper hand. 'Shouldn't your counsel be talking to my counsel? Seems a bit, shall I say, irregular to have the parties to litigation speaking directly to each other. Of course, I'm only a criminal hack and wouldn't know about the niceties of high-level negotiation.'

The president is trying to be firm. 'It's not an ordinary matter, Harry. I'm sure both sides want to avoid any unnecessary embarrassment.'

'I'll take that to mean embarrassment to the Bar Association. I think I've already suffered mine. Anyway, I take it that you're looking for a compromise?' Harry looks at his companions and winks.

The president's voice changes. 'Well, let me be frank. There's nothing in this for us. I shouldn't have let that silly bastard chair the hearing, of course.'

'And,' Harry butts in, 'you don't want any publicity of the fact that three senior counsel demonstrated total unfamiliarity with the concept of natural justice, never mind procedural fairness?'

'Look, Harry, this is all in-club, isn't it? Without prejudice? Privileged? Of course it is. And no, I don't want that prick at the *Herald* to have a field day at our expense. So for Christ's sake come in and see me as soon as you can, and we'll see what we can hammer out. Eleven o'clock be all right?'

'We're on our way back down the coast, Frosty. I can make it by four.'

'Thanks, old boy …'

'Frosty? At the coffee shop, not your chambers. Neutral ground, okay?'

The call ends and Arabella, who seems to have been holding her breath, exhales.

Surrey says, 'I'll bet he didn't realise we were listening.'

Arabella doesn't understand. 'Why are they giving up, Harry?'

'Pretty obvious … the Chief will have read the decision, where they held against me my supposed further offence of insulting O'Kelly last year. They weren't entitled to do that — I wasn't charged with it. I had no chance to defend myself on that, so the whole thing miscarried. Not too impressive, is it? Three barristers, charging $7500 a day for their coruscating legal brilliance, and when they sit in judgment they fuck it up totally.'

'So you think the Chief told them to back off?' Surrey asks.

'Well, he used to be the president of the Bar himself. I imagine words like "idiots", "embarrassment", "publicity" and "see sense" featured quite prominently in his call.'

Surrey doesn't have the full picture yet. 'What's this about insulting O'Kelly?'

'Nothing at all. I had a jury trial, some piddling drug supply matter, and there was evidence from a policeman about the accused running away and making a right-angle turn.'

Arabella grins. 'You didn't hear about this, David? I thought all Sydney knew.'

'Not a word.'

Harry enlightens him. 'Well, the copper gives evidence that the bloke ran north for fifty metres, then turned a right angle at the corner of a fence and ran west, getting away. And O'Kelly looks puzzled and says to him: "What do you mean — a right angle?" And the sergeant says: "Ninety degrees, your Honour." And O'Kelly says: "But if he turned west, he was going to the left." And the sergeant agrees with that, so O'Kelly says: "But don't right angles go to the right?"'

Surrey groans.

'And the jury couldn't believe it. So I said to him: "Your Honour wouldn't by any chance be Irish, would you?"'

Surrey gapes. 'You didn't?'

'He did.'

Surrey has caught up. 'So the committee wanted to kick your arse for that one, too?'

Harry overtakes a semitrailer. 'And they were foolish enough to refer to it in their decision.'

Arabella looks ahead. At least there are no more trucks in the way. 'Harry one, Bar Association nil.'

All three smile to themselves for a few kilometres. Arabella breaks the silence. 'So, Harry, do we take all your books and stuff back to your room? It's only cluttering up your living room.'

Harry's smile fades. 'Not so fast. I haven't decided that I want to be readmitted to practise.'

A few more kilometres are reeled off in silence. Harry turns on ABC FM and listens for a few minutes, then says, 'You know, Bella and David, I've been thinking …'

Surrey holds his forehead with one hand. 'I was afraid of that.'

Harry takes no notice. 'You'll recall that your clients were told not to apply for their costs …'

Arabella nods. 'That would have smacked of ingratitude.'

'But the arrest was unlawful, and they were imprisoned at Ballina lockup for twenty-four hours before they got bail.'

Arabella breaks into a broad smile. 'Stand by, David. I think Harry's got some work for you. Civil work.'

'What I was thinking was that the tofu twins, your innocent clients, might make a quid out of this.'

Surrey is interested. 'What a good idea.'

Arabella looks at a road sign. 'Lunch in Newcastle? Down on the harbour?'

Harry is in favour. 'Another good idea.'

Surrey, in the back, stretches. 'And we can talk about your next case.'

Arabella turns in her seat. 'Don't tell me — you've got another one for us?'

'There is always,' says Harry, 'another case. Sometimes, there's another fee.'

And he turns left at the green sign that says Newcastle, accelerating as he does so.

Not Much of a Terrorist

In a small flat on the top floor of a three-storey red-brick block of units at Liverpool, a long way out on the south-west fringe of Sydney, an Italian man has been sleeping on his aunt's sofa for almost a week. He arrived in Australia six days ago in a state of acute exhaustion. Since then, he's made one trip to the city to lodge an application with the Immigration Department for an Australian passport, providing a birth certificate that shows his birthplace as Mildura, and the rest of the time he's slept. From time to time, his aunt or uncle wake and feed him, then leave him alone to rest and recuperate.

He wakes with a raging thirst and walks into the kitchen in his underwear. He takes a glass from the cupboard next to the sink and fills it with cold water. As he drinks, he looks idly down from the kitchen window at the browned-off kikuyu grass and the stunted gum saplings struggling to gain a foothold in the clay soil beneath the building.

Despite the heat, children dressed as ninjas play among the trees and in the adjoining car park. Dressed in black, carrying toy assault rifles. His still-clouded mind wonders at how big the children are. And their weapons. Perhaps not children at all …

And then the front door of the flat explodes inwards, blown off its hinges, and five black-clad, masked men charge inside, screaming at him in a language he doesn't understand. He does comprehend, though, the nature of their terrifying commands, and throws himself facedown on the vinyl tiles in the kitchen before they can carry out their obvious threat to shoot him. The water glass lies on its side, rolling across the floor and emptying itself. He is instantly handcuffed, lifted to his feet, and almost carried down the stairs and into the car park, where he is thrust into the back seat of an unmarked car, still in his underwear, between two more black-clad men. The car speeds off in the middle of a convoy of anonymous but somehow threatening vehicles of various types.

The man's first thought is that he is still thirsty, and he asks in Italian for a drink. His request is ignored. After a while, he falls asleep with his head on the shoulder of one of the guards as the convoy speeds south. The men are struck by his calm demeanour.

It's dark and raining in Goulburn as Harry Curry turns off the motorway, brakes to eighty and points the Jaguar in the direction of the main street. When he reaches the business district, a few umbrellas move across the road, but there's nobody else about, and he looks at his watch (the car's clock has never worked). Seven, or as close as makes no difference.

David Surrey's office is over the Commonwealth Bank, and the lights are still on. It's much quieter since the Hume Highway bypassed the town, and the cafés and restaurants across the road seem to fill up only towards the end of the week in winter, when the Porsches and Beemers are heading for the snow with the Rossignols on the roof. So now, in April, Harry has no difficulty finding a spot to park the Jag almost right outside. He steps into the rain without an umbrella, and retrieves the Globite from the back seat. Quickly locking the car, he takes a couple of long strides onto the footpath and gains the shelter of the bank's awning.

The front door to the suite of upstairs offices isn't locked. Through it, and past the gold-leaf lettering of 'DG Surrey, Solicitor and Notary' and, below that, 'G Diamond, Dental Surgeon', Harry can see the staircase to the first floor. He shoulders the door open and climbs the thirteen stairs to another glass door. He opens that and turns left. Surrey's waiting room may not look like it, but it has been put together with a degree of subtlety that embraces his clients' tastes: Hans Heysen and Namatjira reproductions, an antique photograph of the majestic Goulburn courthouse, with horses and sulkies drawn up outside, and men in bowler hats, stiff collars and moustaches staring proudly at the camera. Surrey can't claim credit for the colour scheme — pistachio green walls, in bank-issue semi-gloss — but he bought the furniture. There's no receptionist; clients waiting for their appointments can take their choice of the three old but tidy leather armchairs and read the newspapers on the coffee table: just the *Sydney Morning Herald*, *The Land* and the *Goulburn Post*. Beneath them is the current *Women's Weekly*. Everyone catered for by David George Surrey, Esquire, sole practitioner. When he needs documents typed, he engages a contract service from further down the street.

Surrey looks up as Harry appears in the door to his office. 'Made good time, Harry.'

'She's going well. Stopping's a bit of a problem, though, especially in the wet. But we're here.'

What Harry doesn't say is that he fears he was picked off by a radar trap on the way down from Sydney. If he's right, it's going to be a problem — only last week he opened a letter from the

RTA, warning him that he was on the limit with his demerit points, and any more will cost him his licence.

They grin at each other and shake hands across Surrey's desk, which is swamped with unorganised papers, diaries, a dog-eared copy of the *Crimes Act*, and an open packet of Scotch Fingers. Harry sits in a chair plainly chosen for its uncomfortable properties and puts his Globite on the floor beside him. He looks around the room. Nothing's changed in the nine months or so since he was last here — manila folders labelled with numbers and clients' names are stacked along the skirting board in dangerous piles, the small glass-fronted bookcase holding textbooks and loose-leaf legal research services is unequivocally shut, and the three-drawer filing cabinet in one corner still serves as the operating centre for the electric jug. Two mugs stand beside it, one lettered with 'Sue the bastards' and the other decorated with Laura Ashley flowers. Incongruously, that's the one Surrey prefers to use.

Surrey notes Harry's inspection of the room. 'The cleaner'll be in tomorrow.'

'No doubt she'll whip up a couple of filing cabinets and a bookcase.'

Surrey bites back. 'Still practising from a cell, are you, Harry?'

Harry leaves his response for a beat and fabricates a solemn look. 'Not practising at all, Dave.'

Surrey also pauses. 'Sorry, mate.'

They look at each other until Harry slowly and ruefully laughs. He approves of the schoolmaster-turned-solicitor, affecting as he does a carefully constructed persona: thick shock of gleaming black hair (you can still get Brylcreem in Goulburn), Gloster shirt and wool tie, and Harris tweed jacket on the back of his chair.

From where he's sitting, Harry can't see, but he'd win a bet that Surrey's in moleskin trousers and highly polished elastic-sided boots. He's never been on a horse in his life, but very few of his clients would believe that.

There is one very substantial pile of papers on the chaotic desk. Surrey rests his hand on it. Not time to talk about it yet. He asks how Harry is managing.

'Not exactly busy.' A moment of silence passes before Harry speaks again. 'You're looking well, anyway,' he says. 'Sorry we missed your enthronement — Bella really wanted to be here, but that business with the Bar Council and its incompetence knocked me around — a bit of a delayed reaction, I suppose. I couldn't face the drive and I didn't want to see people, least of all country solicitors, saving your presence. To be honest, there wasn't much I *could* face when we got back from the North Coast — certainly not Phillip Street or the Barracks. The Erskineville shops were even something of a challenge for a couple of days.'

Surrey knits his fingers together, leans back in his chair, and puts his locked hands behind his head. 'Well, Harry, you wouldn't have enjoyed it much if you had been able to get here. Election as president of the Southern Tablelands Law Society only rates a dinner at that place you hate — the one you always reckon smells of burnt fat — and some speeches. I know you hate parties, and you wouldn't have liked this one. Arabella would have loved it, of course, and they would have loved her. We don't get much exotic glamour down here.' He looks absently at the window, against which a squall of rain rattles; a door slams somewhere. 'The things we have to do. In the country.'

'How's work?'

'Surprisingly good, really. People are still buying houses and rural properties — I couldn't keep the door open if they weren't. But I've had a string of decent District Court trials — all drugs, fucking and fighting, of course, and all on legal aid — and we've got a murder in the Supreme Court here next month. Speaking of which, what's Cunningham J like?'

'Good reports. Never addressed a jury in his life, of course — did nothing but liquor licensing work at the Bar, and plenty of it — but I hear he's quick and courteous, he's courageous enough to make decisions, and he isn't heavy on sentence. Even more importantly, he's been heard to say that he won't judge cases looking back over his shoulder at the geniuses on the Court of Criminal Appeal.'

'Christ,' Surrey says, 'if the Attorney knew he'd be like that, he'd never have appointed him.'

'What's the client's defence?'

'The usual legal aid strategy — hope that a star witness disappears, or his memory fails, or that the forensic evidence gets lost in the exhibit room. Hope against hope.'

'So the court work's all crime?'

'No, and that's the funny thing. Cockies are suing insurers and banks again, and there are building cases and blues with the council. I know I said I wouldn't, but I've even taken a couple of Family Law matters — they're over there in the corner somewhere.'

'You cannot be serious.'

'Well, no. There are a couple of new girls in town who want to specialise in divorce, and I'll probably flick-pass to them — typecasting.'

'That's what some idiot said to Bella when she started at the Bar:

"You'll be doing Family Court and social security matters, won't you? Adoptions?" Had his testicles handed to him in a paper bag.'

'You can overdo it, of course. When one of my girls was about six, she got so sick of my constant encouragement she said, "I know I can do anything I want, Daddy, but can't I just be a nurse?"' He grins at the memory.

Surrey puts his hand back on the stack of papers. Still not time to raise the subject. 'How is Arabella, anyway?'

'She's fine, Dave.'

'And?'

'And she's been fantastic. Your little conspiracy with her over this consultancy idea is very kind of you both, and I'm in your debt. But you'll both have to give me some time. What I would like to do is bury myself in this Federal Court thing of yours — so long as I really understand what it's about, and so long as there's something I can contribute. See if there's anything I can come up with for you two to run. I'm going to do you the courtesy of assuming that it isn't just a make-work scheme for the involuntarily unemployable.'

'Just as long as we avoid the self-pity, Harry.'

'Easier said than done, but okay. In my defence, I'm going to plead the unreasonable expectations of others. You remember those children's dress-up sets — doctors, bus conductors? My parents had me measured for a barrister's set when I went off to kindergarten. And I did my duty by them, right up to the time I chose criminal law. Defending the children of the poor who'd never heard of the eminent Queen's Counsel Wallace Curry. Down here on the ground, I've only ever been as good as my last jury verdict or my last good behaviour bond.'

'And that was always good enough. You're too hard on yourself, Harry.'

'At least I'm not my own worst enemy. Not so long as the Bar Council's in business.'

'But you did them like a dinner, old boy. They threw in the towel.'

'For the moment. I have yet to be persuaded that I should rejoin them.'

'There's plenty of time for that.'

Surrey lifts the stack of papers and stands them on their end, banging them gently to square off the edges.

'Can we talk about this now?'

'It's why I came, through rain and radar.'

Surrey starts selecting papers from the pile in front of him. 'You could start by reading the Government solicitor's summary.' He holds out a bundle of pages.

'No, you tell me. I've just driven for nearly three hours, and I don't want to read anything except a menu.'

'Fair enough.' Surrey sets the papers back on his desk.

'There's an Italian man about five hundred metres from here, in Goulburn jail, and this is all for him. All about him.' His hand riffles the edges of some two hundred pages of white A4 paper. 'To begin at the beginning: a generation ago, an Italian couple migrated to Australia from Padua. Padova, I'm sure you'd say. He was an interior architect, whatever that means, and I can't remember what she did. Something, it doesn't matter. In short, it didn't work out, even though some of her family were already here and making a go of it. He couldn't get a decent job, and after two years they went back.

'The one thing that did happen for them was that they had a son. At that stage, they were still in love with Australia and intending to make their lives here, so they gave him what they considered to be an Australian name: William. Libero William Paradiso. "Libero" has proved somewhat ironic. Anyway, they went home before he could even walk, and that was the last any of them ever thought about this country. Neither of them ever mastered English, and the baby certainly didn't.

'The boy — this is all about the man over there in our jail, of course — did all the usual things. Grew up, went to school, played football, chased girls, went on to tech to qualify as a central-heating engineer. Nothing remarkable there. But he was a student when Italian students were becoming very politicised. Radicalised. You remember seeing the student riots on TV? They were huge — throwing Molotov cocktails, overturning the professor's Fiat Bambino, painting slogans on historic monuments, that sort of thing. Getting hit with water cannon in the streets. Our William was in all that. His mob had a pirate radio station, and he did a lot of the setting-up electrical work. But he was in the demos as well.'

'To meet girls, probably.'

'Why not? Thanks for the irrelevancy. The point is that William, or Libero, took part in quite a few actions by the radical students. He was a member of some mob called the Army of the Proletariat or something. Can't remember the proper name, but it's in the papers here. You'll read it eventually. One of their targets was the selective high schools in Padua — they wanted to destroy elitism, so they broke into the primary schools at night, took the academic reports out into the playgrounds and burned them. That was supposed to ensure that everyone got a fair go at high school. They also locked some of the teachers in their classrooms for the whole day. Not sure what that was supposed to achieve, but it was a criminal act.'

'We'd call it false imprisonment.'

'Which becomes important, as you'll see. You want some coffee?' He looks at the electric jug.

'Instant?' A nod. 'In that case, no. We are going to eat, aren't we?'

'In half an hour? Let me finish this, and we can talk about it over dinner.'

Surrey consults his file for a few moments, confirming his recollection of the facts.

'There was this flurry of student activism or anarchy or whatever your personal politics would call it, but it died a natural death. And certainly our man backed off and got on with his studies. But then, years later, some politician was kidnapped and murdered. I think he might once have been prime minister. Who wasn't, in Italy? The Italian government, as always, blamed the Red Brigade, and the police set out to solve the case by chasing down every *Brigate Rosse* member and sympathiser they could identify, by whatever means. In the end, it proved to be the right wing who killed the man, but that makes no difference to what we're concerned with.

'It seems that the Italian police's investigative technique is based on the principle of six degrees of separation — you know, Joe Bloggs doesn't know George Bush, but he knows someone who met a cousin of Nicole Kidman's hairdresser, and Nicole Kidman was invited to the White House ... and so on. What the *Carabinieri* did was to stop anyone, practically at random, and ask whether they knew who murdered the politician. When everyone said no, they were then interrogated about what knowledge they had of any radicals, and some people got the police off their backs by naming names. All the pinkos were then on a list, and the cops interrogated the lot of them, and none too gently. All that produced nothing, of course, at least nothing about the murder, but a lot of the people they tracked down had old, forgotten warrants hanging over their heads, including plenty from the student activism period — and they were charged with all those old matters. They got locked up for long periods.

'Libero William Paradiso, our client, the appellant, was one of the people named and a warrant was issued for his arrest. He got to hear about it through the old student grapevine, and he took off. Went to London, with some idea that because Labour was in power in Westminster, it was a socialist country.'

'Silly boy.'

'As you say, Dud, silly boy. Anyway, London was too grey for him. Grey people, grey weather, grey town. One of the English mob persuaded him that Nicaragua was the place to be: it had a Sandinista government, was running the purest form of socialist utopia, all that stuff. And off he goes, with a letter of introduction to the President in his pocket.

'He lands in Managua, and presents himself at party headquarters. Asks not what the revolution can do for him but what he can do for the revolution. The Sandinistas take one look at him — he's tall, fair-haired and blue-eyed — so they tell him he can be a Danish journalist working freelance in Central America. That's his cover, complete with a very authentic-looking Danish passport and a new name, and he's to go to Costa Rica and live there, reporting back on Oliver North's Contra activity along the border. What the Yanks were doing was using the Miskito Indians to feed and support the Contras, paying them a lot of greenbacks. The Miskitos had no interest in politics, and they had no reason to knock the money back. It was all about survival, and no government had ever done them any favours.

'There was something else the Sandinistas expected him to do in Costa Rica — at least, so the CIA thought. There's a report from them in the file, heavily redacted, of course, but you can get enough from it to see that they were telling Foreign Affairs in Canberra that our boy was a spy running an assassination cell. If he got a message that a certain person was in his part of Costa Rica, he had to plan and carry out — or at least arrange — an assassination. Everyone agrees he was never actually involved in a killing, but it's supposed to have been one of his duties. Spying and running a hit squad. But it all went a bit sour. This isn't in the papers, but I saw him at the jail last week, and I got this part of it from him.'

'Why's he all the way down here in Goulburn? Shouldn't he be in Long Bay?'

'I would have thought so, but they've got a new supermax division in the Goulburn jail that they want to use for terrorists.'

'Which he isn't, I assume?'

'Which he isn't. What he told me was that he became disenchanted with the revolution, or the revolutionaries at least, when he saw how brutal they were to the Miskitos. Driving them out of their villages, burning down their houses and killing their animals, all because of the strategic advantage of separating them from the Contras and their Yanqui dollars.' Surrey stands and crosses to the window. He looks across the road at the Paragon, and notes that the rain has stopped.

'He's pretty naive — he was, and he still is, as you'll see — so he went to party headquarters in Managua and told them he was resigning. They were revisionists, or whatever. Betraying the revolution. Brutalising the very people they should be glorifying. He showed them his diaries, in which he was foolish enough to record all the brutality and dispossession he'd witnessed. Strangely enough, he's still got them — here.'

Harry stands. 'You've still got a lot to tell me, haven't you?'

'Hardly started.'

'Can we keep going over dinner? I suppose we're going over the road?'

Surrey shrugs into his jacket. 'Okay.' They descend the stairs. As Harry waits on the footpath, Surrey kills the lights, flicks the lock on the front door and pulls it shut. The rain has left puddles on the road, and a police car splashes past slowly, its occupants throwing a hostile stare at the solicitor who so frequently gives them a hard time in court.

The two men cross the wide main street as the town hall clock strikes eight, climbing over the dividing strip and pushing through the doors of the Paragon Cafe. Only a few tables are occupied, and the owner, in white shirt, black bow tie and black trousers, waves expansively for them to take their pick. Harry seats himself in a booth and picks up the heavily laminated menu as Surrey slides in on the opposite side.

'Two beers and two steaks?'

Surrey withdraws his hand, which was reaching for a menu, and agrees. He calls the order to the nearest waiter.

'So our hero has given his Marxist masters a poke in the eye with a burnt stick. What happened next?'

'There's a subplot. By the time he gets back to Managua, there's another Italian in residence there. But a very different kettle of fish.'

The beers arrive and the waiter pours out two glasses. Harry drinks half of his in one gulp. Surrey sips his and continues. 'This other man is from Milan. Said to be one of the heirs to the Lancia fortune, whatever that is.'

'You bloody philistine! Lancia made some of the finest motor cars ever produced in Italy, peasant. Ascari drove one of them into the Monte Carlo harbour.'

'And what's wrong with the Leyland P76? Don't answer that. The Lancia heir — and I'm going to call him Luigi because I can't remember what his name really is — is a hopeless heroin addict. The family have used their considerable wealth to try to get him off the stuff — everything from prayer vigils with their personal priest right up to clinics in Switzerland, and nothing works.'

'Tell me something I don't know, Dave. If it's heroin, nothing works.'

'Indeed, but their priest finally tells them that maybe the answer is to send him to a place where there's no heroin. He's a Capuchin, and has mates in Managua at some monastery, and he's asked to line it all up for Luigi to go there and dry out. He promises them that while there may be cocaine in Nicaragua, there is absolutely no heroin. Which I gather is supposed to be true.'

'So they pack a very reluctant Luigi off to Central America, but he gives the Capuchins the slip within days and is making noises about going to New York. But the monks hang onto his passport, and he's forced to mooch around the city. As fate would have it, he meets up with William. Libero. And they team up. They're both stuck there, because the Sandinistas have told our hero that he can't leave either — he knows all about their spy network and assassination cells, and the Contra surveillance network, and they fear he could sell all that stuff to the CIA for a great deal of money. So they won't give back his passport. Not even his Danish passport. They tell him — or so he told me last week — that he'd have to stay another year, because it would take them that long to dismantle and replace the networks he'd worked with.'

The steaks arrive, and the men take turns with the tomato sauce bottle. Harry orders more beers and they start eating.

'I've arranged for us to see the client tomorrow, because there's some stuff I think you should get from him. But to cut to the chase …'

'Please, Dave, I'm eating. Spare me the juvenilia.'

'Sorry, it won't happen again. The upshot, if that word doesn't offend you, is that his political masters jailed him and eventually saw fit to charge him with the murder of Luigi, which sparked a long diplomatic wrangle, and the Australian embassy in Mexico City — after two years — extricated him and brought him back here.'

'That's it?'

'No, Harry, that's not it — but I want you to get the rest of the picture from William. It's an unbelievable story, and I won't do it justice, so it's for him to tell. We have an appointment with the Governor at ten, and then they'll bring him to us.'

'Is he going to tell this story in English?'

'No. I had an interpreter, sent up from the Italian embassy in Canberra. But you don't need one, do you? Not after all those summers in Tuscany.'

'I can probably manage.'

Harry pushes aside his empty plate and finishes off his beer. 'Pudding?'

Goulburn jail is as ugly, overbearing, threatening, intimidating and heartbreaking as it was intended to be. Not much more need be said about it. All jails appal Harry, and this one does it in spades. He knows the not-so-distant history of its cages, where men were treated as if they were wild animals, and left out in all Goulburn weathers. The present Governor, under a marginally more enlightened government regime, welcomes Harry and Surrey into his unwelcoming office (and quite effusively, apparently in the mistaken belief that he is dealing with Curry QC), speaking proudly of his prison's new role in the war against terrorism. They are as polite as possible, and wait patiently for the audience to finish and their client to be brought up. They are taken to a comfortable-enough room to wait for him, with a guard at the door. The table is topped with linoleum, and Harry spends the time waiting for his client distractedly digging pieces out of it with his thumbnail. He hates being within the walls of any jail.

There is a flurry of activity and the sound of manacles being released, and a slight, unsmiling man appears at the door, clad in green prison-issue. At least it's not his underwear. Surrey does the introductions in English, and Harry utters some Italian pleasantries. Paradiso smiles tentatively, and they sit. He places on the table a dark book, which Harry picks up.

'A Spanish–English dictionary?' he asks in Italian. 'Why?'

Paradiso responds in Italian. 'I speak quite good Spanish. I get an order in English, so I look it up in Spanish, and translate for myself from the Spanish to Italian. They had this book in the prison library.'

Harry looks quizzical. 'But they didn't have an Italian–English dictionary?'

'No.'

Harry opens his Globite case and extracts a fat book with a bright green-and-yellow dust jacket. He pushes it across the lino table. 'Would this be better for you?' It's a Cassell's Italian–English dictionary.

'Of course.'

'You'd better keep it, then.'

Harry called in at a bookshop in town that morning and bought it. Paradiso pushes the old book aside and takes hold of the bright new one. He smiles. Trust is established.

'Now,' Harry says, 'I've read all the papers from the government lawyers, but there's a great deal they don't explain. Will you tell me, please, Libero, what is this story about the murder?'

Paradiso nods and both lawyers watch him look down at his hands. He has long, fine fingers, and he studies his nails before replying. Obviously he is composing himself, thinking through how he will explain it all to this huge man with the big hands. But, so far, a kind man. Sympathetic. So far.

'You know I came back from the Costa Rica border and I asked permission to leave? And they told me to wait a year?'

Harry says he knows about all that. He takes Surrey's pile of papers from the case and, as he puts them on the table, asks what Libero knows of the Lancia boy.

'Luigi, is it?'

'Guido,' Paradiso says. 'Guido Sissini, not Lancia. We met in a café one night when I heard him speaking in Italian. A junkie. Hopeless. I don't know how, but he had plenty of heroin, and plenty of money. Also a very expensive camera. He said he would take photographs and sell them to magazines — political photographs, but he had no idea of politics. In truth, I did not really like him, but I had nothing to do, and I was sick of speaking Spanish, so we hung out together. We lived in a *pensione* together, and sometimes I would go out with him while he took photographs of the countryside. He would hire a car and a driver, and we had a political commissar come with us to make sure he took no pictures of places with strategic importance. And then one day he wasn't at the *pensione* any more.'

'They said he was dead.'

'They did,' Paradiso agrees. 'But I didn't know if it was true.'

'Keep going, please.'

'When Guido disappeared, his cousin came to Nicaragua with lawyers and a man from the Italian foreign ministry to see if he could be found. The family has a lot of money, and a lot of influence. They interrogated me, but there was nothing I could tell them. They were not satisfied with that. I had his camera, you see. The Nicaraguans pushed me and pushed me, but it made no difference. I couldn't tell them what I didn't know. And the Sissini people kept pushing the government until a body was found. But that was after the Sissinis went back to Milan, and they never came back, not even to bury the body. I was taken into custody.'

'Were you charged?'

'Not then. My mother came to Managua to see me, and she went to the Italian embassy for help. But the ambassador told her they wanted nothing to do with it. Long before that, the government had sent an extradition request to Nicaragua, trying to get me sent back to Italy to face trial on a lot of trivial nonsense from my student days, so long ago, and the Sandinistas had ignored it. The ambassador told my mother I could have come back voluntarily, that I was a criminal, and that now I could look after myself. He said, "Italy washes its hands of your son."'

Surrey says in English that Paradiso should tell Harry how he came to be charged, and Harry translates the request.

'Well, it was like this: our ambassador would do nothing, and my mother was driven to distraction — until she thought of asking Australia for help. I was born here, after all. So she went to the British, there being no Australian embassy in Managua, and they told her to fly to Mexico City and see the Australians there. Which she did. The ambassador came back with her and spoke to the Sandinistas. He said they had to charge me with something or let me go.'

'And?'

'So they charged me with the murder. It was a joke. A murder without a body.'

'But I thought you said they found his body?'

'A body, not Sissini's body. Sissini is smaller than me, and this body was nearly two metres. It was a joke, and the judge said so at the trial. She acquitted me.'

'But that obviously wasn't the end of it?'

'No. The government appealed, and again the court said I was not guilty. But still they would not let me go. The Australian ambassador came back and told them they had to let me go.'

'How long did it take?'

'Three more months. Finally, they told me the ambassador was coming — or someone from Australia was coming — and I would be taken to Sydney.'

'Why not send you back to Italy?'

'Two reasons. The first is that I didn't want to go there to be put on trial in a cage like a terrorist or a mafia don. The second, I found out, is that repatriation means you go to the country representing you. They told me, "We are not a travel agency. You don't get to choose."'

A guard knocks at the door and brings in a tray with cups of tea. All white, all two sugars. Harry says to Surrey, 'They still think I'm a silk.'

'No,' Surrey says. 'They think Libero's a celebrity. Their first international terrorist. He has jail cred.'

They drink the tea anyway.

'In the end I was in prison for two years, and most of it in solitary confinement. I thought I had gone mad.'

Surrey waits while Harry summarises what was said. He puts his hand on Harry's arm. 'Just to explain, Harry: it turns out that Foreign Affairs had told the Italians they were going to bring Libero back here, and that our people in Canberra wanted an extradition request quick smart, so that they could turn him around at the airport and put him on the first flight from Sydney to Rome. The idea was that he wouldn't ever get out of the transit lounge.'

'I assume that didn't happen?'

'No, it didn't — the Italians couldn't get their act together in time, and the request hadn't been sent by the time Libero reached Sydney. So his uncle and aunt took him home to Liverpool, and put things in motion to get him an Australian passport on the basis that he was born here. The new *Migration Act* hadn't cut in at that stage. After a week, the request arrived and they scrambled the anti-terrorist squad. Liverpool's never seen anything like it.'

What the court papers show is that there had been a speedy application to a federal magistrate to ratify the extradition request, and that it had been granted. But Paradiso's uncle was given assistance by court staff to lodge an appeal, and he then approached Surrey to handle the matter.

'Why you, Dave? I mean, no disrespect, but a criminal solicitor in Goulburn? For a major extradition appeal in the Federal Court by an alleged international terrorist?'

Surrey grins. 'No offence taken, counsel, but why not me? Actually, the reason is that I'm the only solicitor the uncle knows. He once had a traffic offence on the motorway near here and had to appear in the magistrate's court in town, and I did that matter for him. He remembered me, once he was told that the boy had been brought to this jail. The family in Padua are putting maximum pressure on him to stop the extradition.'

Harry turns back to Paradiso and explains to him in Italian what he and Surrey have discussed.

The client is looking up words in the new dictionary, and sounding them out to himself, almost silently. He tries a sentence in English.

'We can win this appeal?'

Harry sticks to Italian. 'I can't tell you that yet. I haven't read all the papers, and I have to study the law. But let me explain this: extradition isn't automatic, just because a foreign government asks for it to be done. Before Australia can send you back to Italy, the court has to be satisfied that the charges against you are serious, and that this won't be a political show trial once they get you to Rome. I think that's the point where I might find something to save us.'

'Us?'

'Lawyers always identify with their clients.'

'Yes, but they won't send you to Italy if you lose.'

'I'm going anyway. San Gimignano this year, maybe Lucca. I'll have to pay for my own fare, of course. You'll have that over me.'

Paradiso laughs ruefully. 'Your hotel will be nicer than mine, though.'

Harry stops himself from asking whether his client knows San Gimignano, or Sienna for that matter, or Florence. He is not, despite the forbidding mass of him, an insensitive soul.

'Do you want to ask me anything about the appeal?'

'When the magistrate made the order to extradite me, they did not take me into the court. I was in the cells under the ground. But I know how the court is.'

Harry becomes angry. It is every man's right to be present in court when his liberty is at issue. The magistrate's order smacks of yet another rubber-stamping, and Harry considers taking steps to invalidate the decision on the grounds of a denial of natural justice. He tells Surrey.

'Sure, Harry, no doubt that's entirely right, but somewhat redundant now, surely? We don't need to set the original extradition aside, because the Federal Court hears it *de novo*.'

Libero's ears prick up at the Latin. '*De novo?*'

Harry explains: 'The appeal starts with a clean sheet, as if this is the first time the government's application has been considered.

We ignore any mistakes the magistrate made, just as we ignore his decision and start again. To be quite correct, it isn't an appeal but what we call a judicial review. It's good for you. It gives you a better chance.'

'But at the trial, I will be in a cage with bars, like this prison. Soldiers with guns in the court, and chains on my legs and arms. A terrorist, and no one will believe me.'

Harry leans across the table and puts a big hand on Paradiso's shoulder. He squeezes it quite hard and looks intensely into his eyes. 'Listen to me. This is Australia, and, while there may be many things I don't like about our judicial system, I still believe it's fair. I don't know of a better one — certainly not Italy's. Our courts don't have cages or bars or chains or soldiers or guns. Maybe one prison officer will sit in the court beside you to make sure you don't run away, but you're not on trial. You won't even give evidence. This is a case about whether Italy has the right to drag you back there. That's about your liberty, and it has to be considered very seriously.' Harry is speaking words he believes wholeheartedly to be true.

His client gives every appearance of disbelieving him. 'But how do I prove these accusations are false? That I am no terrorist? Why would the judge believe me?'

'Your credibility isn't the issue. There is an extradition treaty, an agreement between Italy and Australia, which is that a person charged with a crime over here must be sent back if the Italian government can show that there is a proper charge involving a serious criminal offence — that means one with a long jail sentence if you're guilty. We can only win if we can show the offence is trivial, or the charge is not properly brought. If the

Italians have made crucial mistakes in the official papers, you'll win. If not, you'll be on a plane back within a week.'

'Even if I'm innocent?'

'That has to be decided in Italy. We don't try you here on Italian charges.'

Paradiso's eyes flare. 'These are trivialities — the charges are burning school records, throwing a petrol bomb, locking the teachers in their rooms. And they are so old and I was only a boy. The charges are just an excuse to arrest me and interrogate me about the assassination, and I know nothing about that. They did this to my friends, and now they are in jail for childish things they did so long ago.'

'That doesn't make any difference, the age of the charges. What we have to do is look at Australian offences of the same kind, or as close as we can get, to see what punishment you could receive if you committed those offences here. That's how the court judges seriousness. But I'm quite sure that falsely imprisoning someone is a serious matter, with a maximum sentence of several years. Maybe the other matters aren't serious enough, but we might have a problem fighting that one.'

'I can't speak for myself. You will do that?'

'Not even me. Ms Engineer will be your advocate. I will be helping her.'

'Will I meet her?'

'Probably on the morning of the case. That doesn't matter. My job is to get the case ready, to write out the arguments and to find the law to explain to the judge. We have very few of these cases — in fact, I think you are the first person in this situation.'

Libero looks out the window, through cyclone wire, at the

sky. He is trying not to cry. 'If there is a mistake in the papers, they can fix it?'

'Not immediately. And some mistakes can never be fixed. That's the kind of mistake we will be looking for.'

'You have found it?'

'No, not yet. Maybe not at all. But if there's anything we can use to keep you here, we will find it and we will use it. You have to leave that to us — there's nothing for you to do but watch and listen.'

Libero looks from Harry to Surrey.

'And you'd better bring that dictionary,' Harry says. 'A lot of the words in court are harder than the words they use in jail.'

Paradiso smiles. 'Maybe some of the jail words are not in here.'

'I'm sure you're right.' Harry stretches a big rubber band around the papers and puts them back in his Globite.

'If I say nothing in court, and if you can't tell me whether we'll win, I have no more questions. But thank you for coming. It is very kind.'

Surrey says to Harry, 'Just check with him that they're treating him properly.' Harry poses the question.

Paradiso speaks in English to Surrey. 'This is nothing. I was for two years in solitary confinement in Nicaragua. I was kept in six jails. One was an old chicken farm, and they had us in the chickens' cages. Their shit was still on the floor. Men killed themselves there. I wrote it all in my diaries, every day, and I still have them. They didn't know — they couldn't read Italian, or maybe they just couldn't read my writing.'

'I compliment you on your English. Did you speak it before you came here?' Surrey asks.

'No, but I have three months in here to learn. It is not so difficult.'

Harry asks if there is anything else before they leave.

'I would like to see the Sydney Opera House.'

The lawyers smile. 'We'll see what can be arranged,' says Surrey.

They stand and make ready to leave the room. Surrey knocks on the door, and a guard looks through the window before pulling it open. The three men shake hands.

'Court is in one week, in Canberra,' says Surrey. 'I'll speak to your uncle about getting you some clothes to wear. You can't come in those things, and they tell me you were brought here in your pyjamas.'

'No, my underwear.' He smiles.

Manacles are placed on Paradiso's wrists and he is led away, carrying both dictionaries.

There are the remains of a takeway meal on Arabella's glass-topped dining table, and two copies of the papers produced by the Italian and Australian government lawyers are spread out. Arabella's laptop is there too, glowing white with a legal research site. Arabella is reading from the screen and Harry sits opposite her, staring out the window at the lights across the harbour in the direction of the zoo. He is in shirt and trousers, with his jacket and tie thrown on the leather sofa. Arabella wears a large white T-shirt and shorts, her long brown legs folded under her.

'The fellow in this most recent case was wanted for defrauding a bank in Johannesburg. He was in Brisbane, and the South Africans made an extradition request … de dum de dum de dum ... here it is: the law is that the Australian government has to consider the nature of the offence and whether, in all the circumstances of the case, it would be unjust, oppressive or incompatible with humanitarian considerations to surrender the person to the requesting country. Any good?'

Harry pulls his gaze away from the window. 'What's the date of the decision?'

'It's 2004.'

'So it's not apartheid South Africa. What would have been the injustice or oppression of sending him back for trial?'

'That he would have been gang-raped and infected with HIV if he was jailed there. He had evidence of a high likelihood that that would happen, and the Australian government failed to consider it.'

'That should be enough. Did he get a result?'

'Not from the first judge, but the full court granted the appeal.'

Harry stands, moves to look over her shoulder, and reads for a few minutes. He looks also at her legs. 'Well, it's not exactly on all fours with Paradiso's case, but there might be something we can work up. Some analogy ... But you'd better check the High Court — maybe the government took it up there and reversed the Federal Court. That's always embarrassing, not knowing that everything you rely on has been overruled. But tomorrow. Just save what you've got,' says Harry, 'and we'll call it a night.'

'Ooh good, then we can discuss our feelings.'

'I hardly ever hit women,' says Harry, jamming his papers into the Globite. 'But I could make an exception.'

Arabella types a correction into her laptop, then saves it.

'That's all good stuff, Harry. But this is another classic example of what David says about you — all the eggs are in one basket.'

'I'm not saying there's only one tactic, Bella. The strategy is to hold our best point back until they've made all their arguments, so we'll run hard on this South African stuff and whatever else you can find if there's anything in it, and the triviality points, and the juvenile point, and get our learned friends to concentrate all their efforts on those directions. They might not see the killer point coming. It's weird, though, that you can't find any record of any extradition case involving juvenile offences. You'd think there's got to be some law on that.'

'Well,' she says happily, 'there soon will be.'

'I mean, really, it's fair enough that serious offenders should never be able to escape justice merely because they have enough resources, or resourcefulness, to leave the country. But some judge, somewhere, must have had to consider what effect it has on holding a matter to be serious that it was committed—'

'Allegedly.'

'—by a child. Or a minor. There's got to be an argument that you don't actually imprison children, at least in Australia, so a juvenile offence doesn't fall into the category of extraditable crimes.'

Arabella shuts down the laptop and tidies her table. She collects the empty glasses, coffee cups and takeaway Chinese food containers and carries them through to the kitchen, which looks as if she has never cooked there. Except for the espresso machine, of course.

When she returns, Harry is sliding open the door onto the balcony and stepping out. Ignoring a cold sea breeze, Arabella joins him and puts her arm around his waist. He puts both hands on the railing in front of him and Arabella lets her arm fall. She returns to the living room and falls backward onto the sofa. Harry remains outside, watching a Manly ferry slide slowly from left to right. He looks at his watch.

'Probably the last ferry. Time I went.' He leaves the door open as he walks over to pick up his clothes from next to Arabella. The air is soft.

'Sit down for a minute. Please.'

Harry sits, his jacket across his knees. He leans forward, as if waiting for a train. Neither speaks. The night is still, the thick, oily water soundless until a fight erupts between fruit bats in the Port Jackson figs bordering Elizabeth Bay. Car doors slam; someone calls out, 'See you!' from the street, a car drives off, and silence returns, except for the muted metallic slapping of halyards against aluminium masts of yachts that never seem to move from their moorings.

'Lots of sexual tension, Harry.'

'Isn't there just?' He looks at her, almost smiling — but not quite. Arabella picks up a Marimekko cushion and holds it across her breasts. Defensive, Harry thinks.

'I'm off home, Bella. I forgot to feed the cat.'

'You haven't got a cat.'

'I keep forgetting that, too.'

She makes to throw the cushion at him, but stands up and holds out her hand. Harry uses it to pull himself to his feet, almost toppling her, but Arabella is a strong woman. Still holding Arabella's hand, he kisses her on both cheeks. She shuts her eyes after the first kiss.

'Thanks for the dinner.'

Arabella doesn't let go of his hand; she walks with him to the door, picking up the Globite case as she passes the table. At the door, she releases Harry's hand and he takes the case.

'You could leave that here. I mean, it's not as if you're going to take it in to chambers tomorrow and work on it there.'

'I'll work at home until you're free. Will you be in court all day?'

'No. Just a high-range PCA. Company director, important client of an important firm, too important to soil their hands with magistrates' courts and drunk drivers, so it's farmed out to a local solicitor at Waverley, and me. Still, fifteen hundred dollars for fifteen minutes' work. I should be back in chambers in time for morning tea.'

'Unless the grateful client wants to buy you a coffee.'

'Even then.'

Harry stands back, looking at the door. 'I'm not allowed to open it. You have to.'

'Why me?'

'Because I haven't known you for seven years. One of my mother's rules.'

Arabella chuckles. 'My mother could beat your mother into a cocked hat on rules — the etiquette of the village.'

'Which village would that be? Hampstead Garden Suburb?'

Arabella turns the handle and opens the door. 'At least I've now been kissed.'

'In Lucca, I kiss the baker's wife every morning. She has whiskers growing out of a mole on her chin.'

'So nothing special, then?'

'You are very special, Bella. The kiss wasn't.' And he kisses her again. Very gently, and on the mouth.

***

It is 9.30 a.m. and Harry parks the Jaguar in the public car park adjoining the Canberra Federal Court complex and removes a heavy pilot's case from the boot. No sign of the Globite. As he looks at it, Harry judges the modernist seventies building still to be graceful, but he'll find its external marble steps have broken edges and the glassed-in internal atrium around which the courtrooms are circled has become an artless display of dead and desiccated shrubbery. He leads Arabella past the ticket vending machine, ignoring it. Surrey, arms full with a cardboard box of law books, comes from the direction of his own car and asks whether Harry's going to pay and display.

'The owner's in Long Bay for the next ten years,' he responds airily. 'I don't see them having much success in chasing their four dollars.'

Arabella, weighed down with her blue bag, laughs. The three lawyers reach the bottom of the steps as their opponents arrive in two white Commonwealth cars and emerge, retrieving their own cases and papers from the boots. There are six lawyers on the other side.

Harry greets the most senior-looking: a short, squat man with greasy hair, in a rumpled three-piece suit and scruffy shoes. 'A six-pack, Ralph? Surely the Attorney-General doesn't run to such luxury for one small terrorist?'

'The Italians are paying half the bill, Harry. And if you don't behave yourself, I'll see to it personally that they don't give you a visa for your next trip.'

Harry and Ralph were once in the same chambers, but both are too well mannered to mention it. Laurence Ralph QC, for such he is, is backed up by a lookalike junior, to whom Arabella nods, and four solicitors who are so similar they could be cousins, all attending the same Marist Brothers school. Perhaps they are and perhaps they did, Harry reflects.

The nine lawyers involved in *Paradiso v Governor, Goulburn Remand Centre* — it's the prison's boss Surrey's case is aimed at, not the Attorney-General, seeking orders that the jailer release his client — take turns to pass the metal detectors. Mobile phones, cigarette packets, car keys and small change are shuffled around in plastic trays, bags are peered into, and the teams split up once inside the lobby. Arabella heads for the barristers' room to get into her court dress while Harry organises the bags and boxes of papers outside courtroom 2, and Surrey heads for the court officer in charge of security to ask for an escort to the cells. The officer, sitting behind a desk, merely points to the other end of the lobby, where a uniformed prison guard sits next to Paradiso, tieless and jacketless in a white business shirt several sizes too big for him over dark trousers, even worse-fitting, and Dunlop Volleys. He waves with both hands at Surrey, because he is in handcuffs. On the seat next to him is the green-and-yellow Italian dictionary. Surrey points the client out to Harry, and they cross the lobby to speak to him.

'Christ,' says Harry. 'Talk about a dwarfish thief in a giant's robe.'

'*Macbeth.*'

'Nobody likes a clever dick, Dave.'

'I taught it to at least five HSC classes, Harry.'

They reach their client.

'*Come stai*, Libero?'

'I am very well, thank you, Mr Curry.' He is actually shaking with nerves. Arabella emerges from the robing room and joins them to be introduced. She shakes Paradiso's hand, rattling the handcuffs. The prison guard slides a couple of metres off to one side along the curved bench and looks studiously straight ahead.

Arabella is well aware that this is the most important client she has ever had. Maybe the most important she will ever have. She sits next to him, her wig in her hands, and lowers her voice. 'Don't worry, Libero, if you don't understand what anyone's saying in court. Tell Mr Curry — he'll translate. Okay?'

'Okay.'

'We told the court we wouldn't need an interpreter — it just slows things down. Now, you remember: you won't be talking. I will do that. Understand?'

'I understand.'

'And there will be a lot of talking. All day. I talk first, then the others, then I talk again.'

Paradiso nods. 'Does it finish today?'

Harry shakes his head and speaks in Italian. 'No, Libero. The judge has to consider all the law and all the evidence, and what the lawyers argue. Maybe he'll take a few days, maybe a few weeks. Nobody can say.'

'So I shall return to the jail tonight?'

'Yes. One day should be all we need in the court, but maybe some of tomorrow, too. We'll see.'

Paradiso purses his lips and gives a small nod. 'And you have confidence?'

'Ms Engineer is very confident.'

'And you?'

'I'm just helping, Libero. Arabella is your advocate. Nobody knows your case better than she. Trust her.' Arabella looks at Harry. She well understands that *'avvocato'* and *'confidenza'* are about her. He looks at her then back at her client. 'I do.'

Just then, the government lawyers sweep past the group and into the courtroom. Two of the solicitors are pushing shiny chromium trolleys of books and colour-coded folders. The other two carry laptops.

'We'd — sorry, I mean you'd — better get set up,' says Harry. He asks the prison officer to bring Paradiso and they also enter the courtroom, setting out books and folders, pens and pads on the left-hand end of the Bar table — the protagonists' end. Paradiso is given a chair immediately behind his counsel. At the antagonists' end, there isn't room for all the lawyers and hardware, and they're asking the uniformed staff for an additional table to be joined on. There is a delay while court officers head off and return with another table and butt it up against the primary field of battle. When everyone's satisfied, Harry retreats to the first row of public seating, his hands empty. Junior counsel for the Commonwealth gets up and whispers to Arabella, 'No wigs here, Arabella.'

Blushing, she removes the wig and hands it back to Surrey, who places it in the now-empty cardboard box.

The Federal Court is a foreign country to Harry and Surrey. Less so for Arabella, who has appeared in a few migration appeals, an unsuccessful refugee status claim, and a fight over entitlement to a widow's pension, but nothing like this. As 10.15 approaches, the court fills up with reporters — also a first for Arabella. There is another unruly group that can only be administrative law students from the Australian National University. Paradiso looks at the people taking seats, and particularly those with shorthand pads in their hands. He raises his eyebrows at Surrey and then holds up his manacled hands. Surrey instantly signals to the prison officer standing off to one side, who steps forward and unlocks the cuffs. He puts them in his pocket and retreats to the seat nearest the door. Paradiso gently rubs his wrists in disbelief and turns to look at his guard, who returns his gaze, expressionless.

Surrey bends over, speaking softly. 'As I told you: no chains, Libero. No guns, no bars, no cage.'

Paradiso shakes his head slowly from side to side. He looks around the courtroom, the walls of which are gloomily finished in vertical strips of wood stained a dark brown to match the furniture and the unpainted coat of arms, high above the judge's chair. Mounted on these walls is a series of solemn if not bad-tempered portraits of past Chief Justices of the Australian Capital Territory in full-bottomed wigs and regalia, who remind Libero of school plays, of kings in cardboard crowns and old dressing gowns trimmed with cotton wool spotted with black ink to represent ermine. He can't help smiling at the incongruity.

The judge's associate enters from a door behind the raised bench, carrying books. She sets them down for the judge and settles herself in place, then stands and turns to face the door through which she just entered. There are three loud knocks on the other side of the door, and a court officer commands all present to stand. They do, and the judge enters in the regalia of the Federal Court, gowned but wigless. The gown features some strange maroon element, and beneath it Saville J (nickname

Savile Row) wears a dress shirt and tie. Some judge's wife must have designed the gear, Arabella thinks. Some judge's wife who watches American TV.

Arabella has been briefed by Harry on the judge and how to handle him. 'I've never appeared in front of him, Bella, but I was in a long coronial inquest against him about ten years ago, just before they appointed him to the bench. You'll find him a very different proposition from the thugs in the District Court. He's courteous, and he's a bloody good lawyer. Don't fight him. Look for his attitude, and don't flog any dead horses. If he thinks you've got a good point, he'll let you know.'

Everyone, except the judge, stands while the court officer reads a formal message opening the proceedings from a laminated card, which he then replaces in his pocket. Following counsel's lead — it wouldn't do to sit too soon, as if they were in the New South Wales Supreme Court or some such jungle — everyone takes a seat except the associate who reads out the name of the case. 'Libero William Paradiso against the Governor of Goulburn Remand Centre and others.'

That's the signal for Arabella to announce her appearance: 'May it please your Honour, I appear for the applicant.'

The judge looks at a page in front of him. 'Thank you, Ms Engineer. And Mr Ralph, you appear for the respondents?'

'May it please your Honour. With my learned junior, Mr Ralph.' Not 'my son', but 'Mr Ralph'.

'Yes, Ms Engineer?'

Arabella carries her folder to the lectern in the centre of the Bar table and opens it. Her hands are shaking and the words she has typed out swim on the page in front of her. She pours herself a glass of water, straightens her gown on her shoulders and raises her hands to adjust her wig before she realises she's taken it off. Right at this moment, she wants to run from the court. She takes a sip from the glass instead, and some water spills down her chin. She wipes it away with her hand. 'This is an application pursuant to section 18 of the *Extradition (Foreign States) Act* of 1966 and under the *Administrative Decisions (Judicial Review) Act 1977*. My client challenges the validity of the magistrate's decision that he is liable to be extradited.'

Arabella is settling in. Her voice becomes stronger, and the waver disappears. She looks up at the judge for the first time, and makes eye contact as she continues. 'The respondents to the proceedings are the Governor of the Goulburn Remand Centre, the learned magistrate Mr McLucas, and the Attorney-General. Your Honour, only the Attorney-General is taking an active part in the hearing, putting submissions in support of the magistrate's extradition order.'

Justice Saville uncaps his pen and flattens the pages of his notebook with his left hand. He makes a note as Arabella continues.

'The applicant is an Australian citizen, having been born in this country on …'

The Federal Court doesn't believe in morning tea. A longer lunchbreak makes up for that, and Arabella, who has not yet finished her address to the court, is wrung out when the first adjournment of the day is taken. Paradiso is handcuffed again and taken off to the custody area, where a sandwich and a cup of instant coffee are waiting for him. Arabella doesn't even notice him being taken away. All she wants is to talk things through with Harry. Surrey volunteers to cross the road to a takeaway in Civic and get everyone a coffee and something to eat.

Arabella takes off her gown and hangs it on the back of her chair, then follows Harry's hurrying back as he strides out of the courtroom and through the foyer, leading her into a room marked 'Legal Profession'. She puts her folder on the table and they sit. To Harry, she looks exhausted, but her eyes shine.

'He's very interested, Harry. I think we're getting somewhere.'

'Not so fast, Bella. Let's go through your arguments so far and see if we can agree. That first point — triviality. He doesn't agree with you there.'

They spend five minutes arguing about the point before Arabella concedes. 'Well, granted, but I think that'd work on appeal. He's only speaking theoretically about maximum punishments being more than trivial.'

'I don't think we've got time to worry about that one now … that's not going to work.'

Surrey enters with lunch and puts it on the table, but nobody takes any immediate interest in it. Surrey takes the top off a takeaway tea, and sips it. Too hot; he puts it down.

'Okay. Next argument was that the Italian evidence is inadmissible, because a co-accused's confessions can't be used in a trial under Australian law.'

'Yes, Harry, and he expressly agreed with me that only evidence that is admissible at a criminal trial for these offences in this country can be used in the extradition case. In fact, he was even stronger than that — he picked up that none of the confessions that they propose to use against Libero were authenticated. We hadn't noticed that.'

'But, Bella, you have to listen to the "howevers" when a judge is talking. What he was saying, at least as I heard him, was that the evidence would be admissible if the co-offenders were called as witnesses and gave it orally at his trial.'

'Did he say that? David?'

''Fraid so, Arabella.'

Arabella is not yet beaten. 'Yes, I suppose … but he very clearly threw out five of the charges. Ralph had to concede that there simply wasn't a *prima facie* case on those.'

'That was great, Bella. Very, very well done. But there are still three charges that he is quite clear on — there's enough admissible evidence, and they're serious enough for him to be convicted here and sentenced to at least two years' jail on each of them.'

Surrey tries his tea again. Still too hot, so he asks, 'What does that mean, Harry? Isn't that the end of all Bella's arguments? Will he even call on Ralph to respond?'

'Might be the end of those arguments, but there's still mine. Ralph has no idea what's coming, and if we do it quickly and clearly, and keep it short, they just won't have time to think of a rebuttal.'

'Harry reckons there's no possibility of rebuttal, anyway,' Arabella says, unwrapping a salad roll.

'Am I allowed to know what it is, this killer point?' Surrey asks.

'And spoil all the fun?' Harry puts his feet up on an empty chair. 'Let's have a bit of lunch.'

When the hearing resumes, Saville J has something to say. 'I'm most grateful for your assistance so far, Ms Engineer, and that of Mr Ralph and his learned junior, but I notice that there's one point on your outline of argument that you didn't develop in the papers you handed up, and I want to hear you on it.'

'That would be paragraph 33, your Honour? Political character of the offences?'

'Yes. Would it be convenient for you to move to that argument now?'

Arabella looks back at Harry, who tilts his head in a satisfied manner and looks at the ceiling of the courtroom.

'Yes, your Honour, I was just coming to that.'

'Please go ahead.'

Ninety minutes later, the judge courteously interrupts Arabella for the first time that afternoon. The mood at the other end of the Bar table has changed from confident to sullen. 'So, am I right in understanding your submission as being concerned with this, Ms Engineer? That the early English cases, where it was held that the assassination of a member of parliament in Switzerland was of a political character, despite being murder, so that the admitted assassin couldn't be extradited; but where it was also held that French anarchists who set off a string of bombs killing people because they were opposed to *all* forms of government could not claim their crimes to be political and had to face trial back in France; and yet that the 1955 case of the Polish trawlermen ...'

'At least my learned friend could find one twentieth-century decision, your Honour.' Ralph feels he has to say something.

'Thank you, Mr Ralph, yes — those Poles who assaulted and locked up the political officers commanding their ship, and then sailed it to Whitby and claimed political asylum ...'

Arabella reaches for the law report in which the judgment is set out. 'They succeeded, your Honour. They admitted to the assaults and the false imprisonment, but the court accepted that it was an act of political rebellion, notwithstanding that Poland was then a one-party state and none of the men was a member of a political group.' She reads from the law report: '"Having regard to the circumstances in which the rebellion occurred, the prosecution in Poland would have been in fact a political prosecution."'

'But in the present case, your argument, Ms Engineer, doesn't rely on the circumstances of what your client did, does it? I mean, the offences in the warrants — at least the three charges that I'm satisfied could be made out on the evidence, and are serious offences — they're irrelevant, aren't they? You get no support there.'

'I don't need it, your Honour.' Arabella's smile is always disarming, and never more so than now.

'Go on.'

'Can I ask the court to look at the warrants themselves — the ones applying to these offences?'

'I have those.'

'May I read them to your Honour?' And she does:

> *That in complicity with nine others, in execution of a program adopted by the Ronde Aramate Proletarie of which they were members, which program was intended to oppose 'selection' in schools, Paradiso materially committed the acts for purposes of terrorism and eversion of the democratic order.*

'In other words, your Honour, the warrants themselves define political activism — terrorism and eversion of the democratic order — as an essential element of the offences.'

'And you would, wouldn't you, Ms Engineer, draw my attention to section 13 of the extradition law, which provides — I'll read this onto the record — that, "A person is not liable to be surrendered to a foreign state if the offence in issue is an offence of a political character or if the application for extradition has been made to punish him for an offence of a political character."?'

'I was just about to do that, your Honour.' An even broader smile at the judge, who turns to the unhappy end of the Bar table, where all are in whispered conference. Arabella turns back to Harry, leans over and says softly, 'You were right about him throwing me a lifebelt.'

Harry makes a guttural noise meaning that his argument needs no rescue.

'Mr Ralph, I confess that I had to look up the word "eversion" in the OED.'

'As did my junior, your Honour. He tells me it means "overthrow".'

'So even your client — and I refer in the loosest possible way to the Italian government — asserts that the intention of Mr Paradiso in committing the alleged offences was to overthrow it.'

'We have to accept that, your Honour.'

'Hard to come up with a clearer definition of a political offence, wouldn't you say, Mr Ralph?'

Ralph QC chooses not to answer.

Arabella is sitting, but could swear she is floating ten feet up in the air.

Saville J speaks gently. 'Mr Paradiso, would you please stand?' Libero complies. 'Please tell me if you don't understand what I am about to say. I want you to know, now, that you are free. You have won your case, and you will not be sent back to prison, or to Italy. I will have to write a judgment, and that may take some months for me to do — I have a lot of other work to complete. But I don't want you to sit in jail, waiting for me to make a decision. I have made the decision, and I will hand down my reasons later. I am sure that your lawyers will make all the necessary arrangements.'

The prison officer at the back of the court had taken the handcuffs out of his pocket when the judge stood Paradiso up, anticipating his return to custody and the trip to Goulburn jail, but now he walks quietly out of the courtroom carrying the cuffs in his hand as the court officer adjourns the proceedings to a date yet to be fixed — for the formality of the judgment. As soon as the judge disappears through his door, Arabella embraces Harry, and Surrey delightedly puts a hand on each of their backs. Paradiso weeps quietly, sitting in his chair. Surrey takes hold of the man's hand and shakes it. 'No need to cry, Libero. You came first.'

Arabella embraces Paradiso while Harry watches. If anything, he looks embarrassed. Some lawyers' shibboleths die hard, including the one that barristers should never become emotionally involved with their cases. Or is it their clients? Harry thinks to himself that he won't attempt to explain that one to Paradiso's advocate, who seems close to tears herself.

Ralph QC comes over to Harry. 'Your fingerprints were all over this, Curry.'

'You wouldn't be so silly as to advise an appeal, would you, Larry?'

'Hardly. Savile Row's destined for the High Court, they tell me.' He holds out his right hand to Harry, who takes it. 'Hope to see you back on this side of the Bar soon, Harry.'

Harry inclines his head and the defeated team walks out, looking defeated, leaving its books and papers to be cleaned up by a team of clerks. The journalists rush out, the public seats empty, and soon it's just the Paradiso team and a couple of court staff.

'Celebrating tonight, Ms Engineer?' one asks.

'Is there still a decent Italian restaurant or two in Kingston?' Harry asks him. 'It's a long time since I've been there.'

'Sorry, sir, it's a bit out of my league.'

'We'll find something,' says Surrey as they leave the courtroom. 'But I'd better drop you two off at some hotel first. It's a bit early for dinner. Libero, you're staying with us in Goulburn tonight, and we can call your aunt and uncle and get them to come down and collect you in the morning.'

Paradiso looks uncomprehending, so Harry repeats the message in Italian and Arabella goes off to disrobe. A journalist returns and approaches them, but retreats at a look from Harry. '*Rettile*,' he explains.

'What?'

'Reptiles, David. Libero understood me.'

'Thanks, Harry. I could have used the publicity.'

'But you wouldn't have got it. The headlines are going to be "Red Brigade terrorist on the loose in Sydney", and Libero's going to be the only one mentioned.'

'I wouldn't be too sure of that, Harry. A few of those journos looked heterosexual enough to want to impress Arabella.'

Harry responds with a baffled look. That hadn't occurred to him, but now he is suffering from something that hints at jealousy. Or is it a proprietary claim? he wonders.

As they wait for Arabella to return, the lawyers gather the

boxes of books and papers in silence and Paradiso sits in his chair, clasping and re-clasping his hands. He borrows Surrey's mobile phone and calls his uncle. There is a short, excited conversation and he hands the phone back. Libero turns to Harry. 'May I kiss you?'

'You should kiss Arabella, Libero. David and I will shake your hand.'

Hands are duly shaken and Arabella is kissed on both cheeks when she emerges in her street clothes. As they walk outside into the late afternoon light, Arabella steers Harry to one side and whispers to him. 'Thank you, Harry.'

'For what? You won it, not I.'

'Because I've never felt so alive. Will we ever do anything as good as this again?'

Harry stops and looks at her face. 'They're all as good as this, Bella. All you have to do is win.'

'So that's your secret.'

The lawyers load the books into the two cars. Boot lids are slammed and the men remove their jackets. It's warm for April. There is a moment of awkwardness. Harry speaks first.

'I'm going to stay at the university. Why don't we all go over there and have a drink or a cup of tea and kill a bit of time? Then we'll find a restaurant and a bottle of Prosecco.' Arabella doesn't know what to say, but Harry continues. 'Bella, they'll have rooms for both of us.'

She looks at Surrey and raises her eyebrows a millimetre. All he says to her is, 'Patience.'

The Live Dead Man

Sydney Harbour in the hot, dead days after Christmas. A couple of hundred metres upstream of the Bridge, old men are fishing and boys are shouting and jumping off the wharf outside the Sydney Theatre Company building, bombing thin brown arms and legs hard through the slack, oily surface and sending up competing sprays of foam, backlit from the west as the red sun descends into Parramatta River.

And then one boy surfaces to find a dead man wallowing deep in the water beside him.

Two hours later, in the dark, red and blue lights blink sharply along the wharf as theatregoers try to sneak a look past the ambulance officers and police detectives at the mound concealed beneath a bright blue plastic sheet, water spreading out from under it across the concrete. Occasional flashes from the forensic officers' cameras spike into the darkness. The media have stayed away — just another holiday drowning.

But to those present, the body is obviously no mere drowning accident. Its length has been wrapped tightly in orange nylon rope, a great deal of it, and — as the police found when it was winched out of the water — short offcuts of steel railway track had been pushed down the dead man's jeans and held in place by the rope.

A detective lifts one corner of the plastic sheet, takes another look at the head, and drops the sheet. 'That young constable from George Street North identified him — he's supposed to be one of the deros who live in the old wharf buildings. Called the Pom, but he's Polish. Dunno why.'

His offsider is admiring a pretty girl walking into the theatre building in a strapless dress and high-heeled sandals. Summer. 'Dunno why he's Polish?'

'Dunno why the other homeless guys call him that. If he's not. A Pom, I mean.'

The uniforms are ordered to trawl the pubs on the higher levels of The Rocks, and they round up from the public bar stools perhaps a dozen of the men who foolishly admit that they sleep in the wharf buildings. It doesn't take long to build a picture of the Pom's last day. The police computer incident report spells out a narrative of the quotidian pursuits of the downtown homeless: begging from the tourists watching the didgeridoo players or photographing the Opera House at Circular Quay; eating at the charity kitchens and sometimes showering there too; dossing down on rancid mattresses in the old wharf buildings of Walsh Bay; and obeying the imperative of all-day drinking, funded by the tourists' spare change and withdrawals from the ATM accounts into which their disability pensions, or their dole, are deposited every fortnight.

Three men are nominated as having been seen drinking with the deceased at the Palisade four nights ago — the last time anyone admits to seeing the Pom alive. Their camp is in the wharf building across from where the body bobbed up, lifted by the putrefying gases accumulating in its gut. Two of them, hopeless alcoholics, spill out the story. The third, a younger Aboriginal man, exercises his right to remain silent.

At the Homicide Squad briefing, the detective-sergeant in charge reads out his rendition of the Short Facts as told to him by the two cooperative men, rendered into police-speak (Harry is later to comment on the police fixation with the present perfect simple tense) and tendered to the magistrate, who duly refuses bail to all three.

'The deceased is Andrei Jaruzelski, born 1.3.48, a.k.a. Andrew Jones, no fixed address, on a disability pension from a work injury suffered eight years ago. He was a welder. Divorced, no children. The deceased has been drinking in the Palisade Hotel in Bettington Street, Millers Point, with the defendants and a number of other homeless men through the afternoon and until closing time on December 28th. There has been an altercation in the hotel when one of the defendants has accused him of stealing his drink, but the barman has threatened to bar all the drinkers, and things have returned to normal. At closing time, the defendants have bought a flagon of muscat and left together and have walked to the Walsh Bay wharf building — Number 15 — where they customarily sleep. The deceased has followed the three defendants, and joined them inside.

'The defendants have drunk the wine, refusing to share it with the deceased. He has been constantly abused and called a bludger. An altercation has developed when the deceased insisted that he be given some of the flagon to drink, and the defendant Harris, an Aboriginal, has struck him a number of times with an iron bar — a length of reinforcing rod which has been located and sent for forensic examination. Most of the blows have been struck to the head of the deceased.

'The defendants have slept the night in the wharf building. They have woken at about 10 a.m. and found the deceased's body to be cold. One has tried to find a pulse, but there was none. The defendant O'Reilly has located several short lengths of steel railway track, and weighed the body down with them. The defendant Harris has been sent to Woolworths at Town Hall to buy rope. When he has returned with the rope, all three defendants have trussed the body and dragged it to the adjoining wharf building, Number 16, where they have removed a manhole cover and dropped the body into the harbour. Three days later, the body has been seen by some boys from Ultimo, who were swimming between the wharves.

'The defendants O'Reilly and Willingale have been charged as accessories after the fact, and the defendant Harris has been charged with murder. The first two defendants have signed confessional statements, but Harris has refused to be interviewed.'

The police brief, including the signed statements of the co-defendants and eyewitnesses from the pub, are in the fullness of time put together and sent on to the Director of Public Prosecutions.

The DPP is not aware that Willingale is also Aboriginal, which creates a problem and delays the trial. The Aboriginal Legal Service, initially involved after visiting both men at Long Bay jail's remand section, forms the view that there is the potential for a cut-throat defence — where each man blames the other, claiming himself to be innocent — and these cases have both to be flick-passed to legal aid, being what's known in the trade as 'black on black'. That duck-shoving takes almost six months.

Then there is a delay of a further six months while the prosecution solicitors wait for the police to finalise and present them with all the forensic material from the government analysts and the morgue pathologist in a form that can be presented to an administrative hearing before a magistrate. For a month the postmortem report is lost at the morgue. Then the police officer in charge of the brief goes off on long service leave. Or perhaps he was Hurt on Duty or suffering from stress. Same difference, more delay.

Consequently, it is nearly eighteen months after the event that the matter is ready to come on for trial, by which time Willingale and O'Reilly have pleaded guilty to accessory charges and been given light sentences — fifteen months each, of which they have already served half. The only man to stand trial for murder will be Christopher John Harris, aged twenty-three, who has been, since his arrest, a resident at the Long Bay Hilton's remand division — which is where Arabella, Harry and their legal aid solicitor, a harassed-looking young woman, have presented themselves to confer, early on a Friday afternoon in winter, with their client. The problem is that Harry no longer has a practising certificate to produce, which is a condition that the Geordie-accented prison officer expects to be satisfied before any legal visit can take place.

'Look,' says Harry, 'Ms Engineer and Ms Williams have shown you their prison passes, and they both vouch for me. That's got to be enough for your rules.'

The officer looks through hooded eyes at Harry and folds his arms. 'Says here legal visits can only be allowed to legal practitioners and paralegals with prison passes. I don't make the rules.'

Harry's frustration is building, and he's about to put his foot in his mouth, ensuring that they will never get to see Harris, so Arabella steps in. Her London accent gets the officer's back up — she can see that — but he's also used to taking orders from people with those voices. He used to be in the British Army.

'What about this?' she asks. 'We'll just have an ordinary visit — no contact, not a legal. His trial starts on Monday and this is the only time we can see him, but we have to talk to him. We'll go in with the families.'

He thinks about it for a while. 'But you won't be able to take any papers in with you. And you can't give him anything.'

'It's better than no visit,' says Arabella, hushing Harry by putting her hand on his chest, whence the words 'For God's sake …' are escaping in a stage whisper.

Their identifications, including Harry's driver's licence, are recorded and they are finally, forty minutes after presenting themselves at the gate, released to enter the outdoor visiting area. No tables, no privacy. The prison officer can't hide a smile as he ushers them through two locked and barred gates. He's done his bit for the day and made things hard for the lawyers.

In the open air, things are busy. There are multicoloured garden benches on which family members sit, talking to prisoners in white plastic overalls. Children climb on the playground equipment off to one side. Guards move around slowly, speaking occasionally to the visitors. There is grass, pretty sparse in winter, and some struggling plants without flowers in regimented garden beds surrounded by white-painted stones. The sky is blue and cold.

Harris waits on one of the garden benches, as he has been for half an hour. The solicitor introduces Arabella and Harry.

'Which one's my barrister?' Harris asks.

'I'll be appearing for you, Chris,' says Arabella. 'Mr Curry is working with me.'

'Not sure about you, Miss. Nobody in here's ever heard of you. Couldn't Mr Curry do it?'

Harry takes over. 'You haven't heard of Ms Engineer because none of her clients are in here. Her clients are all acquitted. And I can't do it, because I'm not practising at the moment.'

There is a long pause while the prisoner absorbs this. Arabella takes the time to look closely at him. Young, obviously, and brown-skinned against the white plastic clothing. Black hair. Strong white teeth. Tall, slim, nice-looking. Hard to believe he's an alcoholic. The first Aboriginal man she's met. He's noticed that she, too, has brown skin. He's impressed.

'You a Koori, Miss?' He speaks as if he were a schoolboy and she the teacher.

'No,' she says. 'My parents are Indian.'

'Right.' He looks across at Harry and thinks for a moment. 'Are you the boyfriend?'

Harry laughs. Nobody else says anything, and Harry takes over the meeting. 'Are your mates giving evidence?'

'No chance of that,' Harris says with certitude. 'They're not dogs.'

The solicitor says, 'But when they pleaded guilty as accessories, their lawyer blamed you. Said you killed the man, and they only helped you dump the body in the harbour.'

'Yeah, of course. Wouldn't you? Doesn't mean they'd give

evidence. They didn't for their sentencing, either — just let the barrister say it. Whatever. And if they did jump the box, they'd probably have to say that they're just old drunks anyway, and their memory's fucked by the grog. Couldn't remember a thing after all this time.'

Arabella puts her hand on Harry's arm. 'Jump the box?'

'You'd say "enter the witness box". Give evidence. Blokes like Chris master the argot pretty quickly in here.'

There is only an hour available to them to confer with their client, so they get on with it, but he isn't much help. It takes half their allotted time to persuade him to tell them the truth and that he can trust them, and the other half-hour is occupied with him blaming the other men, claiming that they actually wielded the iron bar, and that he, in fact, was the mere accessory. All very unsatisfactory and unhelpful, and they head back to the legal aid solicitor's car without any comfort about the possibility of a successful defence.

As Harry slams his door, he asks the solicitor about the alleged confession. Harris refused to answer the detectives' questions, but there is another homeless man who provided a statement to police, saying that the young Aboriginal man had confessed to him one night outside the Matthew Talbot Hostel at Woolloomooloo that he'd killed the Pom.

'Do we know anything about him? Drugs? Alcohol? Criminal record for offences of dishonesty? Anything we can discredit him with?'

Ms Williams from Legal Aid takes her eyes off the road to look at Harry ruefully. 'Not going to get much on Mr Quinn. They won't give us any money for private investigators — budget's all spent months ago. I've issued a subpoena to the cops for his criminal record and to the prison hospital for his medical reports — they might show his substance abuse profile. Can you think of anything else?'

Harry shakes his head. They're passing the Maroubra shops and he hasn't had any lunch. 'Do they have cafés here?'

'Not so you'd notice,' says Arabella. 'Let's wait till we get back to chambers.' She thinks for a while. 'Can't think of anything else on Quinn? No guarantee that's even his right name, I suppose.'

Harry brightens. 'If Mr Quinn — what did Chris call him? The Guru? — if we can get the jury to see him as a ratbag, or an alcoholic, or an alcoholic ratbag, maybe the confession won't be much use to the Crown. You know, Bella: "You wouldn't hang a cat on that man's word." But the client, if we can accept what he says, seems to revere the man — says Quinn's been all over the world, and has all sorts of insights mere mortals wouldn't understand.'

'Hence "the Guru", I suppose.'

Ms Williams drops them in Macquarie Street promising to meet them in court on Monday morning, and they sit at an outdoor café where Harry orders a sandwich and a pot of tea. Arabella makes do with a short black. The deep shadows and cold wind make the experience unpleasant. Arabella tries to persuade Harry to come to her chambers to work on the case, but he won't go any nearer Phillip Street than a block's distance.

'Harry, I made notes of all that palaver Chris gave us about the Guru and his powers of observation. I'd like to work that up a bit.'

'Could work. He's all they've got to hang their case on. The judge has to warn the jury that Chris is perfectly entitled to say nothing, and they mustn't hold that against him. If he's right and his mates won't testify — and that's got to be right when you think about it, because we haven't been served with any police statements signed by them — all they've got is the eyewitnesses from the Palisade …'

'And all they prove is that they were drinking together, and the Pom lit out after them at closing time …'

'Yep, so there's the pathologist from the morgue. Have you read the postmortem documents?' He looks impatiently for their waiter.

'Not yet, Harry.'

The food and drink arrive, and Harry despatches the thin ham and tomato sandwich — white bread, English mustard — in seconds.

'Okay, then I'll go through that stuff over the weekend. Might be something there. Maybe he died of a heart attack, or AIDS, or something.'

'Well, someone killed him. We know that much.'

Harry finishes his coffee in a single gulp.

The wind blows a plastic bag against Arabella's ankles and she looks disgusted. 'Or aliens did it. Can we go?'

'Sure.' Harry leaves money on the table, putting the teapot on top of the notes to stop them blowing away. Pointing at the money for the benefit of the waitress, he leads Arabella towards Martin Place. Her blue-black hair blows across her eyes.

'Will we work on this in chambers on Sunday?'

'You can, Bella. I'll work at home. But can we have dinner together on Sunday night and see what we've got?'

'Be still, my beating heart. What are you doing tomorrow?'

Harry is standing on the kerb, waiting for a break in the traffic so that he can cross the road and collect his car from the sick judge's parking spot next to Sydney Hospital. The sheriff's men still let him use it when he's in town. 'Taking my father out for a drive. He won't enjoy it, and he probably won't know who I am, but I still have to do it.'

'I'd be happy to come.'

'I wouldn't wish that on you. Old men smell funny. Wait till I'm in a wheelchair.'

'I'd happily push your wheelchair.'

'So you say. I'll call you on Sunday night. Work hard.' And he sets off at a trot between a blue-and-white bus and a taxi, carrying the Globite. Arabella blows out her cheeks, gently shakes her head and turns on her very high heels — she must top six feet in those shoes — and walks down Martin Place to her chambers, where she catches up on other cases for a couple of hours before taking a taxi home to Elizabeth Bay, grilling Emmenthal on toast with mango chutney and going to bed, Classic FM playing softly beside her as she falls asleep.

On Saturday afternoon, the Jaguar drives Harry to see his father. He has made the journey so many times that he lapses into autopilot control, listening to European current affairs on the ABC's radio news network. At St Ives, a man with little children in his car, travelling in the left lane, tries at the last minute to force his way in front of Harry's car, but Harry implacably maintains his speed, looking straight ahead, and the other car is forced to yield. As he makes the turn at Turramurra, Harry checks the mirror and sees the man's agitated face. He follows the Jaguar all the way to the nursing home, tailgating.

Outside the nursing home, Harry parks in his usual spot and leaves the car. As he locks the door, he sees the man's car is still there, stationary behind him. Harry walks to the driver's door and stands there, silent, inviting the driver to do something, say something. The man lowers his window and opens his mouth to speak, but looks at the tall man standing above him in his Harris tweed jacket and corduroy trousers and thinks better of it. As Harry crosses between the two cars to walk into the building, the man drives away, his children's faces at the windows, staring at Harry.

He climbs the stairs with their figured pastel carpet past the striped pastel walls and finds Wallace Curry QC sitting in a pastel living room with the Saturday *Herald* spread across his knees, open at the editorial. Harry pulls up a chair with a floral pastel pattern in its upholstery.

'How are you, Dad?'

'Never better, sir.' He lifts the paper as if to read the leading article, and squints at it. Harry hands him his glasses from the table alongside. The old man puts them in his breast pocket. He, too, is in a tweed jacket, but with a checked Viyella shirt and a silk tie. Nothing is said for some minutes. Then Harry asks if his father would like a cup of tea, which he says he would, and so Harry asks a nurse for two cups. Again, there is silence between the two men until the tea and two Monte Carlo biscuits are placed on the side table. They sip the tea, still in silence, and the old man eats his biscuit fastidiously.

Harry decides not to offer to take his father for a drive.

For no reason that he would be able to explain, Harry recalls a monochrome photograph of his father in the family album: a dark-haired man in an old-fashioned woollen bathing costume, navy or black, with a white belt threaded through its loops. In profile, Brylcreemed hair and a disciplined moustache, looking out to sea. Short and stocky, but quite handsome in the style of Ronald Colman. Harry does not resemble him in the least.

Holidays. The family seemed always to take them at bizarre times — renting a house at Austinmer one cold Easter and being told to enjoy the beach, no other kids there. Staying in his father's cousin's house at Orange one Christmas. The timing always had to fit with Curry QC's big court cases, weeks or even months spent preparing and then leading a big team in an assault on the Taxation Commissioner for the benefit of some monolithic corporation that sold cigarettes or imported machine parts. Textbooks about import duty on the dining table. Discussion between his parents about 'refreshers' which, when he was little, Harry always thought of as scented towelettes such as they gave you on Ansett flights. It wasn't until he was fifteen that he understood it meant the reduced fee paid to counsel for subsequent days' appearance in court once a matter was being tried. The more refreshers the better. By the time Harry came to the Bar, everyone simply charged a daily fee. Even today's Legal Aid rates are a mere fraction of what Curry QC commanded twenty years ago.

Their tea drunk, the men look at each other.

'I suppose you have places to go, people to see?'

'You know how it is, Dad.'

'Chambers busy?' So it's one of his lucid days.

'Very.'

The old man nods and retreats into his memory of a long career, solicitors constantly demanding his advice or his representation. A steady supply of cheques from grateful clients.

'Will you be putting in for silk this year?'

'Not this year, no.'

'A good idea, though, if you're going on the bench.'

Harry laughs. 'Unlikely, Dad. You never did.'

'Couldn't afford it. Dreadful money. Suppose it still is?'

'Dreadful.' A pause, and Harry wonders if $300,000-plus a year, all expenses paid, is all that bad. 'You seem well, Dad. On top of things.' Harry recalls his last visit, when the old man had no idea who he was.

'Doing the crossword. Keeps the mind active.'

Harry collects the cups and puts them in an adjoining kitchen, then returns to kiss his father and descends to the foyer. Outside, he exhales and realises he was holding his breath all the way down the stairs.

There's no sign of the angry man when he unlocks the car.

On Sunday night, Harry doesn't phone Arabella — in chambers or at Elizabeth Bay — but she turns up at Erskineville anyway. Neither of them mentions his unreliability, or her unscheduled appearance. Arabella tells Harry she's as ready as she can be for the next day's trial. The case left undiscussed, he cooks them an omelette and opens a bottle of Wirra Wirra Church Block. They watch a BBC bonnet drama and at 10.30 Arabella drives herself home in her shiny two-door BMW.

Harry arrives first at Taylor Square, Darlinghurst, on Monday morning. The wind is blowing grit and pages of the *Sunday*

Telegraph across the forecourt of the Central Criminal Court building, and rolling empty takeaway coffee cups in arcs around the outdoor seats. Rain threatens and the state flag stands out from its mast on the lawn behind the hedge that effectively keeps secret the courthouse — which Harry has heard called 'Sydney's finest Greek revival building' — and its history. Everything from the original sittings of the High Court before it moved to Canberra, through the Charles Kingsford Smith Royal Commission, to the trial of Don Lane (late of the Channel Nine *Tonight* show) for inadvertently importing a single marijuana cigarette. And countless murder trials since then, not a few of which involved H Curry as defender. Jurors, or at least citizens summoned for jury duty, huddle about uncertainly, waiting to be told what to do. They are unknowingly mingling with, and indistinguishable from, the two antagonistic groups always found outside the courthouse before trials begin: the friends and family of the accused, and the friends and family of the crime victims.

Harry strides, as he has done so many times before, towards the barristers' robing room at the eastern end of the facade, and then realises he's not carrying his blue bag. The horsehair wig, the Bar jacket and gown, and the still-unlaundered jabots are in the spare bedroom at Erskineville. Harry veers away before pushing through the massive doors to join his former colleagues as they hang suit jackets in the battered lockers. Instead of entering the building, he consults the daily court list in a glass case on the exterior wall, and sees that the matter of the Queen against Christopher John Harris is to start at 10 a.m. in Court 5, in front of Justice Moses.

Neither Ms Williams nor Arabella has arrived yet, so

Harry enters the courtroom where he is greeted with a nod of recognition by the sheriff's officer, who is busy placing Bibles along the rail in front of the jury box and filling carafes with water for the witnesses and barristers. Bet they haven't washed the glasses, Harry thinks.

He sits in one of the pews set aside for the public, taking in the unaccustomed perspective as if examining the room for the first time as architecture rather than as his workplace. It strikes him that he has never seen the big room as it really is, but always operated in a zone of what mattered: the central cocoon of personalities, that irregular-sided figure, the cardinal points of which were himself at the centre, the judge opposite and above, the Crown prosecutor alongside him, and the two focal points of the witness in the box and the silent jury. Everything else was in a penumbra, as if unlit, the perimeters some vague cyclorama, out of focus.

His eyes descend from the clerestory, down the recently redecorated walls. All very authentic, in what is judged by the government architect's office to be heritage colours: parchment from the ceiling to about five metres from the floor, then thin bands of deep green above a solid green wall down another two metres, then thin bands of burnt umber above a solid coat of that colour all the way to the carpet — deep green with red clocks, reminding Harry of the sort of socks worn by government clerks. But all of it redolent of the rituals that have taken place here and around here for so many years, and that are still taking place. Today included. At least they aren't still hanging people in the old jail behind the courthouse buildings, only very bad paintings — it is now the National Art School.

The timber panelling gleams softly in the artificial light. There are descending tribunes of varnished pews on both sides of the room and in front of the bench, making little enclosed cubbies labelled with gold-lettered identifiers: Jurors in Waiting; Jury; Sheriff; Reporters; Associate; Witness; Governor of the Gaol; Inspector of Police. They should have one saying 'Judge', thinks Harry, for the avoidance of doubt — and one labelled 'Accursed' across the front of the dock, although there's never any uncertainty about that. The gold signwriting reminds Harry of the honour boards in the Shore assembly hall, only those were headed *Dux*, *Proxime Accessit*, and Captain of Boats.

Harry is reflecting on the trial judge's greatly elevated position and the British coat of arms in high-relief polychrome on the wall above. Soon after he was called to the Bar and decided on a life of crime, Harry developed an address to the jury that he used in hopeless cases; he is rehearsing now the familiar words in his head that he has, in his deep and confident voice, directed at so many juries over the years, including those in this very room:

May I ask you, ladies and gentlemen, to look above his Honour at the coat of arms?

The jurors always cooperated with this suggestion.

As you've already noticed, that's not *our* coat of arms — neither that of New South Wales, nor of Australia. No kangaroo, no emu. That is the British monarch's coat of arms, with its two mottos: *Honi soit qui mal y pense*; and across the bottom, *Dieu et mon droit*. We'll come back to what those mean in a moment. So, and particularly in these times when we speak of an Australian republic, what's that doing there? Well, it certainly isn't there to be decorative. That coat of arms represents the most important thing for you to consider when you decide this case. The verdict you reach. It reminds you of what you received as your birthright, or what was guaranteed to you when you became an Australian citizen — British justice. It's one element of our colonial heritage that nobody would wish to change.

Well, what does that mean, British justice? Much more than the wigs and gowns, and the bowing and scraping and all this formality and tradition. *Honi soit qui mal y pense* — meaning 'Evil be to he who evil thinks' ... in other words, Shame on this prosecution for twisting the facts as it has done, putting the worst possible meaning on what I submit to you was ...

And here, Harry inserts the words 'simply self-defence' or 'simply an honest mistake' or 'simply not the act of my client'.

And then, even more importantly as a statement of what British justice is, and setting out the rule you must follow: *Dieu et mon droit*, meaning 'God and my right hand'. Equally, 'God and my right' ... my client's right, and yours too should, God forbid, you ever be accused of a crime ... your fundamental legal right to be judged by a jury of your fellow Australians, with all their knowledge of the world out there, understanding that you don't have to prove yourself innocent. It's the Crown, with all the resources of the government, that must prove you guilty beyond any reasonable doubt.

That's the essential meaning of British justice. Australian justice. Our justice. The justice to which you, and my client, are entitled: my client stands before you, presumed to be innocent. He is entitled to the benefit of that presumption right to the end — unless and until this prosecution, with hard evidence, has proved beyond the shadow of any doubt that …

Harry pauses to consider what Arabella is going to say to the jury in her final address. What's Chris's defence? Reasonable doubt as to who struck the fatal blow? Reasonable doubt as to the cause of death? Sympathy for the disenfranchised and dispossessed? Something about the Stolen Generation? Perhaps not. And, just then, Arabella lays her hand on his shoulder and he looks up to see her, wigged and gowned and nervous.

'Different perspective back here,' she says.

Harry thinks she looks stunning. 'Indeed. Ready to go?'

'Well, the Crown's not here yet, and I want to talk to him about the order of his witnesses. They sent an email to my chambers this morning to say they have to put the pathologist in first, unless we object. Does it make any difference?'

'I dunno, Bella — did you find anything in his postmortem?'

'Maybe, but maybe it's unimportant. Let me try it — even if I'm wrong, it won't affect your strategy.'

'So I just have to trust you not to stuff it up?'

'Harry, I can't just be your parrot. I'm the one taking responsibility for Chris's liberty, and I have to back my own judgment — in the final analysis. I'm going to tell them we don't object to the changed order of witnesses.'

'Granted, Bella, it's your case. But you don't want to share whatever it was that you found?' He grins very slightly, but Arabella doesn't notice. She has seen the prosecution team enter the courtroom, and moves to speak to her opponent.

Harry isn't displeased. Arabella's right — she won't be able to excuse any error she makes by passing the buck to a non-practising strategist. And Moses J isn't going to let Harry into the arena. He'll be stuck here among the public, powerless.

By ten o'clock, the court is full, with the spectators — Harry included — shepherded off to one side, and the jury panel-in-waiting filling the rest of the seats. Murder trials can be lengthy, and a number of the citizens summoned for jury duty will not want to be kept away from work, or their long-planned holidays. For half an hour the judge hears applications from jurors to be excused, three of which he rejects. Harry scribbles a note — 'Make sure you challenge those three, they don't want to be here' — and beckons to Ms Williams. She takes the folded page and hands it to her counsel. Arabella reads it, turns to Harry, and nods. She thought of that anyway, but she well understands that Harry needs to be involved in the decision-making.

The associate stands and arraigns Chris, who stands to hear the charge.

'Christopher John Harris, you are charged by that name that you did on 28 December murder Andrei Jaruzelski at Walsh Bay. How say you — are you guilty or not guilty?'

The accused looks at the jury, fear all over his face. 'Not guilty.' Spoken so softly they can hardly hear him.

Arabella stands to announce her appearance. 'May it please your Honour, I appear for Mr Harris.'

Harry has insisted that she never refer to her own client as 'the accused'. 'You're not accusing him,' he says. 'Let the Crown do that. The jury shouldn't think of him as some sort of abstract. The more human he is, the better for his defence. Try to make them think of him as Chris.'

'Thank you, Ms Engineer. Empanel the jury.'

Justice Moses doesn't know Arabella, but his associate's job is to bring him the names of counsel, so that the fiction of judicial familiarity can be maintained. He certainly knows Harry.

The process is quite swift. This isn't America, where jury selection can take weeks, with jurors being interrogated as to their attitudes on racial minorities or the death penalty or the religion of the accused. Arabella makes a quick note as each juror's number is called — names are withheld to prevent media contact — and the juror makes the short walk from the pews to the jury box: MW (middle-aged woman), OM (older man), YW (young woman). She draws a tick beside those she'll accept, and crosses against two OWs. Too old, she assumes, and too compliant to the dictates of the MMs, who characteristically attempt to dominate the decision-making. When twelve people fill the jury box, the judge's associate repeats their numbers and they stand to take the Bible or indicate that they will make an affirmation. This is the moment when the opposing counsel voice their challenges, and there is a kind of breath-holding among the lawyers. Getting challenges right isn't as easy as it looks. Arabella turns to her client and raises her eyebrows. *Anyone you don't want?* she silently enquires. He shakes his head.

The prosecutor rejects two young men wearing T-shirts, one

with an anti-war slogan on it, and Arabella challenges the two blue-rinses. Four more numbers are drawn out of a box and read out. Two youngish women and two retired-looking men take their places. No challenges when they are brought to the book to be sworn or affirmed. The jury is set, eight male and four female. Harry's own view is that Arabella will do best with a jury of mainly men.

Moses J sends the balance of the jury panel away, and makes a short speech to the jury as empanelled about housekeeping matters. Then his Honour launches the trial.

'Yes, Mr Crown?' The judge uncaps his pen to note the main points of the prosecution's opening address.

'May it please your Honour. Members of the jury ...'

Arabella and her solicitor are taking a full note, even of the part where the prosecutor explains what murder is. As the accusations against him are laid out, their client is darting panicky stares all around the room, as if planning to leap from the dock and run past the police guarding him out into the Taylor Square traffic. Harry is looking at the back of the Crown's head. As the journeyman employee of the Director of Public Prosecutions drones on, Harry mentally counting the mispronunciations and grammatical blunders, rain starts to beat against the clerestory windows, and the electric lights, which hang from the ceiling, burn brighter. After an hour, the prosecution's opening draws to a close and the judge notes the time.

'We'll take the short adjournment. Members of the jury, we usually break for a cup of tea at about 11.30, then we take luncheon from one to two o'clock — you will be given sandwiches — and we adjourn for the day at four.' The court officer instructs all present to rise, and the scarlet-gowned judge sweeps out through his own door. Then the jury are led out, and the public retreat to the foyer. It's too wet to stand outside. The smokers are unhappy.

Harry joins Arabella at the Bar table and sits beside her. Unlike the defence, the prosecution have their own room and their own electric jug. There isn't time to cross the road to a cafe, and the instant coffee and tea bags available at a shiny urn managed by some well-meaning volunteer is unappealing, so the defence team drink water and say little. Arabella, tentatively, raises a problem.

'Harry, Moses looked pretty unhappy about you passing us notes.'

'A note. Anyway, I'm going upstairs for the rest of the morning. You won't have to worry about me.'

'Upstairs?'

Harry gestures to the far end of the room, where there is a little-used mezzanine gallery. 'If I need to communicate, I can do so at lunchtime. The pathologist's going to be in chief until then, anyway.'

Ms Williams wants to speak to Arabella about the admissibility of the postmortem report, so Harry moves back. The two women have their heads over a document for some time, and eventually, as people start to fill the courtroom again, Harry catches Arabella's eye and points at the ceiling before leaving the room to mount the stairs. He climbs the spiral staircase, emerges some metres above the action, and takes a seat in the centre of the public gallery, the only person there. When the judge resumes the trial, the first thing he notices is Harry's presence, at a level even higher than his own. He is displeased.

Moses J is the Supreme Court judge whose question Harry

had answered with what he took to be an obscenity, which was causal of his separation now from the fray.

The government pathologist is a beefy man with a thick Glaswegian accent, which is enough to raise Arabella's hackles, and a suit two sizes too small — all exposed shirt cuffs and straining buttons. He is difficult even for the prosecutor to handle, because he exhibits a high opinion of the dignity of his own written expression in the postmortem report, which impenetrable jargon the judge allows him to read onto the record. Plainly, the jury hasn't a clue what he's talking about, and the efforts of the Crown to have him put it 'in plain language, that the jury can understand' provoke only an uncomprehending intransigence from the witness. This unedifying spectacle drags on until ten past one, when all present are happy to head off for something to eat.

Arabella reassures Chris that nothing harmful has happened, at least not yet, and he is taken down to the cells for an hour. The defence team runs across the road through the rain to the barristers' habitual greasy spoon, once responsible for the halting of a trial for two days because the prosecutor and three defence barristers all contracted food poisoning from the soup. They take comfort from the intractability of the expert and the opacity of his evidence.

'What you'll have to be aware of,' Harry says, 'is that Moses isn't entitled to explain the medical evidence in his own words when he comes to sum up, just because the Crown couldn't get the pathologist to do it. There's a recent case on it in the Court of Appeal reports — I read it at the weekend — it's a civil matter and one of the parties is called Singh, and the appeal was upheld because the judge used his own experience of medical evidence in personal injury cases to interpret the expert reports. So make sure he doesn't do it.'

Arabella smiles broadly and squeezes Harry's arm. 'So you're still reading the reports?'

Ms Williams looks doubtful. 'But if that's a civil case, it wouldn't apply, would it?'

'Oh, yes it would,' says Arabella. 'Even more so. If you can't do that in a civil matter, you certainly can't do it in a murder trial.'

'Will that fit with whatever it is you've found in the postmortem?' Harry asks.

'Well, we'll have to wait and see, but I think it can stand alone, Harry.'

'I can't wait.'

'Singh, was it? We may be related by marriage.'

They finish up, Harry pays for the lunch, and the solicitor forgets to thank him. He notes that. The rain has eased, and they cross lawfully at the traffic lights.

Before the court is reconvened, Arabella asks the sheriff's officer to hold the jury back for a moment. She has a question she wants to raise with the judge. When he comes out, she rises.

'Is there some problem, Ms Engineer?'

'Not at all, your Honour. What I wanted to do was to let you have a recent authority relevant to Dr Maconachie's evidence. Your Honour may not yet be aware of it.'

'Yes, Ms Engineer. I have been thinking about that. It's going to require some explanation for the benefit of the jury.'

'That's the issue, your Honour. Mr Crown having completed the evidence in chief, it's not the responsibility of the defence to seek explanations from the witness of all that technical material. And, of course, neither does it fall to your Honour to assist the prosecution by providing your own interpretation.'

Justice Moses looks up at the lone figure of Harry in the gallery. He glares, quite sure who's to blame for this slight. 'Isn't that precisely my job? To ensure that the jury fully understands the expert evidence?'

'With respect, no. That's the responsibility of the learned prosecutor. May I hand up to your Honour a copy of *Strinic v Singh* in the Court of Appeal? It's just been published.'

The judge nods, and Arabella hands a sheaf of papers to the court officer, who hands it to the associate, who hands it to the judge. Arabella gives a second copy to her opponent. The judge and he start to read.

'Your Honour will find the relevant part begins on page seven.' Arabella would have to say she's enjoying this. Harry looks down to hide his grin. The foxy bugger! She knew that case all along — she's even brought copies of it to court. And all she did was make a joke when he told her about the judgment. Some girl.

Moses puts the superior court's judgment down, making no further reference to his near blunder, narrowly averted by Arabella (for which he should be and is, in fact, grateful — being unloaded upon from a great height by the Court of Criminal Appeal is no pleasure, least of all for a Supreme Court justice who is paid to keep abreast of his betters' rulings). District Court judges may be expected to be 'quick, courteous and wrong', as a member of the House of Lords once put it, but expectations of red judges such as himself are considerably higher. He takes another look at Harry, who stares back, expressionless. Despite the construction of his bench, Moses thinks that he is being looked down on, and there's nothing he can do about it. To a man who habitually refers to it as '*my* court', it's distressing. He has the jury brought back, and the pathologist put back in the witness box.

'Cross-examination, Ms Engineer?'

'Thank you, your Honour.' She turns to the witness, who wasn't following the previous exchange. 'Dr Maconachie, your report suggests that this man drowned, doesn't it?'

'Drowned?' The Scots accent is stronger than ever.

'Yes, drowned. You found water in the lungs, didn't you?'

'Water?'

Arabella rolls her eyes at the jury. 'You have read your postmortem report, I assume?'

A hostile glare in response, but no words.

'I'll have you handed a copy. Turn to page three, please, under the heading "Pulmonary System". Do you have that?'

He finds it with some difficulty, flicking back and forth through the pages.

'Please read it to yourself.'

'On examination, the lungs —'

'To yourself, please, doctor.'

Harry could swear that the man's lips move as he silently examines his own document.

'What was the question?'

'If he had water in his lungs, he must have been breathing when he was first submerged, surely.'

'Yes.'

'And if he was breathing, he was not dead when he first entered the water?'

'Yes.'

'So he drowned.'

'Presumably, I suppose.'

'Then it cannot be the case, can it, doctor, that he died of a fractured skull and his dead body was later disposed of by dumping it in the harbour.'

'But I was there right after the body was pulled out of the harbour.'

'Perhaps you're not listening, doctor. I don't suggest that he wasn't dropped into the harbour, but that when that happened, he must still have been breathing.'

A long, long pause during which the expert looks hard at the unresponsive prosecutor before answering. 'If he had seawater in his lungs, he must have drowned.'

'And you analysed the water?'

'I had it analysed, yes.'

'And the analysis showed salt water, didn't it?'

Another long pause. The witness drops his eyes. 'It did.'

'I'm sorry, could you repeat that a little louder? The jury may not have heard you.'

'It did.'

Again, Justice Moses looks up at Harry, who looks right back at him. Harry thinks, Why's he looking at me? This is nothing to do with me. It's all her own work, and bloody good work it is, too.

Just then, Arabella turns away from the witness and looks at Harry — and winks.

'I notice the time, your Honour. Would that be a convenient point at which to adjourn?'

'Ten o'clock tomorrow, members of the jury. I'm going to assume, Ms Engineer, that you've finished with this witness.' She nods, and the pathologist is excused.

Nine o'clock that night, day one of the *Queen v Harris*. The rain has started again, and is washing down the windows of Arabella's flat. All the lights are on, and they have just finished reading eighty pages of the day's trial transcript of the prosecutor's turgid opening and Dr Maconachie's evidence.

'Why doesn't the Crown throw in the towel, Harry? I mean, all the evidence can prove now — given the pathologist's stuff-up — is that Chris thought he was disposing of a dead body. Honest and reasonable mistake.'

'Not so fast, Batman. They've got Chris confessing to bashing his skull in with an iron bar, and then dropping him in the drink. The jury can still find him guilty of manslaughter.'

'Oh. Causing death by an unlawful and dangerous act.'

'Correct. It ain't over till it's over.'

'But it wouldn't be murder because Chris had no intention of drowning him – no *mens rea*?'

'An essential element.'

'And, of course, your friend the judge can sentence him to exactly the same sentence he would have given him for murder, can't he?'

'And will, if he can.'

'Same difference then.'

Neither says anything for several minutes. Harry drinks his coffee and looks at the rain. He stands up and walks to the window, trying to see through the darkness, speaking over his shoulder. 'Your problem remains the alleged confession. If you can get them to disbelieve that, the Crown's got nothing, not even manslaughter. If Chris did no more than assist in what he thought was the disposal of a dead body, he can't be convicted because they didn't dispose of a dead body. If he believed the Pom was dead, he lacks the mental intention that the Crown has to prove he had.'

'So it's the Guru or nothing?'

'Your Honour puts it better than I could ever do.'

Arabella goes to the kitchen. 'Can I buy you a drink?'

'I hope you don't intend to have your wicked way with me.'

'Chance would be a fine thing.'

An awkward silence follows. Arabella takes short, shallow breaths and decides to ask. 'Please stay with me tonight, Harry.'

He looks at her beautiful face. 'I haven't got a clean shirt for tomorrow.'

'I bought you one.'

He smiles. 'I trust you bought a tie, too. I can't wear the same one tomorrow.'

Arabella throws a cushion at his head.

Tuesday morning is cold, with a light breeze at Darlinghurst. But the sky is Wedgwood blue and cloudless. When Arabella and Harry alight from the taxi outside the Courthouse Hotel, mynah birds are chasing each other into the hedge behind the railings along Oxford Street. Fewer spectators have shown up for the second day of the trial, and the atmosphere in the courtroom is quite different. The excitement of the first day of any murder trial has gone, and it feels like a workplace.

Day two is spent calling to the witness box a series of drinkers from the Palisade Hotel. One by one, their names are called and they amble into the court under the gaze of the jury to take their seats. All appear old before their time. All are alcoholics. Someone has cleaned them up a bit and they seem presentable enough. The police haven't been able to get them along to court in the order planned, with the result that the prosecutor begins his evidence in chief by saying, 'You are Kevin Joseph Burke?' only to be answered 'No'. After several such confusions, Moses J suggests to Mr Crown that he should let the witnesses give their own names, and then find the evidence statement for that witness before proceeding. The prosecutor agrees, relieved.

The drinking witnesses mostly tell the same story: the Pom was universally disliked, being a bludger. He had as much money as any of them, but never paid his way. He was in the public bar of the Palisade on the night of 28 December, and so was Chris Harris. Chris left with his two mates when everyone was chucked out, and the Pom followed them towards the wharves. Nobody saw where they went, but everyone knew they were camping there.

Arabella has offered to accept the evidence of any one of the drinking witnesses without the need for formal corroboration, because Chris doesn't deny any of it. She doesn't cross-examine any of them, thereby conceding that there is no contest about events at the pub. But the police have spent many thousands of dollars finding the witnesses, taking statements from them, even bringing some of them back from the country or interstate for the trial, and they have to justify all that expenditure. So they are paraded before the increasingly restless jury to remember, in greater or lesser detail and not without contradicting each other on certain essential points, what they saw and heard. Some of them are so hopeless that they deny the Pom was even there. Others, with a sense of loyalty to the brotherhood, deny that Chris was there. It would have been wiser for the Crown to take up Arabella's offer, but the day drags on with very little established that is controversial. So much for day two.

Had he been asked, Harry would have agreed to stay another night at Arabella's, but she announces over a coffee with him and Ms Williams that she's off to a Women Lawyers' dinner at the Hilton. Harry finds himself a little miffed, and heads home to Erskineville where he cooks chops and listens to Telemann.

Day three is the big one — make or break. Today the Crown will close its case, unless it can produce O'Reilly and Willingale, Chris's companions on the night the Pom died. Or, more correctly, the night before he drowned. Harry and Arabella have spent many hours preparing for the eventuality that the men, now serving their sentences for the lesser offence, may change their minds and agree to give evidence against Chris. After all, it's a day out of jail. Not only that, but they were given a degree of leniency in their sentences on the presumption that they would be prosecution witnesses at Chris's trial.

The judge wants to know what's planned before he brings the jury back and resumes the evidence.

'We have one witness who will give evidence of a confessional statement made by the accused, your Honour, and possibly two more eyewitnesses.'

'The confession was, you told the jury, made to a man outside the Matthew Talbot hostel a few days after the death, is that right? Is this that witness?'

'It is, your Honour.'

'And the other two — the possibilities?'

'Mr Willingale and Mr O'Reilly, your Honour. The co-offenders.'

'Have they given statements to the police?'

'No, your Honour, they haven't.'

'Ms Engineer, what's your attitude to that?'

'We would object in the strongest terms, your Honour, to the Crown attempting to call witnesses when we have no notice of what they may say in evidence. Your Honour would not permit trial by ambush.'

Moses J is a man like any other, and as prone as any to admire and even wish to please a beautiful woman. Further should he be grateful to Arabella for stopping him before he fell into embarrassing error by making himself an expert medical witness, as he had intended to do, in order to render sensible the otherwise impenetrable and incomprehensible evidence of Dr Maconachie. Arabella well knows that if this judge had to answer truthfully, he would have to say that he places greater importance on his own judicial reputation than on the Crown's ability to bring to justice the alleged killer of a person of no importance.

'I have a duty to ensure fairness to the accused, don't I, Mr Crown?'

'As your Honour does to the Crown.'

'It's a matter of my discretion, isn't it? I can first allow you to call these witnesses and get them to tell their story without the jury being present.'

'That would certainly inform the defence of the case they have to meet.'

'Or I can refuse you leave to call them, on the ground that you are seeking to take the defence by surprise.'

'Yes, your Honour.'

'Are these men here? Do you have them in the cells?'

'No, your Honour, they're still at Long Bay and refusing to come to court. They would have to be brought here once your Honour ordered it.'

'Brought here by force?' Moses looks very doubtful.

'I suppose. If necessary. Reasonable force.'

It doesn't take long for Moses to decide that the jury will hear from neither Mr Willingale nor Mr O'Reilly. It feels strange, exercising his discretion for once against the Crown. He decides he quite likes it, and muses that it won't do his reputation any harm, being well aware that he's known as pro-prosecution, and a heavy sentencer.

So Mr Crown calls his last witness, the Guru. The legal aid solicitor is later to say that had the prosecution engaged a theatrical agent to find them someone whom the jury would instantly dismiss as a nutcase, they could have done no better: when the court officer intones three times the name of Bernard Barry Quinn, the man led into court looks as if he is going to a fancy dress ball as Rasputin, the Mad Monk. His eyes, to Harry, appear to be revolving in opposite directions; he sports a straggly beard, matted with food; his clothes are so filthy they could stand up by themselves; and his feet are bare. He glares at the jury and smiles at Chris as he passes the dock.

The judge leans forward. 'Swear the witness, please.'

The court officer guides the Guru into the witness box and tells him to remain standing. 'Will you take an oath or an affirmation?'

'An oath, of course.'

'Do you swear by almighty God that the evidence you shall give will be the truth, the whole truth, and nothing but the truth? Please say "I do".'

'I swear.'

To Harry's surprise, the Guru is remarkably normal. Lucid, even, or so it seems from his vantage point in the gallery. As he looks down, listening to the evidence, Chris swivels around in the dock, looking up at Harry and beckoning him to come down. Harry does so, and Chris signals to him that he needs a pencil and paper. Harry indicates to the solicitor, and she hands her client a block of yellow Post-its, on which he starts writing a series of tiny notes.

By the morning-tea adjournment, the Guru has given the jury evidence that he approached Chris outside the homeless hostel and expressed his anger that Willingale and O'Reilly were arrested for the murder, but that he knows Chris did it. After the break, the prosecutor returns to that evidence.

'And what did he say, if anything, in reply to that?' the Crown asks.

'He told me that he did it, and that he would kill me too if I told anyone else.'

'I object.'

'Yes, Ms Engineer? What's the objection?'

'Form, your Honour. The witness is not giving evidence of what my client said, but his summary of what he says was the effect of his words. It must be given in the first person.'

Arabella is making a mistake, Harry thinks, because all she is doing is getting the witness to give the evidence in two separate forms. Twice as effective with the jury.

'A very technical objection, Ms Engineer, but I'm sure you can handle it, Mr Crown.'

'Yes, your Honour. Mr Quinn, will you please try to use the words Mr Harris spoke to you, as if you were speaking lines in a play?'

'He said: "Yes, I killed him. And I'll do the same to you if you tell."'

Harry groans inwardly.

The accused takes little notice of all this. He's still furiously writing notes, peeling them off the little pad and lining them up along the edge of the dock. Then he gathers them together and hands them in a sticky bundle to the solicitor, pointing at Harry. She hands them to him, and he separates and reads each one.

Harry looks at the clock. No adjournment is due for more than an hour, and Moses has just called on Arabella to start her cross-examination.

'Bella!' he calls her over.

'Please pardon me a moment, your Honour.' Arabella walks over to the rail that divides the body of the court from the legal arena.

'Bella,' Harry whispers. 'Chris has given me these notes. You're going to have to read them before you cross-examine — we have to get the jury to treat the Guru as a loony.'

'He went pretty well in chief.'

'Yes, he did. But this stuff's good, if you can get him going with it.'

'Harry, he isn't going to give me an adjournment to prepare my cross-examination.'

'He has to. Tell him we haven't really had a proper conference with the client — all we could do was speak to him for half an hour at the jail on Friday. This stuff is all new.'

Moses seems no longer to want to impress Arabella with his fairness. Her application for an hour to prepare is brusquely rejected, with the judge looking pointedly at Harry and declaring over Arabella's protests that the defence has had eighteen months to prepare its cross-examination. The prosecution team looks gratified. Moses is back in character.

Harry beckons again to Arabella. 'Okay, bugger him. Just take it very slowly. Think each question out before you ask it, and make sure the jury follow. If you can show them he's Captain Rats, they won't wear the confession. I'll hand them to you, one by one.' And he hands her the first tiny piece of yellow paper bearing Chris's scrawl.

Arabella takes a deep breath. 'Well, Mr Quinn, you've certainly had a colourful life.'

'True.'

'You say, don't you, that you spent five years walking across the deserts of India in the footsteps of Jesus?'

'That's right.'

Arabella looks at the jury and asks the next question with her eyebrows raised, still looking at the jury. 'I wasn't aware that Jesus ever visited India.'

'No, not many people know that. I do, however.'

Arabella takes the next Post-it note from Harry's hand and reads it. She turns back to the jury, not making eye contact with the Guru. 'And you also say, don't you, that for those five years, you had nothing to eat or drink?'

'Yes.'

'But can that be true?' Still looking at the jury.

'Yes. The Buddha had only one grain of rice a year.'

'That's five square meals more than you had in that period, isn't it?'

Most of the jury laugh. They're getting into it, Arabella gratefully notes. I mustn't make fun of him, she tells herself. Make him do that. She accepts another yellow note. 'They call you the Guru, don't they?'

'It's an honour.'

'But why? Are you a teacher of mystical secrets?'

'I am, yes.'

Arabella is handed the rest of the notes, but can see nothing useful in them. The judge is getting impatient. Arabella's mind races. She thinks she can see a line of questions that could work, but she knows that if they don't, Harry will be furious with her for breaking the first rule of cross-examination: never ask a question to which you don't already know the answer. You're handing the witness a blank cheque and a pen.

'Have you finished, Ms Engineer?'

'No, your Honour. One moment, if you'd be so kind.' She smiles at the jury, who are in no hurry. They're quite enjoying this. In the jury room, the men have already expressed their admiration for the defence barrister, but the women are less enthusiastic. Jealousy may have something to do with that. 'It's not a beauty contest in there,' one of them sniffs.

Arabella decides to jump off the high board. With a quick 'Here goes' look back at Harry, she starts. 'Guru, if I may call you that?'

'Thank you.'

'Guru, would I be right in assuming that you are something of an expert in non-verbal communication?'

'You would.'

'Body language, that sort of thing?'

'Body language can be very eloquent to those who can read it.'

'Including yourself among them?'

'Indeed.'

'What about auras?'

'Yes. What about them?'

'I assume that you are skilled in seeing, and reading, people's auras?'

'I can do that.'

'For instance, can you see my aura?'

'I can, Ms Engineer.'

'I don't want you to read it, Guru.' Everyone in court laughs at that, and Arabella goes on. 'Let me ask you this: when you met Mr Harris outside the Matthew Talbot Hostel, did you take note of his aura?'

'I always do that. I can't avoid it.'

'And did you read his body language?'

'Of course. As I said, I am expert in non-verbal communication. It is where you get the truth. People tell lies, but non-verbal communication is where I can read the truth, whatever they say in words.'

Ah well, Arabella thinks, in for a penny, in for a pound. 'So what you tell the jury is this, isn't it? It wasn't any words actually spoken by my client that told you he had killed the Pom and would kill you too, if you told his secret — you read that in his body language, and from his aura?'

'Precisely,' the Guru answers proudly.

Arabella whirls around to look at Harry.

'Sit down,' he says, loudly enough for the jury and judge to hear. Arabella sits, shaking, too frightened to look up.

There is a flurry at the other end of the table, and the prosecutor is heard to say to his solicitor, 'No. Leave it.' The judge asks if the witness may be excused, and no one raises any objection. The Rasputin-like figure proudly strides out of the court, pausing beside the dock to shake Chris's hand, with the jurors trying to suppress their giggles. Arabella is still looking down, still shaking. Has that done it?

'Do you close your case, Mr Crown?'

'That is the prosecution case, your Honour.'

Moses is obviously conflicted. The last witness has turned a murder trial into a freak show, and he has to restore the proprieties. He sends the jury out for an early lunch. When they are clear, he turns to the prosecutor. 'The way I see it, Mr Crown, is that your last witness effectively withdrew his evidence of a confessional statement. Do you agree with that?'

'Unhappily, your Honour, I would have to accept that that was the effect of his answer. I cannot contend that any admission was ever made.'

'And what does that leave you with?'

A short and inaudible (to the defence) argument takes place between the Crown and his instructing solicitor before he straightens and addresses the court. 'I have to accept that your Honour must direct the jury to acquit the accused.'

Arabella is overcome by euphoria. Some defenders slave all their careers and never win an acquittal for murder, but she's going to do it in her first ever.

'Is there anything you wish to say, Ms Engineer?'

'Certainly not,' Harry is heard to say.

'I don't wish to talk your Honour out of it,' Arabella smiles at him.

And that's how the trial ends. Chris is released, there being no other charges against him, and the team forms a group on the tarmac in front of the six massive yellow sandstone columns holding up the building's pediment, watching the paid-off jury head for the taxi rank and bus stop. Two men come over to shake Chris's hand and look shyly at his defender.

'Am I shivering because we won, or because it's cold?' Arabella asks, her blue bag at her feet.

'You're shivering because you know what'll happen to you if you ever again ask a question to which you don't know the answer.'

'But I did know the answer — I read his body language!'

'If you can read mine, you must know how I'd respond to that.'

The victorious client is staring all about himself at the free world at Taylor Square, still having difficulty coming to terms with his acquittal. The cold breeze is to blame for his shivering, which is obvious to all. He has only the flannelette shirt and jeans in which he was arrested, and is hugging himself to keep warm. There has been no one to support him through the trial — no friend, no family member — and there is no one to take him home now. Harry wants to know what he's going to do.

'Go back to the jail.'

'Why, for God's sake?'

'My stuff's there.'

'What stuff?' Harry asks.

'Jumper, some trainers, cigarettes.'

Arabella is amazed. 'You don't want to go back there, surely?'

'Have to.'

'No, you don't,' she says. 'Where will you stay tonight?'

'Matt Talbot, I suppose.'

'Chris,' says Harry. 'You can't stay in Sydney. Those coppers are very bad losers. They'll fit you up with something else. There must be somewhere you can go.'

'Got relations at Kempsey, but how do I get there?'

'Train, mate. You can afford it, and you shouldn't worry about a few clothes. You can buy new stuff.'

'No money, mate.'

'What do you mean, Chris? You were on remand, not convicted, so they had to go on paying your dole money into your account for the whole eighteen months you were at Long Bay. You'd have plenty of money.'

A rueful look from Chris. 'No, mate.'

'No?'

'No. The cops who arrested me took my key card, and they made me give them the PIN. They've been taking the dough out every fortnight. They do it to all of us.'

Arabella is outraged. The solicitor nods knowingly, and Harry shakes his head. 'Jesus Christ!'

Harry pulls his wallet out of his jacket and removes four fifty-dollar notes. 'You take this, get a cab to Central, and catch the next train to Kempsey. I want you out of Sydney tonight. You can get some clothes when you get up there.'

Chris takes the money with no particular show of gratitude. He folds it and puts it in his jeans pocket. As if having second thoughts, he holds his hand out to Harry and they shake. 'Thanks very much for everything,' he says.

'Don't thank me, mate. She did it.'

Chris turns to Arabella, but doesn't know what to say. 'Good on you, miss. You too,' he says to the solicitor. They all smile at him, and he walks out through the open iron gate.

The solicitor speaks. 'He'll take that money straight to the pub.'

'If that's what he wants,' says Harry.

'Harry,' says Arabella, 'we have to do something about them stealing his dole! Report it to Internal Affairs, or the Police Integrity Commission.'

'Nothing we can do, Bella. They've been doing that to prisoners since the Rum Corps ran this town. Let's go over to the pub. If Chris is there, maybe he'll buy us a beer.'

Travelling South

High summer in the Snowy Mountains. Bushfire season, and a high wind in the high country. Somewhere out the back of Delegate, where the electricity authority has negligently failed to inspect its power poles for three years, perhaps five, one of those poles — carrying high-voltage lines across the drought-stricken sheep paddocks — has all but rotted through at the bottom, and the weight of the cables swinging in the southerly is pulling it, pulling it rhythmically. After a day of heavy wind, the pole shears off, and its length topples. But the power cables don't part, and the heavy top of the pole, with its cross-trees, metalwork and insulators, simply bounces, pivoting where the ragged base contacts the ground. The whole remains supported by the poles that still stand to the north and south of the failure.

Running east–west beneath the power lines is a paddock fence of the usual kind: two strands of barbed wire, then rabbit mesh fixed to fencing wire, strung between steel star pickets and hardwood strainers.

The 11,000-volt lines hit the paddock fence each time the pole bounces, and a shower of sparks explodes at the point of metal-to-metal contact. From early in this process, a grassfire ignites but the sparks keep coming. The fire burns, with the wind behind it, across three paddocks, and into the snow gums. Pushed north by the strengthening blow, the bushfire fans out and eventually destroys forty kilometres of country in a broadening triangle that begins at the fallen pole. Livestock, homesteads, farm buildings, fences, tractors are all lost — but no human lives. At least, not on the farms or grazing properties.

Bushfire brigades from the entire Snowy Mountains region and well into Victoria are called out but find themselves powerless, and terrified. They work in the dark in country so rough, rocky and steep, with a wind so strong, that three woefully inexperienced brigades find themselves cut off and praying that they won't die in their trucks. The prayers of only two of the three brigades are answered. Caught on a narrow fire trail at the bottom of a rocky gully, the Black Lake brigade's driver can't turn the truck around and, as the fire front races towards them up the gully, he decides he can only try to punch through the flames with all the speed he can muster from the lumbering tanker, and emerge beyond the fire. He tells his crew to get on the floor and cover themselves, puts the engine in first gear, and flattens the accelerator. At first, they make good progress, bucking and twisting on the rough trail. The steering wheel responds to their encounters with stones and stumps so violently that it threatens to break the young driver's wrists; yet he keeps his vehicle pointed at the flames, which form a wall twenty metres high. But then the smoke cloud engulfs and blinds him, and his truck slams into a huge tree and comes to rest, steam spurting from its ruptured radiator. He shouts to the crew to follow him, leaps from the cab, covering his head, and runs through the fire. His stunned and disoriented crew never make it out of the cab. Four men die in that gully and the sole survivor is catastrophically burned.

* * *

East of the bushfire, on the coast, is Eden. The southerly gale is blowing there, too, and no one went out fishing today. In the public bar of the Australasia Hotel, trawlermen are drinking schooners of beer, as they have been all day, and now that it's dark they watch television coverage of the fire. Despite its proximity, they feel uninvolved. Very few of them are really locals, and the people up there on the Monaro are nothing to do with them, anyway. It reminds one of the men of watching the second plane fly into the World Trade Center on 9/11 — just a television phenomenon, nothing to do with real life. A spectacle. All the same, the drinkers are affected by it. Tempers shorten, and a group of young Danish backpackers desert the pool table and leave the pub, anticipating violence from these hard-looking men, many of whom have knives on their belts and beer and blood in their eyes.

At the adjoining pool table, one of the players — a deckhand by the look of his leathery face — puts his glass on the edge of the table and heads for the lavatory, telling the other players to wait for him to take his next shot. A huge drunken timberworker who has been watching their game and baiting the players asks the remaining group, 'You reckon AntiCold'd be a good ride? Reckon I could ride him? Eh?'

When they ignore him, he moves from the table and positions himself to one side of the door to the gents. He waits there, and when the man, whose name is Dean Antico, not AntiCold, emerges the giant leaps on his back, wrapping powerful arms around the smaller man's neck and shoulders. They wrestle, and the deckhand tries to throw his aggressor off. Without success.

He staggers under the man's weight towards the pool table, still twisting and struggling. One of the giant's forearms is across his throat, cutting off the air. The attacker has both knees bent, keeping his feet off the floor, so Antico bears all his weight, and is buckling. He frees one arm, and grabs at his glass. The beer spills over the blue felt of the table, but he succeeds in getting his fingers around the glass, and brings it down hard on the edge. It smashes, leaving him holding a jagged base. The struggling man slashes at the upper arm that is crushing his neck, and the drunk releases him, bellowing in pain. Four or five drinkers leap on the drunk and hold him on the floor, bleeding and roaring.

The publican is already on the phone to the police station. The broken glass and all its pieces disappear. An ambulance arrives first, but the paddy wagon isn't far behind. The deckhand is handcuffed and taken out.

Seven pigeons, no, eight, clatter past the open window in a steep diagonal dive from Harry's left to his right. First thing in the morning and the old girl's feeding them stale bread again, three floors below in the square. Except that the square in Lucca is oval in shape, and encircled by tenement buildings of roughly matching height. Harry's already stripped the bed and packed his bag, and is checking the apartment now for any forgotten items. The next holidaymaker is welcome to the paperbacks — Elmore Leonard and Henry James — but the opera CDs are coming home with him. Nothing else? No. He pulls the shutters closed and latches them, then shuts the window.

Leaving the keys on the table, Harry bangs the front door shut and descends the stone stairs to ground level, where the tiny scarlet Fiat still stands beside the No Parking sign where he left it last night. The car doesn't seem to have been booked, but that wouldn't make any difference anyway. His bag goes into the ridiculous boot and his linen jacket is draped on the empty passenger's seat. Harry climbs behind the wheel, feeling not for the first time like a tall clown in a midget car at the circus. His thighs fit beneath the wheel only with the greatest difficulty. Maybe the diesel in the tank will get him to Fiumicino, and maybe it won't. And so what, if it doesn't? It's not just regret that his three weeks are up; Harry is depressed, and unable to discern any benefit from his escape from Australia. Maybe it would have been a very different matter if he'd let Arabella join him in Italy.

Arabella's plane has already left Heathrow, heading for Dubai and a meeting with Harry before they fly the last leg, to Sydney, together. Her feelings as they turn south-east and trundle over the English coast are nothing like Harry's. She feels the kind of happiness that she knows is hers alone … no one else on the plane is feeling this. No regrets at all about saying goodbye to her parents and her sisters as they waved from the back seat of the Vauxhall. It was pretty well impossible to explain to her mother that she could stay no longer, that she was meeting her friend — her man friend — in Dubai. A man who holidayed separately from Arabella. Married? Not married. Never married, no children, also a barrister. His family? Yes, very good family. She smiles and accepts a glass of champagne from an over-friendly attendant. Happy, really very happy.

Harry joins the autostrada just south of Lucca, and in a tick over half an hour he's passing south of Florence. Speeding, of course, but so's everyone; this is Italy. He's gaining a measure of respect for the little red car, as are several BMW drivers and a *Tifoso* in a distressed Ferrari struggling in Harry's wake as he accelerates away from a toll plaza. Once he moves across to the A1, it's pretty well a straight shot down to Rome, barring accidents. As he drives, Harry spreads the Michelin map across the steering wheel and adds up the distances: 283 kilometres to go. At 120 kilometres per hour, two and a half hours will be plenty. Harry looks at his watch. That gets him to the airport forty minutes before his departure time. Excellent.

As the car beetles at alarming — though not to its pilot — speed south through Umbria, Harry amuses himself by putting frames around real-life Jeffrey Smart roadscapes: workmen in orange overalls; pitch-black roads with white markings, red plastic spheres strung on cables; white arrows on brilliant circular blue signs; modernist water towers on the horizon; truckdrivers in dark overalls climbing down from prime movers in lay-bys, pastel-painted containers on their trailers; backdrops of deep forest-green forests bordering the roads. And then the Lazio signs are rushing at him, and he has to concentrate on leaving the autostrada to pick up the ring road going west to the airport.

He makes it, more by good luck than competence, and, without encountering any accidents or even minimally zealous *Polizia Stradale*, hands back the car with its tank bone-dry, and strolls with his bag to the first-class counter just as the 'flight closing' signs begin to flash. Not that Harry has a first-class ticket, but he's always found it the shortest queue. On such occasions, his Italian appears to desert him. His passport is examined and his bag labelled 'SYD' before it disappears on the conveyor belt. For the first time in his travelling life, Harry is upgraded from tourist to first class, at least for the Rome–Dubai leg. Noting the width of the smile and the Roman flourish with which his boarding card is handed over, he infers that he has been given a prize for presumption. Harry's own smile says that he shares the joke, as does his suddenly fluent Italian expression of gratitude. His depression lifts, and instantly he thinks of Arabella and pictures their meeting. In six hours, is it? He looks at his watch as he hurries through the final passport check and down the aerobridge, the last to board, and is shown to a big leather seat in the sharp end of the jumbo.

Arabella is in her tourist-class seat, trying to read a book her youngest sister gave her. Three years ago, it would have been a good choice — a glib commentary by a Sunday newspaper columnist on English politics — but that's a subject she has made no attempt to keep up with since committing to Australia, and she is having trouble with the names of both the protagonists and antagonists. She closes the book without marking her place and stares out her window at the cloud they are travelling through. Or is the plane stationary, and are the clouds being blown past it? Equally plausible. It doesn't matter — in another four hours, she'll be back with Harry. She didn't fight him about the separate holidays; to be fair, Harry had booked his annual trip to Tuscany before the catastrophe of the Bar Association's suspending him, and he simply went ahead with his plans. Solo, as ever. Arabella may not have fought Harry about the separation, but she did try to persuade him that she should spend at least one of the three weeks with him in Lucca. 'Not this year,' he told her. 'I think better alone, and there's plenty for me to think about.'

As the clouds outside her window darken, Arabella finds herself assuming — or is it praying? — that Harry will be less unhappy than he was when he left Sydney. At that time, despite the disciplinary suspension being withdrawn, he hadn't returned to practice and was still playing the part of strategist in criminal defence briefs from Surrey, which were marked with a subtly increased daily fee that the solicitor well knew would be shared between strategist and advocate. She wonders, is that relationship going to continue, or will Harry have spent his time working up to a decision to find a room somewhere, have his gown dry-cleaned, and get back to work? It would mean the end of all those briefs marked from Surrey, of course, at least for her, and Arabella would have to fend for herself again. If that happens, will she mind? And what will it mean for them? She decides that a great deal is going to depend on the reunion in Dubai.

Two jet trails among the many slowly softening and self-erasing chalk marks in the sky. Finally, having disembarked and positioned herself outside Harry's arrival gate, here he comes. Arabella shoots to her feet; she's been waiting for almost an hour in this cavernous city-as-airport. She stands awkwardly still, letting Harry see her, then come to her, peeling off from the other passengers emerging from gate 45. As he strides across, breaking into a slow smile, putting down his cabin bag, she holds both hands out towards him and he slides between them to fold her into an embrace that begins with Arabella being lifted off the ground for a second, and then kissed on both cheeks. 'You're not in Italy now,' she laughs, and kisses him on the mouth. She knows, just from the embrace, that everything's going to be as she would have wished. Neither lets go for a long time.

The trip to Sydney takes half a day, but at least it's non-stop. Harry expects some form of rebuke about their separation, and doesn't look forward to having to admit that he was wrong in insisting that he be alone in Italy. But it doesn't come, and he can't feel it under the surface of Arabella's happy detailing of the inconsequentialities of her family's life.

'They're channelling *The Kumars at Number 42*,' she says. 'Dad even appeared at breakfast every day in his jacket and tie. The details were perfect, right down to Mamaji. Granny, to you. Had I not known better, I would have believed the whole family was put together by Central Casting.'

'You didn't escape the matrimonial cross-examination, did you? On the subject of matrimony, I mean.' Harry's been dreading this.

'Once I told them about you, I did. That silenced them.'

'So what did you tell them about me?'

'That you were light-skinned and short-tempered.'

'Sounds like one of those marriage advertisements in Indian newspapers.'

'They're in the Indian newspapers over there, too.'

'Been reading them, eh?'

'It's possible.'

'Any likely prospects?'

Arabella smiles in a way that she hopes he will read as enigmatic.

'I see,' says Harry. 'No answer, but an enigmatic smile.'

She leans across and kisses him, then retrieves a book from her shoulder bag — not English politics this time. 'And with that,' says Harry, 'she buried her nose in yet another book about the Mitfords.' He produces a Frederick Forsyth paperback about a heroic British army officer single-handedly defeating Al Qaeda and turns to his bookmarked page. The plane grinds ahead through the darkness. They hold hands, only disengaging to turn pages.

At Kingsford Smith Airport, the very tall couple — noticeable for it — emerge from customs into the too-brightly-lit arrivals hall at 6 a.m. The hall is crowded with a confusion of families preparing for emotional welcomes, and the air is dotted with a barrage of silver balloons on strings. Some have escaped from the small plump hands that were told to hang on to them, and wails can be heard through the shouted greetings. Arabella's eyes scan the men in dark suits at the back of the crowd and Harry tries to negotiate the luggage trolley through the crowd without running over unruly children, overexcited by being woken so early and brought in from Lakemba to meet the plane from Dubai.

'You're not expecting to be met, are you?'

'Ah,' she says. 'There he is.' She nods at a man in a suit and chauffeur's cap, holding a shirt cardboard with the name 'Ms Engineer' scrawled on it.

'I thought you'd sent all your personal staff on holiday,' Harry says as the driver takes over his trolley.

'Just a skeleton or two left. On light duties.'

Then, within minutes, they're in a big black Benz speeding away from the airport.

'Did you see the queue for taxis?' asks Arabella, looking back. 'Ever since they privatised the airport, it gets worse every year.'

'And they charge us more,' the driver contributes over his shoulder.

'You two can stop all that socialist propaganda,' says Harry. 'You never know who's listening.'

The driver laughs. 'Well, certainly not the state government. They never listen to anybody.'

They pass an illuminated sign showing the temperature. 'Eight degrees!' says Harry. 'When's the next plane to Tuscany?' Arabella punches his arm. 'Where are we going, anyway?'

The driver turns briefly to look at him. 'The booking's for Erskineville. First time for everything, they say.' Harry looks at Arabella, who appears to have become very interested in a closed-down factory beside the road.

'Why my place?'

'Because we have a conference there at nine o'clock. With David.'

Harry turns to face her. 'About what?'

'Two matters on the far South Coast. One at Bega, one at Eden.'

'When was this set up?' Harry's deep voice has gone up an octave.

'David and I have been emailing each other the whole three weeks I was in London. He's trying to develop his South Coast work, and he's picked up two matters. They're both interesting. And you were incommunicado, weren't you?'

'No, I was in Lucca. Communicado's in Sicily.'

A very slight smile from Arabella.

'He didn't email you the briefs, did he?'

Arabella shakes her head. 'One of them, he did. The other's for you. He'll have it with him this morning.'

Harry looks out the window. 'So you two have organised that I'm going to come out of retirement.'

'Something like that.'

The rest of the journey is made in silence, while Arabella bites her lower lip, and Harry, as he always does, looks for changes that have been made in the neighbourhood while he was away. He can't see any. Despite Arabella's apprehension, he's not unhappy with the prospect of running a defence again. It's been almost ten months since he addressed a court. By the time the car stops outside his house and double-parks as if it's beneath its dignity to be seen there, he's enthusiastic about it.

The driver lifts their bags out of the boot, and Arabella searches her wallet for the right credit card. As the men wait, the driver looks at Harry.

'You're Mr Curry, aren't you? The barrister?'

'Yes, mate.'

'I was on your jury once, about three years ago. At Parramatta. A Lebanese guy who took drugs into the jail for his brother.'

'We lost that, didn't we?'

'Yeah. I think you had some argument with the judge about some of the evidence. We weren't allowed to hear that. We were in that bloody awful jury room for two days.'

'Sorry about that.'

Arabella finds her card and the driver finalises the fare. He still has something he wants to say to Harry. 'Once we heard that evidence, your bloke had no chance. But you know what one of the jurors said? He reckoned, even though you lost, he'd want you if he was ever in trouble.'

'That's nice to know,' says Harry. He can't think what else to say, so he tips the driver, and they enter the house after the usual wrestling match with the front door. No changes there. Very little mail has been pushed through the slot during Harry's three-week absence; Arabella picks up what little there is and heads for the kitchen.

'If you're making coffee,' Harry says, 'I'll have to go to the corner shop for some milk and the paper. You can have the first shower.' He heads out the door again.

At the shop, he picks up 250 grams of coffee, three bananas, a *Herald* and a litre of skim milk. Rosa from Calabria, who runs the shop with her husband Franco, wants to know how things are in Italy, and they talk for a while about Berlusconi, the dishonest government, the weather and the price of food there. Harry uses the clock behind the cash register to reset his watch — it's five to seven — and walks back to the house. As he enters, he can hear the shower running upstairs, and the kettle whistling in the kitchen. He makes the coffee, and reads the newspaper at the kitchen table. The front page is dominated by a report of a District Court judge who is alleged to have taken bribes to delay and adjourn hearings, and to withhold her judgments for as long as three years. Having read that with his eyebrows permanently raised, he turns to the sport and reads an analysis of the Wallabies' demolition of England in Perth over the weekend. By the time Arabella comes downstairs, wearing his dressing gown, he's on his third cup of coffee and second banana. He separates the two sections of the newspaper and hands her the news pages. 'Have a look at that — Holden's found a new way to make money.'

Arabella takes the paper and stares at the headline: *Judge accused of corruption — cases held back three years.* 'Holden?'

'Holden DCJ. Late of your chambers. Didn't you know her?'

'She was appointed not long before I joined. She was supposed to be one of the new breed — young, female, clever, no political baggage. I don't get it; how is delay proof of corruption? Most of the Supreme Court would be in jail if that was the issue.'

'Well, why don't you read it?'

Arabella gives him a hostile look over the top of the paper.

'All right,' he says, holding up both hands. 'These three journalists got a tip-off from a disgruntled litigant, and have analysed all her cases for the five years she's been a judge. The article's about what they say is a pattern they've found: two property developers had a string of actions in which they were both plaintiffs and defendants, depending on the matter, and the extraordinary delays in getting the matters heard, and the judgments delivered, have given them enormous advantages …'

'Financial advantages?'

'Yes, financial advantages. It's let them pay no rent for years, but to keep possession of factories and rural land while they tried to bribe the government into rezonings. Even when she has to give judgment against them, she takes as long as three years to do so, and they hang on to their money or move it all out of that company and let it go under.'

'Any proof that she was paid off?'

'Just two home units in the names of her children, each worth close to a million. One from each developer. If you look on the second page, they've got the documents.'

Arabella turns the page and studies the reproduced transactions. 'God help her.'

'There's even a libel case she heard against one of them. Pretty straightforward issues, hopeless defence, but she held that one back for more than two years.'

'Well, she wouldn't be the first judge to be slow. Defamation's very technical.'

'True, but the defendant was the donor of her daughter's property, and she didn't give judgment until the plaintiff had died of cancer. Which meant that the case died with him, even though he won.'

'But she may not have known that. About the cancer.'

'Oh yes, she bloody well did. The case was the subject of an expedition order, made on the basis that he was dying.'

'So she must have known.'

They sit in silence until Arabella gets up and makes another pot of coffee. When that's finished, she sends Harry upstairs for his shower and sets about emptying their cases of dirty laundry, which she separates and stuffs into the washing machine. She's on her third load when Surrey knocks at the front door. The pilot's bag he's carrying is obviously very heavy.

'Where's the *signore*?'

'Probably asleep. I'll call him.'

A voice comes downstairs from the bedroom. 'Not asleep. I was trying to finish my book, but people keep making noises. Be down in a minute.'

Arabella, still in the dressing gown, is suddenly embarrassed about it and excuses herself. Surrey has to take a seat in the kitchen and read the paper until they join him, both wearing jumpers and jeans and complaining about the cold. Still more coffee is made, and they sit around the table relating their reactions to the news about Judge Holden. When that's exhausted, and it takes some time, they make small talk about London, Lucca and the trip home.

Eventually, Surrey steers the conversation to work. 'And, Harry,' he says, 'spare us the accusations of conspiring against you. Arabella and I kept in contact, and there's work to be done — for both of you. You're still entitled to appear, aren't you? Your practising certificate's still current?'

'Until the thirtieth of this month.'

'Thought so. What I've got is a District Court trial in Bega — that one's a stabbing in the pub at Eden, a couple of fishermen — and a bushfire inquest from the Monaro. That's being held in Eden, because the Cooma courthouse is being restored, and they've rushed it on before the state election. The fire was only last Christmas.'

'A bit silly, isn't it?' says Arabella.

'What is?'

'Holding the Eden trial in Bega.'

Harry adopts an expression of extreme patience, as with a simple child, and waves his hand at Surrey, indicating that he'll deal with this. 'No jury trials at Eden, Bella. Ever seen that courthouse? It's a little weatherboard shed, perched on top of a hill, looking out to sea. I suppose they might have had a jury trial there somewhere in the dim distant past, but that'd be well before my time.'

'Mine, too,' says Surrey, bending down and opening the locks on his bag. He pulls out two white plastic folders with surnames on their spines. He reads the names, and hands Harry the one labelled 'Hain' and Arabella the one labelled 'Antico'.

Harry turns to his first page. 'So I'm doing the inquest?'

Arabella holds her brief, but doesn't open it. 'Well, we thought the best thing, in all the circumstances ...' She pauses. 'Look, would you rather do the trial?'

Surrey looks from one to the other. 'Christ, this is like one of those dreadful fundraising dinners where people swap the overcooked beef for the rubber chicken. The inquest client asked for you, Harry, or at least his family did, so you've got that. And it's a private payer, Doug Hain. The Bega trial's on legal aid, and Arabella's already read the prosecution statements. I emailed them to her in London. She should be ready to go. You won't have any trouble getting on top of the evidence that affects Doug — you don't have to run the whole thing.'

'Who's assisting the coroner, Dave? Do we know that yet?'

'Your mate Moses.'

Arabella looks shocked. 'The judge's son?'

'No, Moses from the Bible. Of course, the judge's son.'

'No, Bella. He's all right.' Harry is unfazed.

'I thought, given the complaint by his father to the Bar ...'

'No, he hates his father.'

'Which doesn't make him Robinson Crusoe,' Surrey adds.

'If we could talk about the stabbing trial for a moment ...' Arabella opens her brief and turns to a summary on the first page. 'There's still no evidence statement from the victim. Alleged victim.'

'No,' says Surrey, 'but you'll find a record of interview with him. The detectives did it on tape, but all they've given us is the transcript, unsigned. It's so long that I didn't email it to you.'

'So that would be the thirty-seven pages in here headed "Electronic Recording of Interview with Suspected Person"?'

'Indeed.'

'Surely the stabbee is the victim, not a suspect?'

Harry smiles. 'Police-speak. They label it with their little acronym, ERISP, and never consider what it means. All taped interviews are ERISPs, as far as police are concerned. Obviously, the Crown believe you've got sufficient notice of the victim's allegations from that transcript. The presumption is that when he's called as a witness, he'll stick to what he told them.'

'It's a good sign,' Surrey adds.

'Why?'

'Because he's uncooperative. You'd expect someone who was stabbed to be only too willing to sign a detailed statement about what happened. He must have been reluctant to do that, so they made him answer questions, even if he wouldn't sign up to the story. It's good for your cross-examination because he won't bother reading thirty-seven pages of disjointed interrogation so that he can give evidence consistent with it. I'm not going to give you a lesson in sucking eggs, but you'll be able to present the jury with a list of self-contradictions and inconsistencies. The bloke's possibly illiterate, too. That's something else you need to consider. Could be the reason for no statement.'

Harry, who knows nothing about the Bega trial, takes the brief from Arabella's hand and locates and reads the Short Facts — the original police summary of the allegations against the accused. When he finishes, he hands it back and turns to Surrey. 'What's the defence, if I may be so bold as to enquire?'

'Self-defence,' Surrey is quick to assert.

'Ah, Dave,' says Harry, 'Ms Engineer will now explain to the class why there is no such defence. Not just in this case, but in any criminal trial.'

Arabella smiles. 'What Harry means, David, is that the onus

isn't on the accused to raise or prove self-defence. If the facts would possibly support that argument, the onus falls to the prosecution to disprove it beyond reasonable doubt before the accused is called on to answer.'

Harry joins in. 'And unless the prosecution produces that disproof, the judge has to take the case away from the jury and direct them to acquit.'

'And if the judge won't stop the trial?'

'Doesn't mean that I can't try to persuade the jury that my client lacked any criminal intention in stabbing the aggressor, because all he was doing was trying to defend himself.'

Harry looks doubtful. 'What about proportionality? You can't respond to a slap across the face by using a shotgun. What happened?'

Surrey says, 'This huge timber worker jumped on Dean and had him in a headlock, so our hero smashed his schooner glass and ripped the bloke's arm open. That certainly made him let go.'

They all fall silent and think about whether Arabella's client overdid it.

'Much known about the victim?' Harry asks Surrey.

'We haven't got the print-out of his criminal record yet, but the detectives told me he's got a string of aggravated assaults.'

'Might be some good stuff there, Bella. I can see some juicy hearsay sticking its head up.'

'You'll have to explain how I can get that kind of hearsay in front of the twelve good men and true, Harry.'

'In the fullness of time, I shall. Actually, there'll probably be more good women than men on your jury. This is a Bega trial, you know, and men in the country can always get themselves excused. Milking or crutching.'

'The fullness of time might not be all that substantial, Harry,' Surrey says. 'Both these cases start on Monday. And there's one more interesting thing for you to consider, Arabella.'

'A problem?'

'You tell me. It's the judge.'

'Go on.'

'Judge Holden will be presiding at Bega.'

Arabella looks shocked. 'How can she, after today's front page?'

Harry adopts a very stern look. 'Even District Court judges, Ms Engineer,' he intones gravely, 'are entitled to the presumption of innocence.'

Winter on the far South Coast of New South Wales can be cold. It usually is, which is fine with Harry and Arabella's colleagues as they thrash their Porsche 911s down to Thredbo for a weekend's skiing before thrashing their way back to Phillip Street late on Sunday night to prepare Monday's equity motion or another gentle exchange of views with the intellectual titans of the Court of Appeal. But on this weekend, Harry, Arabella and Surrey arrive somewhat unprepared in Bega, far from the fashionable slopes, to learn that there are no rooms to be had in any of the town's motels — not for ready money. Everything's been taken by a motor rally and the best the Surrey–Curry–Engineer defence team can manage, while Jamie and Crispin settle down in front of the fire in their ski lodge on the distant horizon, whiskies in hand after a hard day on the *piste*, is two adjoining cabins on the sand dunes in the Tathra Beach caravan park. It's almost deserted. They drop their bags and Surrey advises them to turn on their camping gas stove and light all the burners, as he has already done; at least the cabins will be warm when they return from a counter tea at the pub. Far from objecting, Arabella finds the accommodation charming. It reminds her of childhood cubbyhouses. She finds the tropical-fish theme in the little bathroom particularly touching, given the temperature.

Harry's up at dawn in his pyjamas and jumper, feet bare, to watch the sunrise from the little verandah facing the sea. Looking across to his right at the restored Tathra wharf, where the steamers used to dock, he sees that the tide is high. For some reason he would not be able to explain, high tides always make Harry optimistic, and he takes this one as a good omen — for his case in Eden, for him and Arabella, and for his future in the law.

There is absolutely no wind and the sea is perfectly flat, just the very slightest swelling and sighing where the wavelets stroke the cold, wet sand at the water's edge. The light low in the east is stained with a soft pink in an unbroken sky, above it something closer to green than blue, and across the unlimited horizon the steely grey of the sea. The dunes are white, held in place by native sea grasses and succulents. From the village behind him, Harry can hear the milkman's truck stopping to unload at the little supermarket, a door slamming, and greetings being shouted in the still air. The sun starts to climb into view and Harry shields his eyes with his hand. Ever the iconoclast, Harry looks back into the cabin over his shoulder to check that Arabella's still in bed, and urinates off the verandah. Not feeling at all cold, he goes back inside to wake her, promising her a bacon-and-egg roll at the café up the hill if she'll let him take the first shower.

After an early breakfast in the village with Surrey, they split up. Harry takes the Jaguar and drives south to Eden, where Surrey has arranged for him to meet his client, the Black Lake bushfire brigade tanker driver, and family outside the post office.

Meanwhile, Surrey drives Arabella the seventeen kilometres west to Bega, parking behind the courthouse. Their client, the accused, is waiting on a bench in the town's main street, in front of the Victorian stone courthouse, smoking and talking to some Aboriginal men who have also to face trial in the current sittings. Arabella's trial is the first on the list; after Surrey introduces her to a nervous Dean Antico, she tells the client that he can count on getting a start soon after ten o'clock. He says he doesn't know whether that's good or bad. They stand in the street answering his questions until the courthouse doors are opened by a clerk at nine o'clock, and they move inside, carrying law books, court dress and their evidence folders, to occupy a room with the words 'Legal Profession' in gold on a polished cedar door.

Dean Antico has worn his best clothes, as advised by his solicitor — 'No jury ever convicted a man because he was clean and tidy' — a freshly pressed shirt with red and black checks and pearl snap buttons, and a new pair of black jeans. Blundstone boots, polished. The room is cold, and Surrey can't get the gas heater, high on the wall, to light. Dean doesn't seem to notice the cold — he is a trawlerman, after all.

Once they are all seated, Arabella opens her notebook. 'You didn't agree to a taped interview, Dean?'

'It wasn't that. I wasn't asked. I was still a bit pissed when they arrested me, and they said they weren't allowed to. I'd been on it all day — it was too windy to fish, so we'd been in the pub since it opened. Been like that all that week — no work, no money.'

'David, they never asked him to make a statement once he sobered up?'

'As far as I know, no. I wasn't acting then — there was a local solicitor. I've taken a proof of evidence from Dean in my office — you've got that — but Harry's always told me that you never hand that over to them.'

The client tells them he wasn't informed by his original solicitor of any further invitation to speak to the police, but he doesn't understand Surrey's reference to a 'proof of evidence'. Surrey explains that it's the narrative he prepared after they conferred in Goulburn. 'Your statement, to put it another way. You've still got your copy, haven't you?'

Dean unsnaps one of his shirt pockets and pulls out three folded pages, obviously much-consulted, which he opens out.

'And you've read it through lots of times, like I told you? Learned it?'

'Well, not off by heart, but I know what's in it. It's all true.'

Arabella looks at the unfolded pages. 'May I look at that? I've got my own copy, but you've made some notes on it.' There are pencil markings in the margins. The client passes it over to her, and she reads the notes.

'What's this about "cook at Black Dolphin"?'

Surrey speaks first. 'I think you'll find, counsel, that that's the hearsay evidence Harry thought you might be able to use.'

Arabella looks from Surrey to the client. 'Never as simple as it seems, is it?'

* * *

Fifty kilometres south, quite a crowd has assembled outside the Eden courthouse. In fact, it's not the weatherboard shack Harry depicted, but a graceful cream-painted timber building, single-storeyed, with a grey corrugated-iron roof and a classic verandah facing the sea from its high position among casuarinas and tall eucalypts. It boasts the date '1858' on the gable and looks as if it has been recently repainted. A flagpole stands on the small browned-off lawn in front of the building, today without a flag, and that's where most of the crowd has gathered. They are being filmed by two television news crews, and reporters stand off to the side holding their shorthand pads, recorders and polystyrene coffee cups.

The Hains stand near four other tight groups on the verandah, their posture indicating uncertainty as to whether they should greet the families of the men who died in Doug's tanker. They attended all the funerals, but this is different. Before they can make a decision, Harry emerges from the door of the court office with another man in a suit, who moves off to speak to several older men in Rural Fire Service uniforms standing near the front gate.

Harry joins the family to explain the nature of a fire inquest. Doug Hain has both arms covered with pressure bandages protecting his burns, and there are others that can't be seen under his clothes. His face bears the scars of further burns, and he is wearing sunglasses. He is obviously very nervous. Harry's manner on the verandah may surprise some observers of his take-no-prisoners courtroom style. He speaks softly, listens courteously, nods frequently, maintains eye contact, and takes care to ensure that what he's saying to them is clearly understood.

'Nobody's charged with anything. Nobody's on trial for anything, and certainly not you, Doug. All the coroner has to decide is the manner and cause of death of your mates in the tanker. You and I know that's pretty straightforward — they were asphyxiated when they couldn't get out after the truck hit that tree.'

Doug's father says, 'So why do we have to have a court case? Can't he simply write a report based on the medical stuff and the fire investigator's opinion? We've all seen those.'

'I agree, George,' says Harry. 'Everyone knows the manner and cause of death. But, over the centuries, coroners have come to play what they like to call an "educative" role. They like to make recommendations, with the best will in the world, aimed at avoiding such deaths in future. There are many recommendations by coroners that have improved safety for the volunteers and the professionals, and not just in bushfire cases. But we have to go through it, and there'll be a lot of time taken with fire and safety experts. It won't be quick, and we'll probably be here all week. Still, you're right — the actual medical evidence won't even be examined. It's not controversial at all.'

Mrs Hain pipes up, 'Mr Curry, we have a lot of confidence in you. You might not remember that you looked after my brother in Queanbeyan years ago?'

Harry doesn't remember, but nods. 'How is he?'

'Not so good, I'm afraid.'

'I'm sorry.'

'Yes. But about Doug. What exactly can you do for him in there?'

'Well, Mrs Hain, my job is to protect him. I object to any evidence — and that means any question, or any answer, or any document, or any lawyer's submission that might be made when the evidence has all been heard — that might suggest, even with the greatest subtlety, that anything he did was in any way blameworthy. But there's another thing: it's my duty to warn Doug that, theoretically — and I emphasise it's only in theory — a coroner who believes he has heard or read evidence that would justify putting someone on trial for a criminal offence is required to halt the proceedings and refer the matter to the Director of Public Prosecutions for consideration of criminal charges.'

Doug doesn't speak, but his father says, 'Such as?'

'Such as, in theory, manslaughter.'

The family are stunned.

'That, I promise you, isn't going to happen here, and, believe me, I try never to promise anything about the outcome of court cases unless I can be absolutely certain, but in this case I promise you, there will be no criminal charge.'

Doug speaks. 'Not your decision, though, is it?'

'No, Doug, it isn't. But you have the right to make submissions about what findings of fact the coroner should make, and I make those for you, and I know enough about this case and this coroner to be confident that you're in no danger. Maybe I won't be called upon to even argue it.' Doug starts to speak again, but stops, so Harry continues. 'Maybe you'll find some comfort in this. You should. This coroner is a magistrate that I've appeared in front of for many years. I think I can read him. He's coming up for retirement, so he's not looking over his shoulder about what anyone expects him to do. He'll do what he thinks is right. That's the first thing. Next is that I have always known him to be sensible. That doesn't mean he always agrees with me, by the way. And perhaps this is the most important thing of all — he's a bushie. He's not some townie counter-jumper who worked his way up through the Local Court system, taking ten or fifteen years to get a law degree at night, to become a magistrate and coroner, with precious little knowledge of the real world and of country people. Lots of them are like that, but this bloke was a solicitor in Bathurst, I think it was, before he packed that in and was appointed to the Local Court up there. Maybe it was Orange, maybe it was Young — I don't remember. Somewhere in the Central West. But his clients were people like you — people who volunteered for their local bushfire brigades and sold lamingtons and had raffles to keep their equipment up to date.'

'You seem pretty sure of that.' Mrs Hain wants to believe it.

'Well, Mrs Hain, this isn't like other court cases. The parties aren't really opposed — it's not supposed to be adversarial. So there was nothing stopping me and Mr Moses — he's the barrister who's running the inquest — from having a meeting with the coroner. That's where we were a minute ago, before I came out here. Counsel assisting isn't looking for any finding against Doug, or anyone else, except maybe the politicians and the hierarchy of the Fire Service in Sydney. He's concentrating on asking for recommendations about maintenance of power poles, safer vehicles for the firefighters, better communications and lightweight flame-resistant clothing. And the beak gave a very strong indication that he won't be talking about any kind of criminal charges.'

They think about it for a few minutes. George Hain looks out at the crowd, still harassed by television cameras and newspaper photographers who are pointing their cameras at the families of the dead men. 'But what about the other families? They've got lawyers, too. Won't they want someone to be punished?'

Harry looks at those people, dressed in just the same way as his client and his family, their faces deeply etched by the sun and wind and cold in which they work every day.

Conservative and respectful clothing, almost a country uniform. Most of the women and a couple of the men hold handkerchiefs bunched in their hands. 'If you were one of them, Mr Hain, would you want to see anyone punished?'

'No, Mr Curry. But I'm not one of them, am I? Doug's here, with us. Thank God.'

Harry checks his watch. Time to go in. Ten o'clock.

At Bega, things are a little less prompt. Holden DCJ has been shut in her chambers since 8.30 and is trying to summon up sufficient courage to take her place on the bench. She believes that it's the hardest thing she will ever have to do. Her associate, an older woman with vast experience of everything that can go wrong for a judge — well, maybe not everything — is ferrying cups of hot, sweet tea to her, trying to get her into her wig and gown and to take charge of the business of the court. The judge was happy to be assigned to the South Coast circuit months ago, but has not sat in any court in the four days since the *Herald*'s catastrophic front page appeared. The Chief Judge has made it known in a phone call to her home at the weekend that he expects her to run the Bega criminal list, as planned, starting today. Still incapable of action, Judge Holden sends her associate out to speak to Arabella, who is in her court dress, sitting at the

Bar table talking to the prosecutor about the order of the Crown witnesses.

'Ms Engineer, the judge wonders if she could have a word with you?'

Arabella gets to her feet, closely followed by the prosecutor.

'No, Mr Crown, the judge hasn't asked to see you.'

Baffled, he resumes his seat, remarking to his instructing solicitor about this being 'irregular'.

The associate ushers Arabella down a short corridor, knocks on another beautiful cedar door, and shows her into the judge's chambers, where the first thing she notices is that the bookshelves are strikingly empty. Invited to take a seat, she then notices the haggard eyes of the woman on the other side of the desk.

'Good morning, Judge.'

'Arabella, is Mr Curry going to be here this week?'

No pleasantries, and the use of the first name of a barrister she's never met before. This woman's in trouble, Arabella can see that. 'Well, yes and no, judge. He's got a bushfire inquest down the coast at Eden, but we're staying at Tathra. He'll be in Bega by five o'clock, I should imagine.' No point in disingenuousness — Holden obviously knows of the relationship. Arabella draws an inference as to the reason for the question about Harry. 'Do you want to see him?'

'Yes, I do. This stuff in the *Herald*. I think I need some advice.'

'I won't be able to ring him, Judge — he's famous for not having a mobile phone — but he might borrow one and ring me at lunchtime and, if he does, I'll ask him to come and see you.'

'Thanks. See if he can get here at five o'clock, will you?'

'Certainly.'

'This trial of yours — how long's that going to take?'

Embarrassed, Arabella smiles and says, 'Perhaps it would be best if you asked me and the Crown that question in open court, Judge.'

The judge colours. 'Of course.' And closes her eyes.

Undismissed, Arabella leaves the room and rejoins the prosecutor, to whom she offers no explanation.

A few minutes before one o'clock, the coroner adjourns his court at Eden for lunch. The morning has been taken up with what the lawyers are pleased to call housekeeping matters: noting the appearances of the legal representatives of the families of the four men killed in the fire, Harry's appearance for Doug Hain (which the coroner records without comment, ignoring the passive-aggressive stance of at least one barrister who mistakenly suspects that Mr Curry lacks a practising certificate, from what he's heard around the traps, but isn't game to raise the issue), the New South Wales Fire Brigade, the Minister for Emergency Services, the Rural Fire Service, its insurers, the insurer of the tanker truck, and the insurers of the electricity authority. He also had to rule on applications to participate in the inquest made by lawyers retained by three non-government environmental protection associations and landholders whose properties suffered damage in the fire. The coroner heard the applicants' arguments for a place at the Bar table (which had to be doubled in size to accommodate counsel and, in some cases, solicitors appearing as advocates), and heard also the counter-arguments of the already-approved. There was a late break for morning tea, and the rest of the court's time was taken in negotiations over the witness list, and the order in which those people would appear to give evidence and be cross-examined.

Harry and the Hain family emerge into the winter sunshine and stand in a small circle on the courthouse lawn, as all the others head for cars parked along the narrow street separating the courthouse from the cliff and head down to the town for a sandwich or, in some cases, for the pub.

'All those lawyers, Mr Curry. Why do they all want to get involved if it's only about the cause of death and whatever the coroner wants to recommend about safety?'

'Not to put too fine a point on it, Mrs Hain, it's about money.'

Doug wants to know what that's supposed to mean.

'Well, the first thing is that the families of the men who died have to be compensated — or, at least, the families where the man was the breadwinner, or one of the breadwinners. There are three of them — not the young fellow, Tim, your neighbour's boy. Eventually, the families will sue for what's called Compensation to Relatives, and it's supposed to cover the wages their men would have contributed for the rest of their lives. And it could involve damages for psychological or psychiatric harm suffered by the families. Putting it all together, that could be in the millions.'

Mrs Hain asks, 'So Tim's family get nothing?'

'Probably not. It could only be if they claim psychiatric problems.'

Doug's father looks alarmed. 'But the others — who do they sue?'

'Not you, George, and not Doug. For a start, you haven't got any money, or not the sort they're talking about. There wouldn't be any point — they're looking for people with very deep pockets.

Insurance companies. Actually, that's the only reason the families are here with all these expensive lawyers — they want to see what the evidence is likely to be if there has to be a claim for damages, by which I mean who is the best defendant: the insurer of the truck, the third-party insurer, the Fire Service itself, the state government … whoever appears to have done the wrong thing, no matter how minuscule the negligence. Maybe even the company that sold the bushfire brigade that truck. They'll certainly want to sue the electricity authority for negligent maintenance of the power pole, and I can see them carrying the lion's share of any settlement or, if there has to be litigation, the verdict. What they'll probably have to do is sue as many defendants as they can, because in those circumstances all the insurance companies normally get together and fight out their various shares of the blame. That's why they're here, all lawyered-up: the real fight is going to be between the big insurance companies, and they'll all be trying to make a case that their share of the blame is nil, or as close to it as they can get. What you'll find is that everyone turns on the electricity authority, and expects them to carry the whole lot — compensation, damage to the properties that the fire went through, even the loss of the bushfire tanker.'

'Pretty horrible, isn't it?' says Doug.

'What, son?' his father asks.

'Well, this is supposed to be about why my blokes died. That's what Mr Curry says. But it's really just a shitfight — sorry, Mum — just a shitfight between big bloody insurance companies that can afford just to pay out all the families today, no reason to wait, and Tim's too, without any court case or anything. Everyone knows who's to blame. Makes me sick.'

'No, Doug, you're right. Anybody with any sense would agree with you. But I think we'll find that the coroner keeps them under control, and doesn't let them turn this into a Royal Commission that runs for a year.' They are all silent, and Harry starts walking towards his car. 'Let's get a bit of lunch — we've got to be back at two.'

'We can all go in the Landcruiser,' says George, and they walk the hundred metres to where it's parked. Following his wife's directions, he drives down the steep hill to the Eden Fishermen's Co-op wharf, where they buy rolls and bottles of fruit juice at the takeaway. None of the others from the court are there, which is a relief to them all. Doug walks off across the long wharf, looking at the trawlers that are tied up alongside. The others sit at a picnic table and eat their lunches. A mechanic can be heard working on an engine somewhere. Harry finishes eating and throws half his bread to the seagulls, who fight noisily over it and then pester the group with upraised red beaks until they suddenly burst into flight and wheel out over Twofold Bay, alarmed by the noise of a nearby trawler's big diesel engine bursting into life in a cloud of black smoke. The engine is immediately shut off, but the birds have gone, and the three people on the bench sit in silence. Mrs Hain watches her son, who has started to walk back to them.

'It's hard enough on him that he's going to be questioned. He's scared, but he's also very upset about what you've said, Mr Curry. The thing being just about money. I mean, they were good men, doing the right thing, and nobody's talking about them.'

Harry keeps his eyes fixed on Doug. 'Don't worry, Mrs Hain. I'll be talking about them. And Doug.'

On the way back up the hill, Harry asks to borrow George's mobile phone.

'Making any progress, Bella?'

'Hardly. We haven't even empanelled the jury. She's temporising, calling through the list of appeals from the Local Court for next week, arguing with counsel about the length of the trials in her list and refusing to give priorities for hearing. She's dragging out applications by jurors to be excused. Morning tea was an hour and a quarter. Doing anything to avoid starting a trial. She's in a bad way.'

'Well, we're doing a bit better than that, but not much.'

'She wants to see you, Harry.'

'Who? Holden, do you mean?'

'Yes.'

'What for?'

'She wants some advice. You're the most senior barrister in the vicinity, I suppose. Will you do it?'

'What do you think?'

'I think you should. She's not functioning, Harry. Maybe you can help. She asked me to get you here as soon as you can after court.'

'Okay.'

'Okay what?'

'Okay, tell her — or you'd better tell her associate — I'll see her about four-thirty, five.'

At 2.15, Holden DCJ comes back on the bench at Bega, having taken three Valium tablets in the space of two hours. The court is still crowded with all the lawyers, and their clients, and the police, who've been there since before ten that morning, because still nothing has been dealt with. The jury panel in waiting, more than twenty local citizens, are standing in the sunshine out in Carp Street. The Crown prosecutor, whose experience is limited to country circuits, where matters are conducted with somewhat less pressure than in the smoke, has spoken during the adjournment to one of his superiors in Sydney, and has been told to take charge of things as much as he possibly can without offending the judge. Deferential by nature, he's going to have to become assertive, or the three weeks of planned sittings will turn into chaos and the Director's office will have to take part of the blame. His hands are shaking as he remains standing after bowing to the judge. Everyone else sits.

'Your Honour, may I be of assistance?'

'Mr Crown?'

'May I respectfully suggest, your Honour, that you stand down the list of Local Court appeals until Monday next week — to be called over then — because I have at least three trials that my learned friends for the defence tell me are going to be defended.'

'Is that right, Mr Crown?'

'Yes, your Honour, it is. The remaining three trials in the list are, as we understand it, going to take a certain course.'

'By which you mean those accused will plead guilty?'

'Quite so. Now your Honour will want to hear those pleas before sentencing, of course, and that should take place before any Local Court appeals are dealt with, in the usual way, but after the defended trials. If I may be so bold as to suggest that.'

'Yes, Mr Crown.'

'Which would allow us to start the first trial in your Honour's list — the matter of Antico, in which my learned friend Ms Engineer appears for the accused. He is here, your Honour, and we are ready to commence that trial.'

The judge is gathering some confidence.

'Ms Engineer, what's your estimate of the length of that trial?'

'Three days, your Honour. No more.'

'The Crown agrees with that, your Honour.' The prosecutor, who sat while Arabella answered the judge's question, gets back to his feet as Arabella sits.

'Very well,' says the judge, looking out over the courtroom. 'This is what we'll do. I'll stand all Local Court appeals over to next Monday at 9.30 a.m. Pleas of guilty in the three matters referred to by the prosecutor will be taken on Tuesday and Wednesday of next week, subject to all the defended matters being completed by then. The order of the three trials for this week will be as on the list, starting with Antico. People involved with all other matters are free to go.'

Perhaps it's the Valium, or the lead given by the prosecutor, or perhaps both, but Holden DCJ is starting to sound like a judge again. The courtroom empties, except for the judge, her associate, the sheriff's officer, the two counsel and their instructing solicitors (Surrey moves forward to sit beside Arabella at the Bar table), Antico and the detective in charge of the brief. As the last of the uninvolved people withdraw, Arabella leans across and congratulates the Crown. He grins with relief.

The prosecutor stands again. 'Will your Honour empanel a jury this afternoon?'

'Any objection to that, Ms Engineer?'

'None at all, your Honour. I would have thought, with respect, that we could select a jury and the learned Crown prosecutor may be able to open his case to them before we adjourn this afternoon, also. We could pick up some time.'

'Do you intend to make an opening following the Crown's, Ms Engineer?'

'Possibly. May I reserve my right to do that?'

'As you wish. Officer, will you bring the panel in, please?'

The sheriff's officer leaves the courtroom, bowing as he does. Within a few minutes, he returns, shepherding in the twenty-odd citizens of Bega and the coastal towns of Eden, Tathra and Merimbula who were served with jury summonses a month ago and had excuses insufficient to warrant their being excused from service. A vivid cross-section of the community, they shuffle in and fill the seats in the public gallery at the back of the court.

Judge Holden goes about managing the jury selection with something approaching her customary efficiency, despite a subdued affect. She tells those summonsed that the trial should take no more than three days, and she has the Crown read out the list of his witnesses. He complies, but does not read out the name of Michael Kevin O'Grady, the man who suffered the stabbing. Arabella and Surrey both note the missing name. The judge then tells the jury that, if they know the accused or any of those persons, they should let her know and she will excuse them from this jury — but they will have to remain available for another trial later in the week. Only one potential juror holds up her hand, and says that she knows the detective in charge — their children are in the same class at the local Catholic primary school. These things happen in the country. She's told to stand down.

Since some mischief worked by a law-unto-himself shock jock on Sydney commercial radio after a gang-rape trial involving

Muslim teenagers — he had the names of two of the jurors and interviewed them live on air about their deliberations — reforms to the jury law have the effect that jurors are identified in court by numbers, and any attempt to interrogate them about the discharge of their function is a criminal offence. Harry believes jury anonymity is unconstitutional — 'Any man is entitled to know the identity of his judge' — and certainly a disadvantage to the defence — 'You can tell a lot about a man from his name. Especially his middle name.' But Arabella and Surrey have to make the best of it, and they adopt the strategy of challenging their allowance of up to three jurors on the basis of their ages (sixty-plus) and appearance (two are assumed to be shopkeepers and one a housewife). As it turns out, they were neither shopkeeper — one was a teacher and one a school bus driver — nor housewife — she was secretary to one of the local solicitors, recently retired. Not that the challenges do them or their client much good: the plainly disappointed rejects' places are taken by two women of even greater age and a bald man of extremely stern appearance wearing an RSL badge in his lapel, and the defence has used up all its rights of challenge. The Crown makes two challenges of its own, both to young people whom he judges to be anti-authority on the basis of their clothing: a 'solar not nuclear' T-shirt on the boy, and a gothic uniform on the girl (black jacket over long black velvet skirt, lots of silver chains topped by black lipstick and black fingernails). Pretty, though.

The judge releases the balance of the jury panel, and instructs them to return on Wednesday morning. She then explains the trial process to the jury that has been selected to try the accused, telling them finally about the timing of each day. 'I'll now invite the prosecutor to open his case to you, members of the jury. You should remember that this is merely a summary of the evidence the Crown expects to adduce from its witnesses. What the prosecutor says is not itself evidence, and you should not treat it as such. Yes, Mr Crown?'

The prosecutor gets to his feet and, like a batsman coming out to take strike, goes through his own preparatory routine. He adjusts his wig, hitches his gown up on his shoulders, spreads his folder on the lectern and straightens his spectacles on his nose. He delays even further by pouring himself a glass of water from the carafe on the Bar table, and taking a sip.

'Members of the jury, two days after Christmas last year there was a fight in the public bar of the Australasia Hotel at Eden. The victim …'

The judge interrupts by tapping her pencil on the bench. 'Mr Crown, I won't allow you to use that word, victim. Not at this stage of a trial. It's pejorative and judgmental. Your job is to summarise the facts, not characterise the participants.'

Arabella turns to make eye contact with Surrey. She's impressed.

'Please start again, Mr Crown.'

The prosecutor is thrown. He riffles his papers, clears his throat, pulls at his gown, and begins. 'The … um, Mr O'Grady, was …'

'I think you should start again at the beginning, Mr Crown.'

'As your Honour pleases. Members of the jury, two days after Christmas last year there was a fight in the public bar of the Australasia Hotel at Eden. One of the men involved in the fight, Michael Kevin O'Grady, suffered a deep stab wound to his left forearm which we will call evidence to show was inflicted by the accused in this matter, Dean Antico, using a broken beer glass. He stands indicted for the offence of assault occasioning grievous bodily harm. It is the Crown's intention to call four witnesses to the stabbing: one of the barmen working in the hotel that night and three drinkers who were watching the fight. We shall also call Dr Tierney to give evidence of the seriousness of the injury that he treated that same night by inserting twenty-eight stitches in the wound. The last witness will be Detective Sergeant Howard, who interviewed the accused. On that occasion, the accused exercised his right to silence. Her Honour will direct you as to the law in this case, and I respectfully anticipate that one of the things she will tell you is that the fact that the accused refused to answer police questions may not be held against him, or used in any way to suggest that he is guilty of this crime.

'My task — the task of the Crown on behalf of her Majesty — is to put before you evidence that satisfies you beyond reasonable doubt of the two elements of the offence of assault occasioning grievous bodily harm: first the criminal act itself — that the accused stabbed Mr O'Grady with the broken glass, and the injury caused by that stabbing was very serious in nature; and second — the criminal intention of the accused. We have to prove that the accused intended to cause that injury, or was reckless as to the injury he was going to inflict. Recklessness in this case, as her Honour is bound to tell you, involves foresight of the risk of really serious injury, and a decision to go ahead in knowledge of that risk.

'I note the time, your Honour,' the courtroom clock shows five to four. 'I would ask that I be permitted to call my first witness at ten tomorrow morning.'

'Well, Mr Crown, before I let the jury go, there are two things

I want to ask. First, are you not going to call the man who you say was stabbed?'

'He can't be found, your Honour.'

'That's a challenge, then. And, second, does Ms Engineer intend to open her case in the morning, or after the prosecution evidence has closed?'

The Crown sits and Arabella stands. 'I can open now, your Honour.'

'What? In less than five minutes?'

'In less than two minutes, your Honour.'

'Please do.'

Arabella surprises the Crown, whose seat is next to the jury box, by walking the length of the Bar table and standing behind him. He rises, intending to yield his position. Arabella puts a hand on his shoulder. 'Stay there, Ian. I won't be long.'

Arabella is now at the same eye level as the front row of the jury, who sit in two lines of seats, the closest not much more than a metre away from her. 'Ladies and gentlemen, just two words for you to take home and think about. Maybe only one word, depending on your attitude to hyphens.' At least two jurors smile. Arabella pauses. 'The words are "self" and "defence", or — if it's to be read as one word, hyphenated — "self-defence". What we say is very simple: yes, my client hit his attacker with a broken glass. Yes, he wounded him, and yes, the wound was sufficient to meet the legal test of grievous bodily harm. I'm not going to insult your intelligence on any of those issues, and my friend who appears for the Director need not prove them in anything but the most formal sense. But what we say, and this is what the case is all about, is that this was a clear case of self-defence. If you sit on a jury every month for the rest of your lives, you'll never see a clearer one. Dean Antico had every right to defend himself from a bully and a thug who attacked him without provocation. Just as you would, were you ever in the same situation. God forbid. May it please you, ladies and gentlemen. May it please your Honour.' And she returns to the far end of the table to be grinned at by Surrey. She sits and looks at the jury, many of whom are leaning forward to get a better look at her.

'Thank you, Ms Engineer. Well, members of the jury, a quarter to ten tomorrow for *Hamlet* without the prince. That's a reference to Mr O'Grady, who we're told won't be joining us, although he's the star of the show. Maybe we won't need the three days. Oh, and you'll remember that I asked you to choose your representative — foreman or forewoman — before you come back, and that person should take the seat in the jury box closest to me. Thanks. See you tomorrow.'

The jury is led out, apparently intrigued, and the court is adjourned for the day. The judge returns to her chambers and her associate stands, gathers her papers and looks enquiringly at Arabella. 'As soon as he can get here,' she says.

Things have run on a bit in Eden, because the pathologist whose report covers the deaths of the four firefighters has asked that cross-examination should be completed today — he's needed back in Sydney tomorrow. Harry has arranged things so that he's the last to cross-examine all witnesses — aside from Moses, the barrister assisting the coroner, who has the right of final re-examination on any points left hanging — and there's just one area he wants to make clear to the families.

'Doctor, can we just be quite clear on the point at which these men died?'

'They were asphyxiated, Mr Curry, as I have recorded in my final conclusions.'

'Yes, thank you. No question has been asked on that matter, and you may well feel that the families of the men, who were always told that they were burned to death, may get some comfort from knowing the actual mechanism.' Harry gives him a long look.

'Yes, I see what you mean. Well, your Honour, the photographs show that the bodies were almost totally destroyed. Those pictures are very distressing, I should imagine. But that destruction happened a considerable time after death.'

'If we assume, from the interview with my client, the driver, that he instructed his crew to get on the floor and cover themselves, and if we further assume that they complied, and if we make a third assumption that they were at the very least stunned if not knocked out by the truck's impact with the tree, what in your opinion can be said about the moment of death?'

The doctor nods. 'I believe that most of the oxygen would have been sucked out of the truck's cabin well before the impact. That, and the impact itself — for which they were not prepared — would in all probability have rendered them unconscious. In that condition, I believe they would have asphyxiated in perhaps ten minutes, but something between five and ten minutes, before the flames reached their bodies.'

'There would not have been a stage at which they were in pain?'

'Not at all.'

'Thank you, doctor. I have nothing further, your Honour.'

'Thank you, Mr Curry. Any re-examination, Mr Moses?'

'No, your Honour. May the doctor be released?'

'Certainly. You're free to go, doctor. I'll adjourn until ten tomorrow. But let me just say something to the families before that: Mr Curry asked a question that I would myself have wanted answered. I hope, as he indicated, that what the pathologist was able to tell you was of some comfort. I think you can be sure that your loved ones did not suffer.'

It takes some time for the court to empty out. Mrs Hain comes to Harry, threading her way through the withdrawing people, and simply squeezes his arm. When Harry reaches the outside, the mother of one of the deceased comes over to thank him. 'It's a help,' she says, 'to know that.' Her handkerchief is squeezed very tightly in her hand. Harry simply nods.

Harry takes his leave of the Hain family and says he'll see them back there at a quarter to ten the next morning. He asks Doug to write out any questions he wants him to answer, and says he'll do it then. Then he hurries to the Jaguar and drives it too quickly up the Princes Highway to Bega, stopping outside the courthouse just before five o'clock. Arabella is waiting there as he gets out of the car, her blue bag on the footpath at her feet.

'She still here?'

'It's safe to assume.'

'I really don't know how I can help her, Bella. It's hardly my sort of thing — advising disgraced judicial officers.'

'Why don't you go and see what she wants? I'll wait in the car.'

The court office is now closed, and Harry has to knock on the side door to be admitted. The associate is brought out, and escorts Harry back to the judge's chambers. She leaves them, promising to bring tea.

'Bearing up, Jean?'

'Barely. Barely bearing up.' The judge twists her wedding ring on her finger, looking at it and not Harry.

'Got your list under control?'

'Did Arabella tell you? I nearly lost it this morning.'

'No, she really said nothing. Just that you wanted to see me a.s.a.p.'

'You read it, of course? The *Herald*?'

'It was on the front page the morning I got back from Italy last week. But they don't seem to have followed it up. The story said there was more to come.'

'I imagine that the letter my solicitor served, promising to sue, pulled them up somewhat. But it won't hold them forever.'

'What can I do, Jean? You know libel's not my field.'

'No, but strategy is, Harry. I learned that to my great cost on more than one occasion.'

Harry smiles slowly. 'You won't hold that against me.'

'No. But my solicitor says I have no choice. I must sue.'

'All I know is what Oscar Wilde said: Never sue if you're guilty. And don't look at me like that — I don't know if there's any truth in it.'

'Well, please accept from me that not one word of it has any foundation.'

'Good. Still, the little I know about defamation law is that you don't sue simply on what they published — you sue on what the meaning is of what they published. What it implies.'

'Yes, sure. Defo 101.'

'Why don't you tell me what you think the article's saying about you?'

The judge pulls her briefcase over to her desk, takes out a manila folder and extracts what Harry can see is a photocopy of the front-page story about her. She reads it for about a minute and then looks up. 'To me, it imputes that I am corrupt, that I am in the pay of these property developers, and that I betrayed my oath of office as a judge by manipulating cases to favour them. They've used a photograph taken of me outside the church service for the beginning of term, when I'm screwing up my eyes against the sun. They've chosen it to make me look repulsive.'

Harry holds his hand out for the article, and spends more time reading it than the judge did. She knows it by heart, anyway.

'Yeah. I think you've got the allegations pretty right. There might be more in it than that, more meanings, but that's certainly the sting of it.'

They sit in silence and look at each other until the judge speaks.

'So the solicitor's right? I have to sue?'

'I know of no other way you can be vindicated. I would've thought the Chief wants that.'

'You and I know that will drag on for two years.'

'There's always the psychiatric express, Jean.'

'The what?'

'Didn't you follow the Royal Commission into police corruption? All those corrupt coppers who got tame psychiatrists to certify them Hurt on Duty with a smorgasbord of psychological conditions? Post-traumatic stress disorders, anxiety disorders, borderline personality defects? The Royal Commissioner came up with the title. He reckoned the psychiatric express was the best way to get out of the police force with some semblance of honour.'

'I'm not taking that route, Harry.'

'In which case, you either sue or you don't.'

'To repeat my question: my solicitor's right, in other words?'

'There's only one person in this room who knows the truth. She's not just a lawyer, she's a judge. She has to use her own judgment on this.'

'Certainly the Chief wants to know what I'm going to do. I'm getting murmurs about my duty to the judiciary.'

'Bugger him. He can wait. And forget about any duty to anyone except yourself. And your family. How's Barry taking it, anyway?'

'Not so well. I would have liked him to come down here for these three weeks to support me, but he just can't get away.'

Harry does not respond beyond pulling a sympathetic face. Judge Holden briefly raises both her hands above the desk, turns them up, and drops them again.

'Who are your solicitors?'

She names a mega-firm.

'Well, drop them for a start. They'll take all your super and anything else you've got. If Barry's got anything, they'll take that too. And the kids' moneyboxes. And they're so cap-in-hand to the big media that they're no use to plaintiffs anyway. Wouldn't know how to run a plaintiff's case. I'll ask around for a small firm that knows what they're doing. And you'd better retain Bunter.'

'Seriously?'

'Very seriously. Look, I know you don't like him. I don't like him. But the defendants hate him, for the very good reason that he's just too good for them. I probably don't need to tell you that juries are back in — for everything except damages. It'll be a jury that decides who's telling the truth. And juries, baffling as it may seem to us, love Bunter. He'll knock the *Herald* down at the first mention of the case, and he won't mind kicking them when they're down. You have to have him.'

'They'll bog it down for years, won't they? Vindication won't come quickly.'

'Perfectly true. But the very fact that you're suing proves that you're determined to clear your name, despite the uneven fight. David and Goliath — I always remind the jury who won that one, and so can he. You have to face facts: they'll fight every battle they can provoke, and they'll try to appeal every time a decision goes against them. Money is literally no object to them. They'll make you turn over your bank statements, your tax returns, all the most intimate details of your family's life: Who paid for your holidays? What about the extensions to your home? Where did you get the new car? The school fees?'

'Nobody's going to let them stage fishing expeditions, surely?'

'Question of relevance, isn't it? The issue is whether you're corrupt. They'll go all the way down the money trail. Every cheque butt, every credit card statement.'

Holden looks flattened.

'So, be honest with yourself. If there's anything there that you wouldn't want exposed, anything at all — even if it's got nothing to do with this story and couldn't possibly prove the truth of anything those bastards said about you — is it worth washing that dirty underwear on the ninth floor of the Supreme Court?'

'I don't wear underwear.'

'That's the girl.'

It's a further half-hour before Harry returns to the car. Night has fallen in Bega, and the streets are all but deserted. Arabella turns off the current affairs program she has been listening to but asks him no questions, and they drive through the undulating dairy country towards the coast. They discuss eating at the Tathra Bowling Club. As the car changes gear to climb the last hill into the town, Arabella asks how the judge was.

'At the end, pretty determined. I think you'll find she's on her game tomorrow.'

'I think we might finish tomorrow.'

'Really? How far did you get today?'

'The Crown's opened, and I spent all of thirty seconds telling them Dean acted in self-defence.'

'Did you finish, or will you keep going on that tomorrow?'

'Finished for now. I'll open in more detail when the Crown closes its case.'

'She won't let you.'

'Why not?'

'Because you chose to open today. And the length of your address has got nothing to do with it. You made your election, and you can't have two bites at the cherry. Them's the rules.'

'Bugger.'

'You learn something every time you do a case. At least I do. Is Dave joining us at the bowlo tonight? Chicken Maryland and Porphyry Pearl for three?'

'Jacob's Creek, you mean. I'm not sure, Harry. He said he hopes to get back by seven.'

'Where is he?'

'Merimbula. Interviewing the cook at the Black Dolphin Motel, he said.'

'Ah … the hearsay.'

'As you say, the hearsay.'

Surrey doesn't make it until they're finishing their entrees of *salade de chevre chaud*. Harry admits he was wrong to slight the cuisine. The dining room emptied out by 7.30, leaving them to discuss the *carte* and the *carte des vins* with the French chef. Harry politely declined the *aioli* and chose the *magret de canard*, and Arabella ordered the *poisson du jour* — grilled whiting — for herself and Surrey. While their salad plates are cleared and they wait for the main course, Surrey hands Arabella a single sheet of typing, which she reads at the table and then folds and puts in her handbag. A conspiratorial silence extends between them.

'Do I get to know?' Harry asks.

'Who's robbing this coach, Harry? You or Mr Kelly?'

Harry looks at her, amused. 'You do know where that comes from, Bella, do you?'

'Is there more to it than that?' she asks innocently.

'News to me,' says Surrey.

'Then I'll explain: Ned Kelly bails up a stagecoach near Castlemaine, pronounced Cassle-main, because it's south of the border. And he gets all the passengers out and announces that his gang are going to fuck all the women and rob all the men. One of the men protests and says they'll have to kill him first, whereupon one of the passengers, a woman of a certain age, asks him, "Who's robbing this coach — you or Mr Kelly?"'

'I've never heard you say "fuck" before, Harry.' Arabella is greatly amused.

Harry blushes. They both grin at him.

On their second morning at the Tathra Beach caravan park, Arabella joins Harry on the cabin verandah at seven o'clock to admire the view across the dunes as the sun slides up into another cloudless sky. She clutches his old dressing gown at her throat and shivers, but is enchanted at the sight of three porpoises playing in the surf. 'Were they here yesterday?'

'No surf yesterday. Not in the morning. Which gives me an idea.'

In moments, he has pulled on his Speedos, leapt off the verandah, run across the cold sand and dived into the breaking waves. Arabella watches Harry swim out beyond the break, turn to wave, and then spend a couple of minutes looking for a wave to catch back to the beach. The porpoises have left. She grins widely and shakes her head, but doesn't stop watching. When he makes it back and runs up the dune to her, they are both smiling.

'You're supposed to describe it as invigorating.'

'The water's not really cold. And it's so clear you can see right to the bottom. Bags the first shower.'

'No, you don't. Go for a run up the beach or something. I'll only be ten minutes.'

Surrey appears from next door, coffee mug in hand. 'Do you two have to make so much noise? You'll frighten the fish.'

Harry ducks inside and reappears in an antique rugby jersey with the number five on the back, then sets off north along the water's edge at a fast jog. They watch, expressing unflattering opinions about his mental health. Then they go inside and Arabella makes coffee.

'I had no idea this place was so beautiful, David. It leaves the North Coast for dead, doesn't it?'

'Well, I've always thought so. I'm seriously considering relocating my practice here from Goulburn. The trouble would be hanging onto those clients from up there. Maybe it'd be possible to open an office here, and attend one or two days a week. Something to think about. I'm getting more and more local work.'

'I'm thinking about a hot shower, and breakfast. Are we going to the same cafe as yesterday?'

'Either that or Claridge's. It's a limited choice.'

'Oh, I'm sick of Claridge's. Their bacon-and-egg rolls aren't a patch on what we had yesterday. Meet you up there at eight o'clock?'

'You ready for today, Arabella? Anything else we need to nail down?'

'No, we've done all we possibly could, David. I must say, this is entirely new for me — a prosecution without the victim giving evidence.'

'In murders, Arabella, they do it all the time. Gives you a free hand.'

After breakfast, Harry sets off before the others, and reaches Eden thirty minutes before his inquest is due to resume. He's set up an informal meeting between the solicitors and barristers representing the various families, insurance companies and bureaucracies with sufficient legal interest in the case to entitle them to a slot at the Bar table. The substantial group, only two of whom are women, meet on the courthouse lawn. This morning, someone from the court staff has remembered to hoist the flag, and one of the counsel asks what it's in aid of.

'It's in aid of efficient use of the flagpole,' a colleague explains.

'What I wanted to know,' says Harry, 'is whether we can shorten this thing. I know we've all got different purposes, but those of us instructed by the families, and that includes me, don't have a lot of work to do to set things up for the compensation actions. Needless to say, I've also got to look after my bloke's position from any possible criminal perspective, not that anyone would be game to point any fingers at him. But I know you blokes for the insurance companies — what, that's how many of you?'

'Six, Harry.'

'Yes, well, I know you all want to put yourselves in the best position for apportionment of the damages …'

'You really shouldn't presume that we all admit liability, Harry. Those aren't my instructions.' This is said coldly, with more than a hint of arrogance, by a very young barrister in a very expensive suit. He smiles a lot and is, as one of his colleagues in chambers likes to say, 'pretty happy with the way he turned out'.

Harry stares hard at the speaker. 'You mean, I take it, that the Monaro County Council ignored its duty of care and failed to even inspect the power poles carrying 11,000-volt lines, which fell down in the first decent breeze; an entirely foreseeable bushfire resulted; and these blokes were sent to fight it with inadequate training, second-rate fireproof gear, a death-trap of a truck and an incompetent fire controller … but all your clients, the people who killed these blokes, are all going to deny any liability and—'

'Get off the white horse, Harry. It doesn't suit you.'

'—and you've all advised your insurance company clients to fight this one right out, to the last dollar, because the partners in your mega-firms have all ordered their new Benzes for next year, and someone has to pay for the appalling artworks the managing partner's wife has bought and hung all over your conference room walls? That's what this is about, is it?'

A large section of the group — the people representing the companies holding the money — walk off in low dudgeon and start speaking among themselves, out of earshot of the remainder, casting the odd contemptuous look back.

'That was never going to work, Harry,' one of the remaining barristers says. 'They reckon they can get another eighteen months of revenue out of this. Our people are going to be kept out of their money, just so long as that mob can go on billing the insurers and trying to persuade them that they've got a defence.'

A solicitor, the only woman in the remaining group, holds her hand up for a moment. 'My client can't wait another eighteen months,' she says. 'She's now a widow with three kids, all at school, and they live eighty kilometres from Cooma. She can barely afford petrol to get into town to see the clinical psychologist once a month. The weekly compo payments she's getting don't even cover her food, let alone clothes. She can't work. She's sold the sheep, but she can't sell the property. She has to cut her own firewood. They've been putting up with this since the fire, which is six months ago, and they're going to have to be supported by the neighbours and St Vincent de Paul — for how much longer? Something like two more years?'

The other families' solicitors have similar stories. What becomes obvious is that the human beings (as Harry would call them) and their lawyers are going to be stonewalled by the legal representatives of the government authorities and the insurers. There isn't going to be any sort of accommodation of the immediate problems of the fire victims, and there is no prospect of a compromise until one is forced on the potential defendants by the Supreme Court, which will certainly send the case off for mediation — a process that, well-intentioned as it may be, is not binding and may only serve further to frustrate and delay resolution. And even that is years, and hundreds of thousands of dollars in legal fees, away. The solicitors and barristers in Harry's group won't be paid until it's all over, and in the meantime they're going to have to carry the families by paying their court filing fees, beg the medical experts to provide reports for which they will be paid later, and still go on covering the incidentals and their staff's wages.

Harry singles out the woman and takes her off to one side. She is visibly upset. The families begin to arrive, parking their cars and approaching the courthouse.

'Look at the cars parked there,' she says. 'They say it all, don't they?'

Harry looks.

'The solicitors have their big Mercedes, the barristers have BMWs and Volvos, and my client's got an old people mover. The families have got the utes and four-wheel drives — the dirty ones, not the Double Bay tractors — and the local lawyers drive Fords and Holdens. Says it all.'

Harry agrees.

'And you're driving a Jaguar, aren't you?'

'Well,' says an embarrassed Harry, 'it's not exactly mine. In a strict sense, it belongs to a man who resides at Long Bay. I just get to use it.' She gives him a long look, and Harry changes the subject. 'Country solicitors usually get on well with the local press, don't they?'

'Meaning?'

'Meaning you could talk to the journos from down here and get them to run with our attack on the insurers.'

'Yes, but we haven't attacked them.'

'Not yet,' says Harry. 'Once you've got them organised, that'd be the appropriate time.' He sees the Hain family arriving; Doug is holding a piece of paper — the questions he wants Harry to answer.

In Bega, the trial is moving quickly. The prosecution proves first that the wound suffered by O'Grady was a serious one by calling as its first witness the emergency department doctor from Pambula Hospital, where the injured man was taken by ambulance. The doctor is of the opinion that there was no damage to the tendons, and healing should have taken place without any residual disability interfering with the victim's employment. 'You mean his unemployment,' the jury hear Surrey retort in a stage whisper. Several are amused.

Arabella gets up to cross-examine. 'Dr Tierney, there was just one wound, wasn't there?'

'You mean, he was stabbed only once?'

'Forget the word "stabbed", please. What I'm asking is whether the man you treated suffered a number of wounds, indicating that he was under a repeated attack, or whether there was a single laceration, consistent with an act of self-defence.'

'I object.' The Crown is quick to stand.

'Yes, Ms Engineer. That's rejected.'

Arabella raises her eyebrows at the judge.

'The problem with your question is in inviting an opinion as to what motivated your client.'

'Thank you, your Honour, I shall attempt to correct that.' She turns to the witness. 'Doctor, were there a number of lacerations, or just one?'

'Just the one, yes.'

'A single striking out, as it were?'

'Consistent with one movement of your client's hand, yes.'

'And from your point of view, there was nothing inconsistent with that single blow having been struck in self-defence?'

The Crown is on his feet again. 'I object. Again, my learned friend invites an answer as to motive.'

'No, Mr Crown.' Judge Holden is shaking her head. 'I'll allow the question. Would you answer it, please, Doctor?'

'Well, no, not inconsistent with that. He could have been defending himself.'

Arabella sits, looking happy with the answer she got.

The Crown rises to re-examine, as is his right. 'Why do you say that, Doctor?'

Surrey bends towards Arabella. 'Silly question. Shouldn't have asked it.'

'Well, Mr O'Grady told me that—'

'I object, your Honour. I didn't invite a hearsay answer.' The Crown looks angry with his witness.

'No, Mr Crown. You asked it, and he's answering you. In any event, aren't medical histories an exception to the rule against hearsay? Please go on, witness.'

'As I was saying, and it's here in my notes, if I may read them out?'

'Go ahead.' The judge smiles.

'Thank you. *Patient describes fight in which he held other man from behind, and was slashed up left forearm by broken glass.* Now, assuming that to be correct, we have one man holding and apparently controlling the other, and the man being held uses his right hand — it would have to be his right hand — to strike him with the glass. I can't say that isn't consistent with self-defence. It could be.'

The Crown tries to rescue himself. 'What would be inconsistent with self-defence in such a situation?'

'Where the injury was to his chest or face, I suppose. Something indicating that the man with the glass had got free of the hold he was in.'

The prosecutor gives up. 'May the witness be excused, your Honour?'

'Any objection to that, Ms Engineer?'

'Yes, I'm sorry, your Honour, but there are just two questions arising from the re-examination.'

The Crown has nothing to say.

'Very well, Ms Engineer. But only two.'

She looks across at the doctor again. 'If the account given to you by Mr O'Grady was somewhat less than complete — if, for instance, he wasn't merely holding my client from behind, but had his forearm across his windpipe and was choking him — would that strengthen your opinion as to self-defence?'

'If that was the fact, yes. Of course.'

'Doctor, how long have you been at Pambula Hospital?'

'Eighteen months, now.'

'Is the cook from the Black Dolphin Motel at Merimbula still in a coma there?'

'To the best of my knowledge.'

'I object to this,' the Crown says. 'What possible relevance could that have?'

'Well,' says the judge, making a quick note, 'I gave leave for only two questions, but the third one's been asked and answered. You were a bit slow. And, no doubt, all of us — I, you and the jury — will eventually learn what relevance the comatose cook may have, although for the moment I can't imagine what it could be. Now, can the doctor go back to work, counsel?'

The succeeding witnesses are two drinkers from the pub who saw the fight — one from the front, and one from the side. At least the prosecution has seen the sense in dropping witnesses to shorten the trial, leaving out mere repetition of facts that Arabella undertook would not be in issue, and which she does not, in the trial, dispute. They tell much the same story: O'Grady had been baiting Antico all night, and jumped on his back when he emerged from the lavatory. O'Grady had him in a bear hug (one witness concedes that the forearm could possibly have been across Antico's neck at some stage, but Arabella has to work hard to get that concession), and as they came into contact with the pool table, Antico managed to get hold of his glass, smash it, and use his right hand to slash O'Grady's arm. Everyone, and that includes the witnesses, was drunk by then.

The rest of the day is spent hearing the evidence of the detective in charge, which doesn't add much to the picture presented to the jury. Antico was sufficiently intoxicated to preclude a formal interview, the broken glass was never found, and the public bar that night was well lit. Arabella's turn. 'You received a subpoena from my instructing solicitor, Mr Surrey, didn't you, requiring you to produce Mr O'Grady's criminal record?'

'Yes, I did. I've got it here.'

'I call for that document, your Honour.'

Three pages are handed down from the witness box, with the judge taking a quick look first. She purses her lips. The record is then handed to Arabella, who reads it slowly, occasionally pointing out an entry to Surrey. The third time she draws his attention to something on a page, he mutters, 'No need to overdo it, Arabella. The jury've noticed already.'

'I tender the criminal record of Michael Kevin O'Grady, your Honour.'

'Any objection, Mr Crown?'

'May I see it, your Honour?' It is handed to him and he reads it.

'Yes, your Honour, I object to the tender. In fairness, this can't go into evidence unless Mr O'Grady confirms the accuracy of these matters.'

'A bit hard to do that, Mr Crown, if you're not going to call him.'

The jurors are loving it. Most sit forward in their chairs, making lots of remarks to each other. Surrey whispers, 'He took the wrong objection,' to Arabella, and she nods quickly.

'Accused's exhibit A,' the judge tells her associate, who staples a slip to it and writes the identifier. At Arabella's request, the exhibit is passed to the jury. Each reads it in turn, and they are plainly impressed.

'Any further questions, Ms Engineer?'

'Thank you, your Honour. Detective Sergeant, has any person been charged with the aggravated assault of a James Edward Harding at the Australasia Hotel in Eden late last year?'

'I object!' the Crown shouts, forgetting to stand.

'The question's rejected.'

'Will your Honour hear my argument on that?'

'No, Ms Engineer. Any more questions?'

'Detective Sergeant—' Arabella pauses mid-question. 'No, your Honour, I don't think you'd allow the question I had in mind. I have nothing further.'

'Re-examination, Mr Crown?' the judge asks, and is answered with a shake of the head.

'May the witness stand down, your Honour?'

'Unless the jury has any questions.' A juror puts up her hand. 'Who's James Edward Harding?'

'He's the cook at the Black Dolphin Motel, your Honour.' The sergeant answers before anyone can stop him.

The prosecution team looks daggers at the judge, who pretends not to notice.

'I notice the time, members of the jury. We'll adjourn until ten tomorrow. Is that your last witness, Mr Crown?'

'Yes.'

'Ms Engineer, will you be going into evidence?'

'Yes, your Honour. Mr Antico will be my only witness.'

'Thank you. So I think I can safely say that we should be able to finish tomorrow, members of the jury, if you wish to make your own arrangements about that. Please be here by 9.45.'

**

The old double-decker steamer wharf at Tathra has been restored, albeit on one level only, and there's always someone fishing from the high deck, whatever the weather, or time of day. Rugged up, Harry, Surrey and Arabella walk there from the little restaurant on the beach, where they enjoyed a change of menu from the bowling club. Two old men in fleecy tracksuits, wool caps and jogging shoes have lines in the shiny black water far below, but there's nothing in their buckets. A few lights shine across the expanse of surf between the wharf and the beach, and a cold nor-easter is blowing into their faces. They can hear the waves breaking.

'We won't be here tomorrow night, will we?' Surrey asks.

'I think we will, Dave. But you don't have to be. You'll finish tomorrow, won't you, Bella?'

'We should. One of the Merimbula solicitors has asked me to do a sentence for him, though. That'd keep me here until Friday.'

'Interesting?'

'No. Sexual offence. Not my favourites. He's got a good pre-sentence report from the probation service, though. Should be able to keep him out of jail.'

'But the solicitor wants someone else to blame in case he can't?' Harry asks.

'That's usually the reason, isn't it?'

Harry looks around for a stone or something else to throw into the water, but the windswept wharf has been picked clean.

Arabella threads her arm through Harry's, then loops around in front of him and does the same with their other arms. She hugs him. He lifts his arms clear and hugs her back. Surrey studies the anglers. They turn to walk back to the caravan park and their cabins, for which they now have surprising affection, and Arabella places herself in the centre, linking her arms with Harry's left and Surrey's right. As they walk past the warmly lit windows of the homes of the retired residents, nobody speaks.

It turns out that the last day of the Eden inquest is also the last day of Arabella's Bega stabbing trial. Surrey and Arabella arrive at the courthouse at 9.30 to be met with an atmosphere that communicates, implicitly, the certainty that their trial is finishing and other business will soon take over the judge's time. Three barristers, in their robes, have appeared in town for the first time and are drinking coffee in takeaway cups or talking on their phones or reading briefs on the courthouse verandah. Solicitors are shepherding clients in and out of the interview rooms. Police and other witnesses are making themselves known to those who caused subpoenas to be served on them, asking when they'll be needed. Arabella greets her client. 'Did you have a quiet night?'

'Too right. I read my statement through a million times. That's all I did.'

'So you're happy that you know it all?'

'Best as I can.'

Surrey joins them on the footpath.

'Looking very neat and tidy, Dean. I like the shirt.'

It's another country-and-western special: royal blue with pearl snaps on the pockets.

'Yeah, thought I'd keep it a bit quiet. Listen, about this cross-examination ...'

'Yes, no, and I don't recall.'

'Sure, sure, I haven't forgotten that. But what if he wants me to talk?'

Arabella smiles. 'It doesn't matter what he wants, Dean. We've all got our jobs here. I do the talking to the judge and the jury, Mr Surrey organises the evidence, and you tell your story. I don't want to hear anything new from you, only what's on that piece of paper. There's just one rule: whoever's asking the questions, the answers stay the same. You know that. We've been through it.'

'Yes, but what about trick questions? I'm not that good with tricky stuff.'

'No, Dean. I'll object to anything like that. It won't be allowed. Look, I understand how you're feeling — everyone's scared of cross-examination — but you might even find you enjoy it. Just remember: you're not talking to the prosecutor, and you're not talking to the judge. You're talking to the jury, and they're all people like you. They're locals, they know about the Australasia, and about the deckhands. They know it's not Sunday school down there.'

Surrey grips his client's upper arm. 'The best advice we can give you is to be yourself. The jury won't convict you unless they dislike you, so don't give them any reason for that. Don't be a smart-arse. Yes, no, I don't recall. Okay? For God's sake, if you don't know the answer, don't guess. You're on oath.'

'Okay.'

'Giving evidence isn't like taking a test at school, trying to get the answers right. Just keep it short, and tell the truth. We can do everything else for you, but only you can give your evidence.'

'Okay.'

Twenty minutes later, Arabella calls her client — her only witness. He looks nervously around from the witness box, then across at the jury. Handed a Bible to hold and a laminated card from which to read his oath, he stumbles through the words.

Judge Holden asks him to sit, and he does. She looks at Arabella. 'Yes, Ms Engineer?'

'Are you Dean Antico?'

'Yes.'

'Do you live at Eden?'

'Yes.'

'And are you a fisherman by trade?'

'Yes.'

'Have you always been involved with trawlers?' Arabella is coaxing her client beyond the monosyllables, settling him in.

'No. When I left school I was in the army for seven years.'

'What rank?'

'Corporal when I was discharged.'

'In?'

'Infantry.'

'Your discharge — was it honourable?'

The judge is alert. 'Ms Engineer, do you intend to raise character?'

'Yes, it was.' The client answers anyway.

'Just a minute, Mr Antico, I was speaking to your counsel.'

'My client is a man of good character, your Honour. Mr Crown has no issue with that.'

An almost imperceptible nod from the Crown and the judge settles back. 'Just being sure, Ms Engineer.'

'I'm indebted to your Honour. There may be something else on which the court needs to save me from myself, but not character.' With no response from the bench, Arabella turns back to her client, taking a quick look at the jury as her gaze passes over their faces. Nothing obviously negative.

'Mr Antico, you've heard the evidence of the police and the other drinkers at the Australasia Hotel?'

'Yes.'

'Is there anything they said with which you disagree?'

'Not really.'

The solicitor from Public Prosecutions whispers to his counsel, 'What's she doing?'

The Crown covers his mouth. 'Leaving me nothing to ask him, I'd say. She's not stupid.'

Arabella waits for that conversation to end. 'Is there anything else you think the jury should know about what happened before Mr O'Grady attacked you?'

'I object!'

'That's rejected, Ms Engineer. Put it more neutrally, would you?'

'As your Honour pleases. Before Mr O'Grady jumped on your back as you came out of the lavatory?'

'I object.' Less emphatically.

'No, Mr Crown, I'll allow it. That was the effect of the evidence you called. Can you answer, Mr Antico?'

'Well, he'd been baiting me all night. Calling me AntiCold, like the medicine. Knocking over my beer, bumping the cue when I was taking a shot on the pool table. Getting up my nose.'

'Why didn't you go home?' This isn't a question that Arabella has rehearsed with her client, and it's a serious error of judgment. Harry, had he been there, would have been furious. Arabella is pushing her luck, making a spur-of-the-moment bid to spike the prosecution's guns by asking the question about excessive provocation before it could be posed in cross-examination.

The prosecution solicitor is whispering again. 'Why's she asking that?'

'So that I don't.' But the prosecutor assumes that Arabella knows the answer — or even knows what she's doing — which she doesn't. Risky business. Surrey is trying to cover his panicky reaction by reading the formal indictment to himself. He can't watch.

Antico looks baffled. 'Go home?'

'Well, that would have avoided any trouble. Wouldn't it?'

Again, the Crown gives Arabella more credit than she deserves and assumes this is a planned pre-emptive strategy. If this doesn't come off, she's dug a grave for her client. Surrey is well aware that Antico doesn't have a clue as to what answer he should give.

'How could I just leave?' Antico is still nonplussed.

'What do you mean by that?' Holden J asks. She, too, is at a loss.

Antico looks at the foreman of the jury, a motor mechanic from one of the coastal hamlets. 'But it's my pub!' he says, with feeling. 'He's not going to scare me out of my pub! What would my mates say?'

The foreman nods vigorously in empathetic agreement. He sees the force of that, whatever the lawyers may think. He looks around himself at other male members of the jury, and they obviously share the outrage. A man can't back down. That goes without saying.

Surrey exhales. Crisis passed. Bullet dodged. Arabella takes a quick look at him and shrugs eloquently with her eyes: self-condemnation, apology, relief, gratitude. She exhorts herself to stick to the script. 'You agree, then, that you broke the glass and stabbed him with it?'

'I broke the glass, yes. I didn't stab him, but. I just hit out. I didn't aim, nothing like that.'

'Why?'

'Why what?'

'Why did you hit out with the broken glass?'

'Self-defence.'

'Just tell the jury what you mean by that.'

'Okay. He wasn't going to leave me alone. He'd made that obvious — baiting me, like I said, aggravating me. I could put up with that. But then he jumped on my back, and he was cutting off my air with his arm around my throat. I thought I was going to flake, and he'd put the boot in when I was down. I knew what happened to that cook from the motel.'

'What happened to the cook from the motel, Mr Antico?'

'I object. Hearsay.'

'Yes. Rejected.'

Arabella turns to Surrey. 'But this is about what motivated him, so it's an exception to the rule!'

'Don't argue it with me, girl. Tell the judge.'

She does. 'Your Honour, this has to be relevant to *mens rea* — the accused's intention. Intention is an essential element of this offence, and the Crown has, in this case, a duty to disprove to the criminal standard, beyond reasonable doubt, any possibility that the accused believed it was necessary to defend himself in the way he did, with that degree of force.'

Judge Holden takes a moment to spread the pages of her notebook, using both hands. She waits a beat. 'Ms Engineer, there are three things to say to that. First: I had already rejected the question, and you will not canvass my rulings. Next: counsel in a jury trial should never attempt to argue points of law before the jury. If you want to do that, make an application and I'll have the jury wait outside while I hear your submissions. And third: it is irrelevant what happened to the cook from the Black Dolphin Motel, about whom we have heard so much already. What is relevant, if anything, is what your client *believed* happened to that unfortunate man. And it has to be more focused than that, but I'm not going to do your job for you.'

'May it please you.' A chastened Arabella.

'So, are we clear? The question's rejected. Do you want to have another go at it, bearing in mind what I've just said?'

'Mr Antico, in the few seconds before you broke the glass and hit out with it, what was going through your mind?'

'I obj—'

'It's allowed. His state of mind is central to self-defence, Mr Crown. Answer it, please.'

'Okay. Well, it's like I said before. I was starting to black out, and I was thinking that when I do, he's going to kick the shit out of me — sorry for the language, but it's exactly what I was thinking — just like him and his brother did to that cook bloke, and I knew he was still in a coma in hospital, six months after they bashed him outside the pub. I reckoned then, and I still do now, that I didn't have any other choice.'

'Are you saying to the jury, then, that you honestly believed you had to strike him with the glass to save your own life?'

The Crown is rocketing out of his chair to object, but the judge gets there first, gesturing at the prosecutor to sit down. 'Ms Engineer, I give a prize every year for the most blatant leading question asked in my court. It's only June, but I'm prepared to award it to you now. Surely you know better than that?'

'I apologise, your Honour.'

But the man in the dock isn't following the legal niceties. He knows what he's supposed to say, and he's going to say it. He looks at the jury. 'Yes. I honestly believed that if I didn't defend myself with whatever I had, he would probably kill me.'

Surrey watches the jury. Even the women seem to be nodding in agreement. He smiles to himself, the judge snorts, and the Crown has the good grace to laugh.

When things settle down, Holden J looks over at the prosecution end of the Bar table.

'Mr Crown, are you thinking what I'm thinking? About the utility of cross-examination, and *Prasad*? We've got two other trials to get through.'

'I am, your Honour. Will you give me a moment, please, to get some instructions?' He bends to confer with his solicitor. 'We'll let it go, won't we?'

The solicitor is less than happy — he's spent three weeks organising witnesses and getting forensic reports from technicians who were supposed to be on holiday, booking their accommodation, finalising their evidence statements.

'Yeah, yeah,' his counsel concedes, 'but what's the point? She'd only give him a section 10 good behaviour bond anyway even if we won — no conviction. And we're not going to win. Let's not prolong the agony — I'm not going to get anything out of him on cross-examination.'

Eventually, after a few more home truths, the solicitor accedes, and the prosecutor straightens up to face the bench.

'I'll make the application, your Honour, that you give the jury a *Prasad* direction.'

Arabella has no idea what this is all about. It's a procedure she's never seen before. It's her turn to whisper a question. 'What's *Prasad*?'

Surrey smiles. 'You'll see.'

'No objection to that from the defence, I assume?'

'Oh — no, your Honour.' Still, Arabella has no idea what she's agreed to, but Surrey is still smiling and she assumes she answered correctly.

'Very well.' The judge's voice becomes more formal as she speaks to the jury.

'Members of the jury, the prosecution has made an application — and I'm sure he won't mind my telling you that this is most unusual, coming from the Crown — that I should invite you to consider your verdict now, without the defence adducing any further evidence and without you being subjected to the addresses of counsel or my summing up and my directions of law. This is a procedure that has been approved in certain cases by the superior courts. It was first done in a case called *Prasad*, which is why we call this a *Prasad* direction. So the question for you is pretty simple: you can either decide, without leaving the courtroom, to find the accused not guilty, or you can decide that you want to hear whatever other evidence there may be in the case before you consider your verdict. What you can't do, I must emphasise, is find Mr Antico guilty at this stage. Either you've heard enough, and you want to acquit him now without further ado, or you haven't heard enough, in which case the trial will continue. So, what's it to be, Mr Foreman? Will you consult your colleagues for a moment?'

The foreman speaks quietly to the jurors sitting alongside him, who nod and then lean back in their chairs, after which he turns and checks the mood of the row behind. It takes only a few moments, and then he stands. 'We'd find him not guilty now, your Honour.'

'And that's the verdict of you all?'

All twelve indicate their consent.

'Thank you. I direct that an acquittal be entered. Mr Antico, you're free to go.'

No longer the accused, Arabella's client stumbles on leaving the witness box. Surrey indicates for him to sit beside his lawyers while the judge dismisses the jury and adjourns the court. The jurors are taken out to be paid off, and the defence team retires to the courthouse verandah, where it takes some time for Surrey and Arabella to explain to Dean that it's all over, he's not going to be cross-examined, he's been found not guilty, and he's entitled to have the fingerprints taken at the time of his arrest destroyed. Just as they're about to take their leave of him, Antico is approached by members of the discharged jury who want to shake his hand or clap him on the shoulder. There's little doubt that they all know about the cook, and they even have an exhibit setting out Mr O'Grady's criminal record of violent offences.

'Well, Bella, today you learned about the value of a country jury,' Surrey says, as they head over to the coast for lunch. 'They usually know all about the accused, and all about the victim. Sometimes they even know which of the police witnesses are telling lies. It's nothing like a trial at the Downing Centre in town, where nobody ever knows anyone else.'

'It's kind of you to avoid the issue, David.'

'The issue? What issue would that be?'

'That we may have won the trial, but it was in spite of my total incompetence. I'd never heard of *Prasad*, I went off on a crazy frolic of my own — no, a bloody dangerous one that could have lost us the trial — without preparing the witness, and I won the judge's prize for the stupidest question of the year. In June.'

'Not the stupidest question, the most blatantly leading question.'

'I stand corrected. This stuff isn't me, David. I'm no good at it. Harry will kill me. Or worse, he'll feel sorry for me.'

'Only if he hears about it. All he's going to hear from us is that we won on a *Prasad*. He'll be impressed with that — they're as rare as hen's teeth. I don't know that he's ever had one.'

'Won't Holden tell him?'

'It's just another trial to her, Bella. And she's got problems of her own.'

Arabella looks out the passenger's window at a herd of Friesian cows beside the road. 'You're a kind man, David Surrey.'

As Surrey's car slows to sixty to travel through the village of Tathra, downhill towards lunch, Harry is throwing his blue bag, the Globite, his suit jacket and his tie onto the back seat of the Jaguar before setting off from Eden to meet Judge Holden at the Bega lawyers' pub. The bushfire inquest is over — far too soon for about a dozen of its participants, who will have to find other clients to charge for the two vacant weeks that have suddenly appeared in their diaries. As Harry does a U-turn, finding himself staring out to the blue horizon of the Tasman Sea, he chuckles, recalling a particularly gratifying bit of sledging he worked on the full-of-himself young barrister — the one so keen to ridicule Curry astride his white horse.

The hearing had been under way for less than an hour, and Harry's opponent was getting nowhere: cross-examining the bushfire control centre's radio operator about the Rural Fire Service's policy on logging messages from the tankers at the scene. So pompous were his questions, and so obscure his style of speech, that the coroner had to translate most of them. In any event, the vast majority of the answers given were either 'I don't recall', or 'I don't know — you'd have to ask him'. The questioner ignored the audible sighs from other counsel at the Bar table and refused to take the hint that his efforts were of no assistance to the court. Many of the family members of the deceased firefighters had gone outside in frustration. Having closed his notepad and capped his pen, making it clear that none of the evidence being explored was of any interest, Harry was discussing with one of his colleagues (none too quietly) the somewhat startling suit the cross-examiner was wearing: window-pane checked. Suddenly, as if struck by a blinding revelation, Harry's voice filled a brief pause in the proceedings: 'I know where I last saw that suit! It was at Cirque du Soleil!'

A burst of laughter from the lawyers, and a stern admonition from the learned coroner: 'Mr Curry, sledging went out with Ian Chappell.'

Harry half-rose in his chair and bowed. 'Quite so, your Worship. My apologies.'

'You can't worship me any more, Mr Curry. We're all your Honour now.'

'Just like the real judges, your Worship? Sorry, I should say "your Honour". I trust the court will forgive my solecism — I don't get down here often enough.'

'When you say "down here", Mr Curry, I shall assume you mean the far South Coast, rather than suggesting that my court is at a low level.'

While Harry took a moment to compose his next response, the cross-examiner gave in to petulance.

'If Mr Curry has finished trying to belittle me, and your Honour will attend once again to this tragic and important inquiry, may I be permitted to continue?'

The coroner gave him a long look. 'Well no, Mr Campbell. This interruption gives me a chance to point out to you that you have been interrogating this witness for thirty-seven minutes without obtaining a single answer that assists me in any way to address the issues upon which I am required by the legislation to report. I'm going to have to ask you to summarise for me the subject matters that you propose to cover in the balance of your questions. If I'm not satisfied of their relevance to my function, you won't be permitted to ask any further questions.'

Young Mr Campbell's response was unwise, betraying the fact that his self-confidence exceeded his judgment. 'With great respect, your Honour doesn't have the power to compel me to foreshadow my questions. If the court does not accept that, I would ask that you suspend this inquiry while I seek a mandatory injunction against you in another place.'

The coroner gave him a steely look. 'Do you mean by that that you intend to challenge my control of cross-examination in the Court of Appeal?'

'I do.'

Harry and his colleagues looked at their copies of the *Coroner's Act*, or their fingernails, or the ceiling. No one looked at the coroner or young Mr Campbell.

'Well, your client is free to take the matter elsewhere, Mr Campbell, but I'll make it clear to you that I will not delay this hearing so that you may consider an appeal.'

'As your Honour pleases.'

'And a word of advice, if I may?'

'By all means, your Honour.'

'If you do take this up to the Court of Appeal—'

'Yes, your Honour?'

'Don't wear that suit. I'll take the morning adjournment now, after which I expect any party that wishes to make submissions on the manner and cause of death of the deceased, or as to any recommendations I should make, to do so. I do not intend to adjourn the inquest for that purpose.'

Having left the courtroom to stand in the weak sunshine and consider what submissions he should make, Harry spotted the solicitor from Cooma and walked over to her. 'That was a bit unexpected … welcome, but certainly I didn't see it coming.'

'Didn't you see the local paper?'

'No, have you got it?'

The paper was handed to him, already at the editorial. It was headed 'Stop the Bickering' and the opinion piece that followed was a strong and unusually articulate condemnation of the insurance companies and government agencies for turning the inquest into an expensive blame game, when what the community wanted to know was why the volunteers had been sent into a death-trap, and whether the Rural Fire Service was going to institute changes to ensure that it could never happen again. The expression 'lawyers' picnic' was used twice.

A broad smile slowly spread across Harry's face. 'Your fingerprints are all over this!'

'I decline to comment until my counsel is present,' she laughed.

'Not much they can teach you, is there?'

'All your idea, Mr Curry.'

As Harry returned to his place at the Bar table, the clerk of the Local Court handed him a message from Judge Holden, asking him to meet her at a Bega pub at lunchtime, or as soon as he could be there.

'Isn't she sitting this afternoon?' he asked.

'Apparently her first trial's over. They're taking the afternoon off.'

Harry had a word with Moses, and compared notes on the points he wanted to raise. When the hearing resumed, lawyer after lawyer for the insurers and the bureaucracies declined the coroner's invitation to make submissions. Some mumbled about insufficient time to prepare their remarks, but they sounded unconvinced of that themselves. There was a short submission from a lone QC who had been engaged to speak on behalf of the families of the deceased men, and Harry was the last to rise to his feet before Moses gave his own summation.

'May it please your Honour, I shall be brief. I have spoken with counsel assisting you, and am aware of the points he wishes to make in respect of the court's formal findings in relation to the deaths. I adopt those submissions, with respect. They are plainly correct. As to your Honour's other function, the educative role of the coroner, I would just wish to say this: it is perfectly clear that the Rural Fire Service failed to equip these men adequately before sending them to fight this catastrophic fire. They were neither trained, nor transported, nor clothed with the protection the community would rightly expect them to be given. Their tanker was thirty years old and plainly unsafe. Other fire services have vehicles fitted with sprinkler systems, heat insulation, breathing apparatus and fuel-supply systems that can't fail from overheating lines or vaporising fuel. If the RFS can't ensure the safety of its volunteers, and if the state government won't fund the purchase of up-to-date safety equipment, no one should be sent out to fight bushfires. I submit that your Honour should recommend an expert assessment of the equipment available, and suspension of firefighting until the service has been adequately re-equipped.'

'Thank you, Mr Curry. Is there anything further?'

'Just this, your Honour. It would be wrong for this inquest to be completed without acknowledgment of the sacrifice these men made. We let them down, but that can't diminish their bravery. I represent the only survivor from that tanker. His name is Douglas Hain, and he's sitting behind me. It may be thought that, in their anxiety to please the insurance companies, or the insurance companies' accountants, some of the counsel at this table wanted to hint, however obliquely, that my client bears in some way some blame for the deaths that occurred. None has had the courage to stand up here and articulate that smear expressly. I ask your Honour to give the lie to that cowardly inference by including in your findings an expression of the community's gratitude for the heroism of Douglas Hain. It is impossible for any of us here to imagine the fear he faced as he tried, with all his personal resources, to drive his truck and his men to safety, when he had no hope of seeing where he was going. It is equally impossible for us to comprehend the sense of loss he feels. Douglas Hain ought not to have to face the rest of his life wondering whether he could have done any more for his men. He couldn't, and he deserves to have your Honour put that beyond doubt in his findings.'

From behind him, Harry could hear two women sobbing quietly. He worried that he'd gone too far, but the coroner was nodding his agreement.

'Thank you for that, Mr Curry. There's always a risk that we lose sight of the humanity of these tragedies, but I will adopt what you've asked me to do. Is there anything else before I ask Mr Moses to address me?'

'No, may it please your Worship.' Harry sat. The coroner didn't correct him.

When the proceedings were completed with the coroner's delivery of his formal findings and his restrained but powerful praise of the deceased and Doug Hain, the court was adjourned. In silence, the public filed out and, having gathered their books, the lawyers followed them. The Hains emerged from the building with Harry. As Doug crossed the verandah, the wives and mothers of the dead men embraced him.

Harry avoids the frame of the media's lenses, waves farewell to the Hain parents, and unlocks the Jag. Some gravel spurts from the rear tyres as he departs, still buckling his seat belt.

At two o'clock in the beer garden opposite the Bega courthouse, Judge Holden sits with her associate, waiting for Harry and looking at the glass of red wine on the table in front of her. Lunch plates are cleared away, and people are leaving, going back to work in the shops and offices along Carp Street. Two of them nod at the judge as they pass her table. Local solicitors. There's to be the obligatory dinner at the pub tonight, where the legal practitioners — locals and the barristers and solicitors on circuit — shout the judge a collegiate meal, observing all the pleasantries. Jean Holden isn't looking forward to it. It's all the things that won't be said, all the avoidance, that she dreads. Rather than resent those who refuse to attend such events ('Why should I pay for the bloody judge's dinner? She/he slotted my customer'), she envies them. The judge tries the wine again, finds it hasn't improved, and thanks the work-experience kid clearing her table, who drops the cutlery onto the brick paving. The boy blushes to the roots of his hair, which has been gelled to stand up to a point in the middle of his head. The judge wonders why it should be fashionable in Bega to sport a Newtown hairstyle.

The beer garden is almost empty by the time Harry arrives. He's in jeans and a T-shirt, carrying a schooner of beer and a packet of chips. He puts them on the table and sits.

'Health food of a nation, I see,' the judge observes.

The associate leaves, saying she has some shopping to do.

Harry tears the bag open and stuffs a handful of chips into his mouth. He's had no lunch. 'A bit warmer today.'

'How's your inquest progressing, Harry?'

'Evidence finished this morning, Jean. Submissions, findings and all.'

'Really? I understood it was going to run and run. I was surprised when Arabella said you'd be able to meet me now.'

'A lot of the insurance lawyers made the same assumption, but our learned coroner — God bless him — kept them on a short leash. He had no reason to put up with their bullshit. It's his last matter.'

'Speaking of which …'

They both take a sip from their glasses, and Harry twists in his chair to see who may be in earshot. There's no one. 'Any news from the reptiles' lawyers?'

'Some, and not bad news at all. Bunter is hellbent on exploiting a major scandal at the *Herald*. One of the people writing the story about me has been sacked for misconduct.'

'To do with the story? That'd be too much to hope.'

'No, it's a sexual harassment case that was filed the same day as the story was published. A cadet photographer and a cadet journo have both sworn affidavits complaining that they were groped in the lift by this bloke. He was summarily sacked, but the complainants both want compensation and the talk is that the journo is going to challenge the sacking. It's not going away quietly.'

'An unholy disaster, in other words.' Harry forms the Olympic rings on the tabletop with the moisture on the bottom of his glass.

'Not for us.'

'Apart from falling upon this news with glad cries, what are your people doing?' Harry swipes his glass back and forth, smearing the rings into a shallow puddle. He eats more chips.

Holden takes one from the packet. 'Our Bunterish mate is keeping up the pressure — a barrage of emails from the solicitor, one every three hours, with our settlement demands ratcheting up the scale as they don't respond. An apology and retraction in grovelling terms, twenty thousand for our costs to date, and a quarter of a mill in lieu of damages. And none of it confidential — not even the money. What we're telling them is that we won't tolerate any delay. This has to be done quickly, or I can never recover from the damage they've done. This week or nothing. The apology's got to be on the front page on Saturday.'

'The point being to exploit the fact that this journo won't help them if they decide to defend the thing?'

'Exactly right. They know we know. Our sources tell us that he's a notorious groper, been getting away with it for years because he's just about their top investigative operator, and the staff reaction to the harassment case was so strongly against him that there's no way he can be reinstated. Not even on the *Illawarra Mercury* or the *Gulargumbone Clarion*. There's no way in the world they can defend the story as true, because he did all the work — the other two just contributed sidebars, not about me — and they simply can't call him as a witness.'

'As they say, luck's a fortune. It'd be fantastic to wrap it all up in a week.'

'Part of me wants to fight the case out in court. To prove that none of it's true. But I haven't forgotten what you said about that taking two years, and all the nastiness of the fights over disclosure of my financial records. And Barry's.'

'How could they possibly justify that? Access to your husband's confidential information?'

'Joint accounts. Joint mortgage. Not very politically correct, I know, but I have the feeling they would have fought us for the bank statements even if Barry had his own account. As you warned me, they have this fixation on following the money trail. Anyway, the money's not the point. It's really a matter of the prominence of the apology, and the wording. I'm not going to die in a ditch over fifty grand.'

'I thought you said 250.'

'They've offered 100 plus costs, and I always said I'd take 150 in my hand.'

'So you should. You think you can do it?'

'I do.' She smiles for the first time.

'One thing you haven't told me.'

'What?'

'The gropees at the *Herald* — boys or girls?'

The judge gathers her handbag and stands. 'Quite. And thanks, Harry. It was good advice, and I won't forget it.'

'No, you won't, Jean. You won't forget it, and you won't forgive it.'

She looks at him for a long time, looking at the colour of his eyes.

'It's true, isn't it?' she says.

'That no good deed goes unpunished? Very true, in my experience.'

'Would a bottle of Grange help?'

'It certainly wouldn't hurt.'

Harry finishes the last of his beer, and stands. He holds out his hand and they shake.

Holden shields her eyes with her free hand. 'See you in court, Harry.'

'Probably not, Jean.' And he leaves the pub.

The Set-up

Even before this disaster, Baby's life had not been an outstanding success. The youngest son of a demanding Woolgoolga banana-farming family, he was educated with a great deal of difficulty and expense, his ill-advised marriage produced two extraordinarily beautiful children (now aged six and eight) but was now in the throes of an expensive and unpleasant divorce, and his career as an architect has been characterised more by long periods of unemployment than by any bricks-and-mortar achievements.

And now, as he sits in a cell in the Surfers Paradise watch-house, waiting for his solicitor to arrive and arrange his bail on a charge of rape, Baby feels as if he has finally lost any semblance of control, or even influence, over the direction his life has taken.

It's 5 a.m. on a Saturday. It should have been the dawn of the third day of Baby's brief holiday on the Gold Coast with his children. The three of them should have spent their four-day weekend eating pizza and ice cream, visiting Dreamworld, or Water World, or Movie World, or the Irwin zoo, swimming in the hotel pool and watching DVDs in their room. But the children are in the room alone, or they were alone until Baby told the police about them, and a policewoman was sent to the hotel to make sure that an adult is there to look after them when they wake, which they will do in about an hour, and then wait with them until their mother arrives by the first plane this morning from Sydney. Baby groans. What are his parents going to say? Worse still, what's his wife — ex-wife — going to say? He's got a fair idea. The words 'pervert' and 'criminal' may rate more than a few passing mentions. And he wonders if he'll be spared the usual diatribe about how could she have done anything so stupid as to marry what she is pleased to call 'a bloody Indian'. Baby groans again. These are not the first groans the watch-house police have heard from him.

He tries to think how he's going to explain last night to the solicitor whom the police have been kind enough to contact for him. Baby is not wise in the ways of the Queensland police. He decides that it will be best to tell the lawyer the truth. The whole truth. Which is this: Bruce Booja Singh — Baby's full name — has access rights to his children once a month, and for one week of their Christmas school holidays. Glenda consented to his taking them to the Gold Coast for four days, and last Thursday they caught an early plane from Sydney to Coolangatta. Baby rented a Corolla as part of the package deal, and drove it to their marble-and-chrome hotel at Surfers in time for lunch. The afternoon was spent on the beach, then, after an early meal of Coca-Cola, chips and tomato sauce in the hotel's coffee shop, the kids were asleep by seven o'clock. No daylight saving, and lots of fresh air.

Feeling guilty, but not guilty enough, Baby slipped out of the room with the intention of going clubbing. He looked in at a couple of nightclubs, but the doormen were hardly welcoming to a 39-year-old man on his own, and Baby gave up and was back in the room with Tayla and Jarrod before ten o'clock. Both were still asleep.

Friday was spent marvelling first at trained dolphins and then the spectacle of an American police chase on the Queensland coast, complete with black-and-whites and gunfire in the streets. The kids loved it. So did Baby, for that matter. His cultural targets have never been all that difficult to hit, and *The Blues Brothers* is his all-time-favourite film. Then a couple of hours in the hotel pool, and another evening meal in the coffee shop. This time, calamari rings and chips. Tayla and Jarrod didn't eat the calamari, so Baby ate theirs as well as his own, and had a beer. The holiday was going well.

Feeling even less guilty than on the first night, Baby waited until 10.30 before he made his second attempt at a night's clubbing. When he pulled their room's door shut behind him and headed for the lift, the children were fast asleep, their sunburnt faces peaceful on the pink pillows. Dressed in his black silk shirt, best black jeans and Chelsea boots, Baby walked along the glittering strip of cafes, restaurants, convenience shops and clubs. He loved it — the unrestrained vulgarity. There were queues outside all the clubs and slow-moving shiny cars, full of young men; the air was thick with pounding bass notes and deep angry rumbles from their exhausts.

Turning into a pedestrian area, he saw the flashing neon invitation of the imaginatively named 'Bottoms Up' nightclub, and joined the fairly short queue outside, fenced in by a velvet rope. The queue wasn't moving, but Baby wasn't concerned. There was a girl in front of him — she looked about eighteen, dark hair and dark eyes — and it didn't take long for her to start talking to him with unexpected familiarity. She was dressed in a red halter top and short white skirt, with a sequined purse on a long strap and dangerously high white heels, which she seemed to be having some trouble managing. He thought she looked familiar, but the truth was he had Minnie Mouse in mind. It was the big white shoes that did it. Plainly enough, she had been drinking and showed every sign of disinhibition. Baby had no quarrel with that. She informed him, and everyone in the immediate vicinity, that it was her birthday. They chatted and, after five more minutes, the queue suddenly moved forward and they found themselves under the doorman's appraisal.

'She's been at it a bit, hasn't she, mate?' he asked Baby. 'I mean already.'

Baby, pleased to be identified as the girl's companion, persuaded the doorman that this was the birthday girl, her friends were already waiting for her inside, and that he'd look after her. The custodian gave one of those 'against-my-better-judgment' shrugs and clicked the rope back in place behind them. They then took the lift with two other couples, the girl hugging and kissing a delighted and responsive Baby on the way up to the nightclub, which was all darkness, strobe lights and impenetrable noise, some of it alleged to be music. Not that they cared. They emerged from the lift holding hands, and immediately moved to the dance floor where, after a couple of numbers locked closely together, she managed to insert her hand behind Baby's belt and reach down to make contact with his quickly aroused penis. It was no easy manoeuvre, Baby being a short, chubby person and his jeans having been intended for a tall, slim person. Once she had her objective in her grasp, she didn't let go for another two dances, and then only when Baby suggested that they stop and get a drink. When she agreed, his feeling was that it was not a moment too soon. Not that she needed the drink, but he needed to decompress.

After his beer and her double Bacardi and Coke, they resumed dancing. This time she worked his fly open for easier access. Sweating, emboldened and excited, Baby asked her the question he'd never been game to pose to any woman. 'Do you want to go out and have sex?'

'Yes.' In a New Zealand accent, loudly and happily, as if she feared he'd never ask.

They left the club, Baby struggling to zip himself up in the lift as she kissed him keenly but inaccurately. One overwhelming idea — that all his Christmases had come at once — filled Baby's head. When they emerged at street level, the air was somewhat cooler, but it was alone in that.

'Where's your hotel?' he asked.

'Over there,' she indicated a lit-up tower, 'but we can't go in. My father's here too, and he might come down to my room to check up on me.'

'Well, there's someone else in my room too, so we'll have to use my car.'

They crossed the street towards Baby's hotel, the girl teetering on her heels, and occasionally slipping off. She clung to him and they eventually made it into the foyer, where they waited for a lift to take them to the basement car park. The staff at the hotel's reception desk eyed them doubtfully, and Baby was grateful when the lift doors closed. He found the car, unlocked it, and drove up the ramp into the bright lights.

As Baby drove, the girl kicked her shoes off and again worked on his fly, but the seat belt he'd fastened presented some difficulty.

They travelled for about fifteen minutes, the street lights washing over her face, which looked even drunker than before. She gave up her groping and was pressing buttons, trying to find music on the little car's radio, but kept getting the wrap-up of the day–night cricket from Melbourne. Baby wanted to know the score, but didn't think it wise to ask. She kept pressing the buttons. He followed any sign that referred to a beach, and parked in the darkest place he could find, the sand stretching out in front of the car, a dim line of breakers visible in the distance. The girl was humming along with a song she'd managed to find.

At Baby's suggestion, they got into the back seat. The girl untied her halter top and Baby pulled it down to her waist. She pulled up her short skirt, and pushed her pants down and off. He undid his belt and zip, pushed down his jeans and underpants, and climbed on top of her. She placed him inside her and it was all over in a matter of seconds.

'Where's my shoes?' she kept repeating.

Catching his breath, Baby told her they were in the front. She put her pants on, pulled down her skirt and re-tied her top. Then she opened the back door, got out, retrieved her shoes and handbag, and set off at a fast trot across the street behind the car park. An uncomprehending Baby dressed himself and returned to the driver's seat. He could see the girl about thirty metres away on the other side of the road, talking to a young man and pointing back at the car. She and the man were walking in the direction of a public phone when Baby started the ignition and left the car park, uncertain of the way back to his hotel. It took him the best part of half an hour to find it, and to park and lock the Corolla.

When he got back to the foyer to change lifts, police were waiting for him. They arrested but didn't handcuff him — there were other people in the foyer — brought him to the watch-house in the back of a police car, bullied him a bit but they didn't attempt to interrogate him before he'd made contact with the solicitor they thought would be best for him. It hasn't yet occurred to Baby, who has no prior experience with police, that the lawyer they chose might be a tame one.

Baby looks at his watch. Almost 7 a.m. and still no solicitor. The kids will be awake by now. He groans yet again. What Baby can't tell the lawyer, because he doesn't know, is what happened after the girl left his car, which was this: She ran, carrying her shoes, to the first person she saw, which was a young English holidaymaker. As she reached him, she was weeping. 'I've just been raped,' she wailed.

'Where?'

'Over there. In that car. By him! He's still in it — see? Have you got a phone?'

'No, but I saw one down there. We'll ring the police. Do you know the number?' And he took her to the public phone. As Baby drove past, the young man made a mental note of the car's registration number and repeated it to the emergency operator as soon as he got through. They were collected by a police car within five minutes of making the call. Other police used their computer to trace the car's owner — the rental company — after which it was a simple matter to find Baby's name, identify his hotel and send a car there to arrest him.

And that's how he comes to be in a cell at the watch-house now, wishing a tsunami would come and sweep him, the girl, the police and everything else away.

* * *

A week passes. Arabella and Harry are at breakfast in Newtown, and Harry has just demonstrated that he can read the *Weekend Australian*, including its glossy magazine, in less than ten minutes. In fact, it took eleven minutes and twenty-one seconds by the stopwatch on Arabella's phone, but she doesn't want to hurt his pride. At least he didn't pay for the paper — the café provides that. Arabella mops up the last of her scrambled eggs. 'I've got a brief in Queensland.'

'Really?' He picks up the *Herald*, decides against another speed-reading stunt, and puts it back down. 'Your reputation's growing.'

'Would that it were. No, it's a sort of family matter. A very distant cousin, many times removed, from Woolgoolga.'

'Thought you didn't want to do divorces. Or property settlements, or whatever cruelty married people inflict on each other.'

'It's a rape.'

'Quaint expression. They still call it that in the deep north, do they? What would it be under the *Crimes Act* here — sexual assault category 1A sub-paragraph (e)?'

'Something like that.'

'Don't like the sound of this.'

'I thought you might not.'

'There isn't much that I learned from my father, but I've never doubted that he was right when he said there are absolutely no circumstances in which I could appear for any member of my family.'

'Speaking of whom: were you able to see your father on Friday night? They let you in?'

'Late as it was, yes. Eight o'clock. I actually helped get him into his pyjamas and into bed, which meant he took me for a doctor, or maybe a male nurse. You know what he asked? "How much longer?"'

Arabella puts her hand on his. 'What did you tell him?'

I said: '"Not long now, Dad." He seemed happy with that.'

They are silent for a moment, and Harry signals for another short black.

'Getting back to my family,' Arabella says, 'my mother isn't much concerned with barristers' etiquette. She says I have to defend Baby.'

'You've been discussing this with your mother? And his name's Baby?'

'Hmm. She rang me in chambers last night. It was 7 a.m. in London, and she's not at her best in the early morning. Anyway, she says Baby's innocent, the cousins are distraught — the whole family's distraught — his ex-wife's going to exploit this to the hilt in their property settlement, and the children have been told their daddy's going to jail.'

'Their mother told them that?'

'Their grandmother. The Duchess of Penrith. The Queen, my aunt says, of I-told-you-so. This was one of those unusual marriages where both sides believed their children married beneath them.'

'But you're not going to do it, Bella, are you? Appear for him?'

'It's expected of me. I'm the only lawyer in the family, and no one else would be acceptable.'

'You can't.'

'I know.'

'Is this your subtle, manipulative way of ensuring that I take it on?'

'Oh, Harry, how could I ever hope to deceive you?'

He gives her a long-suffering look.

'Are you going to have any trouble being instructed by a Gold Coast solicitor?'

'Wearing white shoes and a white belt? I would rather think he'd be likely to have trouble with me, Bella.'

'Indeed to goodness.'

And that's how they find themselves checking into the Sofitel at Southport. The Woolgoolga family's covering all expenses. Not a problem, with five good years from the bananas, the continued success of a Coffs Harbour Indian restaurant, and the rents from six holiday homes. Harry looks around their gigantic bedroom.

'On legal aid allowances, even a highway motel would have been a bit of a struggle. This'll just have to do, I suppose.'

As he turns away from Arabella, a huge soft pillow hits him in the back of the head.

'So Baby's not the only violent member of your family? When do we see him, did you say?'

'The conference at the solicitor's office is at 4.30. We can walk there, apparently.'

'Wouldn't it be better at the courthouse? I'm never comfortable conferring in solicitors' offices. In Sydney, it'd be an ethical breach.'

'We're not in Kansas any more, Toto.'

'How very true.' Harry reclines on the gigantic bed. 'Did you see the people out there? Their attire?'

'They're tourists, Harry. Probably from New South Wales. And I'll bet they were equally stunned by your appearance — they can't get many chalk-striped suits and suede shoes at Southport, can they?'

'Most hurtful. As long as the magistrate's not wearing Bermuda shorts and long white socks.'

'Under his gown?'

'Magistrates wear gowns in Queensland?'

'So I'm told. All attributable to American television.'

Arabella takes off her shoes and joins Harry. 'What's the time?'

'Three o'clock. That gives us ninety minutes. Will that be sufficient?' Harry rises on one elbow.

'Possibly. It may not be.'

'Really? Ninety minutes?'

'Oh, sorry, Harry. I thought you said ninety seconds.'

Harry seizes another giant pillow and plants it over Arabella's face. 'Never joke about that! We take our manhood seriously in Queensland, love.'

The solicitor's office proves to be remarkably similar to Surrey's in Goulburn — files spread out everywhere, no apparent system for anything. But the walls are decorated with photographs of the solicitor competing in triathlons, and there are trophies on the bookshelves. A law degree from Bond University hangs in pride of place, and Harry wonders at the wisdom of that. Would you want that to be generally known? Without asking permission, Harry takes the leather seat behind the desk. Arabella and the tanned and athletic solicitor, whose name is Chris, take the clients' chairs. Baby is outside in the waiting room.

'You know, Chris,' says Harry, 'we don't have committal hearings before magistrates in New South Wales any more. Haven't had them for years.'

'Must make life hard.'

'It does, but you can see the sense of it. The lawyers used to drag them out for weeks, cross-examining every witness on every possible issue for days and days. They weren't dress rehearsals for the trial — more like mini Royal Commissions. The solicitors and their tame counsel would bleed the poor old punters dry — the ones who could afford to pay for committals — and then, when the money had all gone, they'd dump the client on legal aid and walk away. That's why our committals are all done on paper now.'

Chris shifts uncomfortably in his seat and opens his copy of the brief on his knees.

'Still do that here, do they? Rip off the hapless defendants?' Harry asks.

Chris looks even more uncomfortable. 'Oh, you know ... you can get a lot of valuable stuff for the trial. Or you can see that it'd be hopeless to defend, and get them to plead.'

'Lots of pleas of guilty, are there?'

'Mostly. The police here are pretty able.'

Arabella looks quizzically at him. 'Really?'

'I was in the police. They put me through my law degree.'

'I see.' It's Harry's turn to study the brief. 'Anything you want to raise before we get Baby in?'

'Umm, can I just understand Ms Engineer's part in it? Is she appearing as your junior?'

'That'd be the best way of putting it, yes. Anything else?'

'What will you want me to do, then?'

'Sit behind us.'

Chris looks a little miffed at that. Arabella, softening the blow, puts her hand on his arm and says, 'What Mr Curry means, Chris, is that we're going to have to play it by ear. When local knowledge becomes relevant, I'll liaise with you. We need you to be present, and involved, the whole time.'

Somewhat mollified, the solicitor leaves the room to bring in the terrified client. He then has to go and borrow a chair from one of his partners' rooms for Baby to sit on.

Baby is visibly sweating, despite the air conditioner. Harry leans over the desk to shake his hand. Baby makes a little bow to Arabella as Harry starts talking.

'Let me explain what's going on, Baby. We're going to talk to you now about what really happened that night. We need to know every detail you can give us — what the girl said, what she wore, what she did, where you went, what you saw. No matter how trivial or unimportant you might think it is. Now I know that you spoke to the police after Chris came to the watch-house on the Saturday morning — we've got a copy of that interview. I wish you hadn't, but you did, so I've got to play the ball as it lies. You've got to understand that you must tell me the truth, but I'll be very unhappy if what you tell me is inconsistent with the police interview. That'll give us real problems. If you're going to contradict yourself, you're going to have to explain why.'

Baby looks nervously at Arabella. 'Yes, I've been told.'

And the next hour is spent going through everything Baby can recall, then raising with him, one by one, the allegations made by the girl in her statement to the detectives. There is also a medical report, obligatory in all rape investigations, but Harry does not discuss that with his client. When the lawyers have covered everything that concerns them, Arabella invites Baby to tell them what worries him.

'Does the jury get to know that I left the children to go out clubbing, with no babysitter?'

Harry looks at Chris. 'Didn't you explain the difference between a committal and a trial?'

The solicitor looks embarrassed. 'I tried to.'

Harry turns to Baby. 'Baby, this isn't the trial. This is just an administrative procedure — yes, it's in a court, but there's no jury, no verdict, and you can't be found guilty or innocent at the end of it. All that's happening here, although it's very serious, is that the magistrate examines all the police evidence to see whether it's good enough to put you on trial. If he doesn't think that a jury is likely to find you guilty, he'll dismiss the charge.'

Baby's face lights up. 'Well, that'll happen, won't it? I mean, the magistrate will see that I'm telling the truth, and that she's a liar.'

'He's not concerned with that. Look, I know this is hard to follow, but he's not concerned with credit — the credibility or the truthfulness of the witnesses — that's for a jury in the long run, unless this girl is so obviously lying that he has to act on it. If he's satisfied that you had sex with her, and you've already admitted that you did, so that's a non-issue, the only question he has to answer is whether there is evidence fit to go to a jury that she didn't consent to it. That's what rape is — having sex with someone against their will.'

'But it wasn't against her will! I asked if she wanted to, and she said yes, so we did.'

'I know. That's what you told the police, and that's what you tell us — but it's not what the girl says. She says she was so drunk, she was unconscious at the time. She told the detectives that she blacked out on the drive to the beach, and woke up to find you having sex with her.'

'She never blacked out.'

'Well, that may be the whole issue at the trial, but not here and not now. Then it's going to be a matter for the jury to decide whether they believe her. She's likely to deny everything you've said about the foreplay at the nightclub and the agreement to go and have sex. You realise that?'

An unhappy Baby acknowledges it.

'I don't want you getting unrealistic expectations, Baby. You had sex with her, that's a given. She says she didn't consent, no matter what you say. Normally, that's enough to commit you for trial in about six months' time, which is when the jury gets involved.'

'Then why can't we go straight to trial now? I don't know how much longer I can stand this. I can't work, the whole divorce is a disaster, she's being a total bitch as only she can, and I haven't been allowed to see Tayla and Jarrod. They've been poisoned against me. I can't cope.'

Arabella takes over. 'Baby, we understand all that, but we're not in control of this. The law has to take its course. You have to take comfort from the fact that your team is working on this, for you, and on nothing else. If there has to be a trial, we'll press for the earliest possible date. This girl's from New Zealand, and it's going to take some coordination of the availability of all the witnesses — the complainant, the police, the doctor, the people from the hotel, even the English tourist. They'll want him back for the trial, so he'll get an all-expenses-paid holiday. Could take more than a year to set up.'

Harry nods. 'It could. But don't think this is a waste of time, Baby, because it isn't. There are a number of very valuable things we can get from this preliminary hearing, things that ought to greatly increase the likelihood of a jury rejecting this girl's story, her allegations. The most important advantage we have, and you wouldn't have got this in New South Wales, is that we get to cross-examine the girl in advance of the trial. It's like a dress rehearsal. So I get to try a few things out, for example I get to decide how tough I can be on her in front of a jury. I don't want to create sympathy for her by being too rough, but I'm not going to go easy either. We'll see how she reacts in front of the magistrate, where I can't really do any harm. It's not pretty, and the feminists hate it, but it's something we have to do.'

Arabella looks out the window and says nothing.

'I don't mind how tough you are on her.'

'I know that, Baby, but it has to be for a forensically valid reason, not to punish her. Anyway, we won't know how much we'll get until the process is complete, and that'll take about three days. Now, is there anything else you want to ask us? Do you follow all that?'

'I think so. But do the police have to tell the court about me leaving the kids unattended?'

'Don't worry about it. The magistrate will think you're stupid and irresponsible, and he'd be right. You were. You know that, we all know that. But it can't affect the decision he has to make ... and if there's a trial, we'll work very hard to keep it away from the jury.'

And, with a few more assurances and words of comfort, they break up the conference. Arabella arranges for herself and Harry to join Baby and his parents at the hotel for dinner in two hours' time. She promises that they won't talk about the case.

'Yes, but can you promise that my mother won't talk about it?'

Arabella can only smile in acknowledgment of the impossibility of that.

The dining room at the Sofitel is very pleasant. Cool, but not refrigerated. It is on several levels and divided into separate areas, breaking up the sight lines and suggesting privacy, which is what this table of five wants. Arabella is wearing a slim black dress, and Harry's in a pale linen jacket and tie, with dark slacks. Baby's mother is in a maroon sari into which a great deal of gold thread has been woven. She looks strong, determined. His father — a tall and dignified man — is in a bright blue suit and a startling tie. He looks thoughtful, interested in his surroundings. Baby is in his favourite outfit, the black silk shirt, black jeans and black boots. After the initial awkwardness, drinks are ordered and the menu scanned. Harry says softly to Baby, 'Have you got any other clothes with you?'

'Yes.'

'Clothes suitable for court?'

Arabella steps in. 'It's all been dealt with, Harry. Baby's got a grey suit and an old school tie. Brisbane Grammar.'

'Chris says the beak's a Protestant, which is rare enough.'

The mother asks, 'The beak?'

'The magistrate, Auntie.'

'And a Protestant beak?'

'Yes. It can't hurt.'

Harry asks Arabella if she and Baby's mother have discussed the sari. She listens in, becoming a little angry. 'How could my clothes possibly have anything to do with this?'

Arabella looks helplessly at Harry, so he picks up the ball. 'I'll have to speak plainly. We want to create as little sensation as possible. There'll be reporters, in all probability. We don't want this to be a notable case, because any jury we get will be from this neck of the woods, and the odds are that they'll read the local rag and remember a story about an Indian raping a tourist. Queensland — and you must know this — isn't noted as the most tolerant state of Australia. They don't mind typecasting any black person — and that's how they'll view Baby — as a sexual primitive. I'm sorry, but we have to think of this stuff. A very ordinary dress would be best, even here where there's not yet a jury. Let's not stand out from the crowd. I don't suspect for the moment that the magistrate would be influenced by race, but we have to play a long game here.'

'Sexual primitive? My Baby? He went to Grammar! He's an architect!'

'Don't shoot the messenger, Auntie. The quieter, the better.'

Baby's father hushes his wife, his only contribution to the conversation. The meals arrive, and all eat in silence for ten minutes.

Having finished his meal, Baby addresses Harry. 'Mr Curry — that's funny, isn't it? An Indian being defended by a curry?' Nobody thought it was funny. 'But you do believe me, don't you? I want you to tell me that, please.'

'It makes no difference what I believe, Baby.'

Auntie's not satisfied. 'But you'll do a better job, won't you, if you believe in Baby's innocence? That must be right.'

'Not necessarily. I believe in the rules, and the most important rule of all is the presumption of innocence. I certainly believe that Baby cannot possibly be convicted if he's not guilty. If I'm not emotionally involved, I can stand back and make a far better assessment of the evidence and the witnesses. It won't do me or Baby any good to make a great show of hating this young woman, as if that proves I believe my client has been falsely accused. That's the very reason why Arabella can't defend your son. She couldn't possibly be objective. She'd want him to be acquitted rather than work to have him acquitted. If you follow me. Counsel has to be objective, and family is never that.'

Auntie won't let go. 'But Mr Curry, you're family, really, aren't you?'

Harry looks sideways at the woman who has changed his life in ways he could never explain. 'Let's just say I want to be.'

Arabella looks momentarily stunned, but busies herself by rearranging the cutlery on her empty plate. News to her.

It's nearly midnight, and Arabella's brushing her hair. Harry's reading the brief in bed.

'Harry …'

'Mmm?'

'That was very sweet. And very unexpected.'

'What was?'

'Oh, you know what I'm talking about. Imagine you wanting to be part of Auntie's family!'

'I don't, not really.'

She feels a knot forming in her stomach. 'Then what was that about?'

'I want you and me to be a family. If Auntie and Uncle, and even Baby, come with that, *c'est la vie*. I promise not to complain.'

She puts down the brush and joins him in bed. 'That's very sweet. And not only that, it headed off Auntie's impending lecture on my coming to live in Woolgoolga, to meet lots of light-skinned, rich young banana farmers, and spend my time doing their books, or their conveyancing, or whatever. Away from the nastiness of the criminal law in Sydney.'

'Far be it from me to stand in the way of such a glittering future.'

'Any more of that and I'll phone down to room service for a heavy-duty cheese grater.'

'For what purpose?'

'To put you out of action for about six months, I would expect.'

'Action?'

'Thank God. I thought you'd never ask.'

The Southport Magistrates Court — opened, according to a plaque in the foyer, in 1987 by some politician who's now in jail — puts Harry in mind of a small multi-storeyed car park. Too many signs directing traffic, too much concrete. His efforts to do the right thing by introducing himself and Arabella to the magistrate, as visiting counsel, before the hearing commences are foiled, because the prosecutor is running late. Baby's parents install themselves in the first row in the public gallery, and the solicitor sits the soberly dressed Baby next to him, immediately behind the barristers. When the flustered prosecutor charges through the doors of the courtroom at three minutes past ten, the magistrate comes immediately onto the bench and kicks the matter off. 'The matter of Singh?' he asks.

'May it please your Honour, I appear for the Crown.'

'Thank you, Ms Novak. Mr Curry, I understand that you appear for the defendant, instructed by Mr Worthington of Worthington Wise?'

'May it please you, and I appear with my learned junior, Ms Engineer.'

'Welcome to both of you, and thank you for asking to see me this morning. Ms Novak, you really must try to accommodate the conventions.'

Good, Harry thinks. She's been put on the defensive already.

'Sorry, your Honour. I apologise to my learned friends.'

'Okay, let's get on with it. Mr Curry, you were served with the brief of police statements?'

'Yes, thank you.'

'Nothing new to be added, Ms Novak?'

'No, your Honour. Mr Worthington served a subpoena for the examining doctor's records, and I can produce those now.'

'Hand them to Ms Engineer, please.'

She does so, and Arabella puts the papers to one side.

'Are there any witnesses whom you'd notified as not required for cross-examination, Mr Curry?'

'There are, your Honour. We don't require any of the hotel staff, or any of the corroboration of the arresting police. In an effort to save the Queensland taxpayers a little money, we notified the DPP of those names one month ago.'

'That's so, your Honour.'

'This taxpayer thanks you, Mr Curry. Before you call your first witness, Ms Novak, can we see if we're all on the same page? I've read the police brief — I know that isn't always done in your home state, Mr Curry, but it's *de rigueur* here in the deep north — and I would have thought that the matters for exploration in the inquiry are to do with the issue of consent only. Would I be right to assume that?'

Harry bends and says quietly to Arabella, 'Contrary to my expectations, this bloke's no fool.'

'And neither is he deaf, Mr Curry. But is that right? Consent's the issue?'

Blushing, Harry agrees. So does Ms Novak.

'Fine. Who do we start with?'

The prosecutor stands. 'The arresting officer, your Honour. I call Constable Hinze.'

'While she's coming in, Mr Curry, you and Ms Engineer might bear in mind the excellent acoustics of this courtroom. Sometimes I hear things that I'm not meant to hear.'

'We'll watch that, your Honour. In future.'

Constable Hinze reads out her statement, haltingly, making it quite obvious that she is not its author. Harry's cross-examination is low-key.

'My client was incredulous when you and your colleague approached and arrested him in the foyer of his hotel, wasn't he?'

'Incredible, do you mean?'

'No, Constable. Incredulous. Disbelieving, taken by surprise, couldn't believe what you were saying?'

'You could say that.'

'But you say it, don't you? He acted as if you'd made a terrible mistake, as if he couldn't believe that anyone could say he'd raped the young woman?'

'Yes.'

'Ever arrested a person who turned out to be totally innocent?'

'Once or twice.'

'They react differently from the guilty ones, don't they? The guilty ones clam up, or try to talk their way out of it. They don't look shocked, do they?'

'You could say that.'

'And you say it, too, don't you? Mr Singh reacted in the manner of an innocent man, wrongly accused?'

'You could say that.'

The beak is growing increasingly amused at the difficulty Harry's facing in getting a straight answer. 'I'm afraid, Mr Curry,' he says, 'that's about as high as Constable Hinze ever puts it. Constable, just try for a couple of yes-or-no answers, would you be so kind?'

Harry tries again. 'So would it be fair to say this: Mr Singh reacted in the manner of an innocent man, and once arrested he complied with all the police directions and was cooperative?'

'You could — yes.'

'And, once he'd been allowed to speak with Mr Worthington here, he was totally cooperative and answered all the detectives' questions without hesitation?'

'Yes.'

'And his account of the events of that night has, to your knowledge, never varied?'

'Correct.'

'Thank you, Constable.'

Harry sits and Arabella comments, 'Doesn't hurt us, at the very least.'

'And you've told me, Mr Curry, that you require none of the other arresting police to corroborate this officer's evidence?'

'That's still the case, your Honour.'

'You have no re-examination, I take it, Ms Novak? No? Then who's next?' Very brisk.

'Ms Oriolo, your Honour. The complainant.'

And into the courtroom, accompanied by a middle-aged woman — the support person from Welfare — comes Bernadette Marie Oriolo. Dressed up to the nines, as if on her way to a wedding and just dropping in for a moment to let everyone in court see her new outfit. Black dress with a white ivy pattern on the sleeves and hem, a white collar, buttoned right up to the throat, a white belt, and even a headpiece (Harry would have been hard-pressed to describe it, but Arabella later named it a 'fascinator' such as the shopgirls wear to the races at Randwick). The big new handbag and shoes match: shiny white patent leather with a matching sort of Rorschach black ink-blot pattern. Four-inch heels. A big slash of red lipstick. Dark glasses, which she is removing as she walks in. Eighteen years old and the spitting image of a shorter, chubbier Joan Crawford. The court attendant's eyes are out on stalks.

Arabella whispers to Harry, 'What on earth?'

But he responds, 'No, Bella, it's her big day. Everyone has to hear what she wants to say. What's that politically correct word — validation?'

Bernadette is sworn in, and the prosecutor takes her through her typed statement. Over Harry's objection, she's allowed to read it out (Harry asserting that it's a privilege intended only for police witnesses), but she's not really reading it, anyway. She knows it off by heart, rather in the manner of an assertive but untalented actor in a school play. All present are used to seeing complainants in sexual offence allegations acting far more nervously than this, but there's a look of triumph on her face when she completes her evidence in chief, with minimal assistance from the Crown. The story she tells is strikingly compendious — it covers the ground but very thinly, with only the barest reference to her initial meeting with Baby, dancing at the nightclub, walking to his hotel car park, and leaving in the car. No mention at all of the sexual foreplay Baby claimed. When she explains the particulars of the sexual assault, Bernadette looks straight at Baby and delivers it as if daring him to challenge her version: 'All I can remember is getting in the car and driving up out of the car park. There were street lights, then I blacked out. We drove for about ten minutes. When I came to again, he was on top of me, having sex with me. I told him to stop, and he did. I said, "Bloody get off" and he got off. I fixed up my clothes and ran over to the first person I saw. He took me to a phone, and we rang the police.'

'Ms Oriolo, when you say he was having sex with you, that doesn't tell the court exactly what was happening. I'm sorry if this is upsetting, but I have to ask you to tell the court exactly what you mean by that.'

Harry stands. 'We don't require that. There's no issue, and there's not going to be any issue, that sexual intercourse took place. We don't want to make it any more difficult for this witness than is absolutely necessary.'

'Thank you for that, Mr Curry. Does that complete your evidence, Ms Novak?'

With a nod, the prosecutor sits down and prepares to keep a note of Harry's imminent cross-examination. He takes his time in getting to his feet, standing while he finishes making a note on his pad. Arabella is keen to draw something to his attention, but Harry indicates with a raised index finger that she should wait. He has this planned, and wants to execute his plan. There's just one little matter before he gets to that …

'Ms Oriolo, I'm going to ask you questions on behalf of the defendant. Do you understand that?'

'Yes.'

'And the oath you took applies to these answers equally, you understand that also?'

The magistrate intervenes. 'Not appropriate, Mr Curry. I'm sure this witness understands that she's under oath at all times she's answering questions.'

'As you please. Ms Oriolo, do you understand what perjury is?'

'Telling lies in court.'

'And you're aware of the seriousness of that?'

'Yes.'

'For instance, it would be a lie for someone to say that he was asleep, but heard a conversation while he was asleep?'

'Of course.'

'Equally, Ms Oriolo, it would be a lie for you to say that you blacked out as soon as my client's car left the car park, but that you were then driven in it for a period of ten minutes.'

'I don't understand.' She looks at the support person and raises her eyebrows as if asking how to answer.

'But that's what you told his Honour — that Mr Singh drove for ten minutes while you were unconscious.'

'I never ...'

'Would you like it played back? Your evidence is being recorded on a tape.'

'No.'

'Will you explain, then, why you swore something to be true when you cannot possibly have had any knowledge of it?'

'Because the police told me?' with a rising inflection.

'Are you asking me that, or telling me that?'

'That the police told me it?' Her eyes are back on the support person. She won't look at Harry.

'Yes.'

'They must of. If I was unconscious.'

'Which you weren't, were you?'

'I've always told the police I was blacked out.' Now she's looking at the prosecutor.

'But you could have told them you tried out for the All Blacks, too. Doesn't make it true, does it?'

'That's rejected, Mr Curry. You're not at Darlinghurst now.'

'Quite so, your Honour.' Turning back to the figure in the witness box, whose headpiece is quivering: 'What I'm putting to you, Ms Oriolo, is that it's either–or: either you lied on oath about the ten minutes, or you were not unconscious at any time you were in the presence of my client. What do you say?'

'I was blacked out. I've always said so.' She closes her eyes and tugs angrily at her earlobe.

'Thank you. We'll leave that for a while.' Harry bends down and asks what it was Arabella wanted him to know.

'You just did it,' she says.

Harry spreads on the lectern the notebook containing the cross-examination scheme he's already planned and written out, question by question. He knows he may have to adapt his carefully crafted questions to the answers he obtains, abandoning great slabs of preparation, but this is what makes him feel secure as a cross-examiner. The very process of thinking through the questions in advance fixes the strategy in his mind. He has a wish list of objectives, and his plan is constructed to achieve each of them in its proper place and at the right time. He expects that the vast majority of the assertions he puts to the young woman will be rejected and, if she's listened to the prosecutor, all she needs to reply is no. As Harry always says, there's not much anyone can do with a straight no.

'Do you have your police statement there, Ms Oriolo?'

'Yes.'

'It doesn't have much to say about your initial meeting with my client, does it?'

'I don't know. The police asked me questions, and they typed up what I told them.'

'Is that right? It's not in question-and-answer form, is it?'

'No, I suppose it isn't.'

'So, strictly speaking, that statement that you learned off by heart and repeated to the court was written by someone else, wasn't it?'

'It's what I told them.'

'Perhaps. We'll see about that, won't we?'

'No comments, please, Mr Curry.'

'As you please, your Honour.' He's being kept on a tight rein.

'Madam, what happened when you first encountered Mr Singh in the queue outside the Bottoms Up nightclub?'

'Can he call me Madam?' Bernadette tries to run a little interference. Never a good idea.

'That's a perfectly courteous mode of address, Ms Oriolo. Don't take offence at it, because I'm sure that none is intended. Now can we have your answer? What took place when you were in the queue?'

'Um, we chatted. I told him it was my birthday.'

Harry resumes his cross-examination plan. So far, he's sticking to the script in front of him. 'You had turned eighteen that day?'

'Yes. My father brought me to the Gold Coast for my birthday present.'

'Was your mother also there?'

'No, they're divorced. Well, he doesn't think so, but they are.'

Now comes one of those momentary side-trips. 'What do you mean by that?'

'Well, my father's a very strict Catholic. He doesn't accept it. He doesn't believe in divorce.'

Back to the script. 'I see. Did you make any physical contact with my client in the queue outside the nightclub?'

'What does that mean?'

'Did you touch him, or hug him, or kiss him, or fondle him?'

'I might of done.'

'Which?'

'I might of kissed him a bit, put my arm round him.'

'Why would you do that?'

'I was drunk, wasn't I? It was my birthday.'

'How drunk do you say you were?'

'Paralytic.'

'Which would make it impossible for you to dance with him, or take a drink?'

'I suppose so, yes.'

'And you caught the lift up to the club with him, didn't you?'

'Must of, because that's the only way to get there.'

'There were two other couples in the lift, weren't there?'

'There were people, I dunno how many.' A look of apprehension towards the prosecutor as she considers the likelihood of the other clubbers giving evidence of what they saw, and contradicting her. 'But yes.'

Harry can see her mental processes. 'The other people in the lift saw you hugging and kissing my client, didn't they?'

'They could of done.'

'I put it to you that they did.'

'All right, they did.'

'You had a number of dances with Mr Singh?'

'Yes.'

'So you can't have been paralytic, to repeat the word you used?'

'Whatever.'

'And, while you were dancing — you didn't give the police any details of what you were doing then, did you?'

'Dancing.'

'A bit more intimate than that, wasn't it?'

No answer. She still won't look in Harry's direction, but is studying the back wall.

'Ms Oriolo, you put your hand inside his trousers and fondled his genitals, didn't you?'

'His what?'

'His penis.'

A long pause, in which she looks at Baby and his parents, and then at two new arrivals taking seats in the gallery. One has a shorthand pad in her hand.

'I could of.'

'It's not a matter of what you could have done, is it? It's what you did. You indulged in intimate sexual foreplay, which you initiated, in front of dozens of people in the nightclub, didn't you?'

A barely audible, 'Yes.'

Arabella points to the clock on the courtroom wall. 11.33. Harry nods. 'Your Honour, I notice the time, but there's just one further subject I'd wish to cover before the short adjournment?'

'Would five minutes be sufficient, Mr Curry? Otherwise, I'd like to give my staff a break.'

'Five minutes will be more than enough, your Honour.'

'Very well.'

'Madam, after you'd had several dances, during most of which time you could be seen with your hand down the front of my client's trousers, he asked you whether you wanted to go out and have sex, didn't he?'

She answers immediately, without the slightest hesitation, 'Yes.'

Harry stumbles. 'I'm sorry?'

'I said yes. Weren't you listening?' Sharply, a nasty streak visible.

'Thank you. And one last question for now: You accepted his offer, didn't you?'

No quick answer this time. Bernadette looks at the people

in the public seats, then at the prosecutor, then sideways at the magistrate. 'I did.'

'Thank you. Would that be a convenient moment, your Honour?'

The magistrate, and everyone else (or so it seems to Arabella) exhales. 'Yes, Mr Curry. Twenty minutes.'

The court adjourns, with the magistrate warning the witness not to discuss her evidence with any person during the break. 'To be absolutely certain of that,' he says after some further thought, 'I'll ask you to wait in the witness room with the support lady. She'll arrange a cup of tea for you.'

After the court clears, Baby is ushered into the sunshine by his lawyers, and Chris crosses the road to buy some takeaway coffees. Baby's parents join them, but Arabella, with as much diplomacy as she can muster, explains that the lawyers will need to speak confidentially to Baby in all the adjournments, and they'll give them a progress report at the end of the day's hearing. They nod and separate themselves from Baby and his lawyers. Then Arabella gives Baby some advice, warranted by things she noticed in the morning session.

'Baby, while this is all going on, don't pull any more faces or put on any kind of show at all. It's not going to impress the magistrate. He's seen all that stuff before. It's best if you just remain as calm as you possibly can.'

'Okay, Arabella. Mr Curry, she comes across very dishonest, doesn't she?'

'Quite the contrary, Baby. She's decided to tell the truth — at least about the things where she's afraid we might have witnesses who support your story. It might be a different matter when she's answering about the one-on-one events at the beach, but we'll have to wait and see.'

'Do you think that's what it's about, Harry? Simply that she's afraid of contradiction by independent witnesses?' It hadn't occurred to Arabella.

'It happens, Bella. I've seen it before. Hard to explain it any other way, with this girl. But, all the same, I was very surprised at her lack of fight, weren't you? It's as if none of this matters to her any more. I've had to chuck out pages and pages of the cross-examination script. You saw it — I got answers that I thought I'd only get, if ever, after half an hour of hard pressing for each of them. And maybe some tough stuff, which this beak doesn't seem to favour. It was just *Yes, Yes, Yes*, wasn't it?'

'She's a complex little person, I think.' Arabella isn't counting any chickens. 'What's next?'

'Chris, with the coffee. Here he comes.'

Resumption of the hearing is delayed for almost ten minutes, with the magistrate, the lawyers, Baby's parents, the court staff and the public in their seats, but Ms Oriolo is nowhere to be found. Baby asks Arabella what happens if she refuses to go on.

'I'm not sure, Baby,' she says. 'That's up to his Honour. I've never had it happen.'

Finally, the support person escorts her back to the witness box. No apology or explanation is offered for her absence.

Harry spreads his notebook out on the lectern again while the magistrate reminds Bernadette that she's still on the oath she took earlier in the morning. He then hands her over to Harry whose immediate objective is to unsettle his prey before proceeding to substantial issues.

'Ms Oriolo, have you over the past half-hour given thought to the matter I asked you about when I started asking questions? I'm referring to you claiming to be unconscious, but also being able to say how long the car trip was.'

'No, I haven't thought about that.'

'Well, will you think about it now? Do you have an explanation for what I suggested to you was an either–or situation: that either you fabricated the ten minutes, or you were never unconscious?'

'No.'

'No what?'

'No, I don't want to think about that.'

Ms Novak stands. 'She has a point, your Honour — the question was asked and answered.'

'No, it wasn't, Ms Novak, not to my satisfaction. And anyway, Marshall Hall asked Oscar Wilde the same question seven times, didn't he? Ms Oriolo, do you have any explanation for the self-contradiction?'

'No, I don't.'

'We'll leave it at that, Mr Curry. Please ask another question.'

'Ms Oriolo, you can't have been blacked out in the car if you were trying to get music on the radio. You accept that, don't you?'

'Are you saying I was using the radio?'

'Please answer the question I asked. If you were looking for music on the radio — pressing the buttons to change stations until you found something you liked — then you can't have been unconscious, can you?'

'I wasn't.'

'You weren't what? Weren't looking for music, or weren't unconscious?'

'Both.'

'Do you really mean that?'

'Yes.'

The magistrate steps in. 'I need to be absolutely clear, Ms Oriolo: are you saying to Mr Curry that not only were you not looking for music, but also that you were not unconscious? I'll repeat that, because it's very important — are you saying, to get to the crucial issue, that it is true that you had not blacked out?'

'Whatever he wants.'

'It's not what Mr Curry wants, witness. It's what the court must have, which is a truthful answer. I'll put the question to you: do you now admit that you were not unconscious in the car?'

'I'll say that if he wants. I just want to go home.'

The magistrate is losing patience. 'Do you wish to withdraw your evidence about unconsciousness?'

'What difference does it make? He raped me. What I told the police is true. I'll stick to that.'

Harry and Arabella put their heads together. 'This is a farce,' he says. 'Her credit's shot.'

'But he can still send Baby for trial, Harry. The easy way out for him is to say that the credibility of witnesses is uniquely a matter for a jury.'

'What I don't understand is why she's doing this. It's as if she wants to be shot of the whole thing, but she's terrified of getting into trouble if she withdraws the allegation.'

'That's exactly what I think,' Chris says from close behind them, leaning forward to hear their conversation. 'She's weird. Why didn't she stay in the land of the wrong white crowd? Why come and expose herself to this humiliation?'

'Maybe her father's got something to do with it,' Harry says. 'Maybe this is all his idea — he's supposed to be a religious nut.'

Chris looks back at the public gallery. 'Is that him back there?' A middle-aged man is standing against the back wall. He looks as if his name might be Oriolo. Ms Novak, who has followed Chris's gaze, asks the magistrate to pardon her for a moment, and approaches the man. There is a short conversation, and he leaves the court.

'That must be the father, and Novak's kicked him out because she still might call him as a witness.'

'What evidence can he give?' Arabella asks.

'Promptness of complaint,' says Chris. 'He'll say that at breakfast the next morning she told him that a man raped her at the beach. It's in the police brief, with the supplementary material. The High Court has held that it can be received as corroboration, despite its fundamentally self-serving nature.'

'Always a good idea to read everything, Bella,' Harry says. She is looking at the young solicitor with new-found respect. Quoting High Court judgments!

'Do you have any further questions, Mr Curry?' The magistrate is back in action.

'That's what we're discussing, if your Honour would give me a moment more.'

'Take your time.'

They go back into a huddle. 'I think we should keep going with the plan — about what she told the English guy, about the forensic evidence … her having no bruising and her clothes not being torn at all,' Arabella says intensely.

Chris offers his view. 'I think we should let it go. Maybe a scattergun question to say it's all a pack of lies, and she knowingly consented, but then leave it at that. You've got terrific stuff to use at a trial.'

Harry takes a moment to think about it. He stands. 'Given the extraordinary nature of the most recent evidence, your Honour, I shall ask the court for leave to defer the balance of my cross-examination until we have dealt with some of the other witnesses.'

'Any objection to that, Madam Crown?'

Ms Novak has no objection. 'Ms Oriolo's not flying back to New Zealand until Thursday, your Honour.'

'Very well. Ms Oriolo, you can stand down but you may be needed tomorrow, so I'm not going to excuse you. The prosecution know how to contact you, don't they?'

Ms Novak agrees. It being close to lunchtime, the magistrate adjourns the committal until two o'clock, when the examining doctor will be called.

Harry and Arabella spend the lunch hour in the legal profession room, going closely through the doctor's records, produced on subpoena and handed over by the prosecutor first thing this morning. Harry's having trouble with the handwriting.

'This woman's obviously a medical practitioner,' he complains. 'No one but a pharmacist could make head or tail of this.'

'Well,' says Arabella, 'I can decipher "Vaginal area — no bruising; upper arms — no bruising" and this part here's plain enough: "pregnant 3/12 and STOP booked".'

'Pregnant?' Harry is baffled. 'How could she be pregnant the morning after she had sex?'

'She wasn't, Harry: 3/12 means she's three months pregnant. Aged seventeen and pregnant. I'll bet her father didn't know.

He wouldn't be buying her holidays on the Gold Coast, he'd be sending her to a nunnery.'

'What's "stop" mean?'

'I think I know, Harry, bless your unworldly and endearing nature, but just to be sure I'm going to ring a doctor friend in Sydney before I stick our necks out. We can't have you upsetting the magistrate with a scandalous question, can we?'

'Scandalous?' Harry doesn't follow.

'The scandal would attach to an ethical complaint, if you ask unduly offensive questions on a false assumption. Let me check first.' She gets out her mobile phone and is starting to dial when there's a knock on the door and the court officer tells Harry that the beak's coming back on. Arabella says, 'See you in there,' and continues with her call.

'I call Andrea Morgan Gibson.' Ms Novak's next witness.

A short, solid woman in a trouser suit, collar and tie and flat shoes enters, carrying a pink file. Chris leans over Harry's shoulder. 'This one bowls from the Paddington end, I'd say.'

'Don't let my learned junior hear you say that,' Harry admonishes him.

The doctor settles herself in the witness box like an old hand. She takes an affirmation, waving the proffered Bible away.

'Are you Andrea Morgan Gibson, and are you a registered medical practitioner?'

'I am.'

'Do you practise on the Gold Coast in family medicine?'

'I do.'

'Have you, though, qualifications in obstetrics and gynaecology?'

'I have.'

'Doctor, did you examine a young woman named Bernadette Marie Oriolo?'

'May I look at my notes, your Honour?'

'You may.'

She opens the file. 'Yes, I examined her on that date.'

'And did she give you a history of having been raped the previous night at Palm Beach?'

'She didn't know the name of the beach, but yes.'

Harry rises and the prosecutor yields. 'May I, probably quite unnecessarily, have it noted that the allegation made to the doctor is not admissible as evidence of the fact, but merely evidence that the complainant made the allegation?'

'Duly noted, Mr Curry.'

Ms Novak returns to her feet. 'To put it in summary form, Doctor, because there's not much controversy about this, were you able to establish that sexual intercourse had taken place the previous night?'

'Yes, I was.'

'Can I now turn to some details of that —'

Harry's on his feet again. 'No issue as to the *actus reus*, your Honour. The sex took place, we've made our position clear on that, and there will be no challenge to the DNA evidence. My client had intercourse with the complainant. That will be formally admitted if there is to be a trial.'

'That's clear enough, Madam Crown. Is this detail necessary?'

'Possibly not, your Honour. I'll move on. Dr Gibson, to be fair, did you find any objective signs of non-consensual intercourse?'

'You don't necessarily find such signs. Doesn't mean it didn't happen.'

'That's a no, then, is it?' Harry interjects, out of turn. The witness glares at him.

Arabella joins Harry at the Bar table. He turns to whisper to her, 'Female complainant, female copper, female prosecutor, female expert witness who thinks she's running the show. This one, at least, is a real man-hater.'

The magistrate frowns at Harry, and Harry thinks that he probably heard the last two words, given the wonderful acoustics. So what?

'Mr Curry?'

Harry stands. 'Yes, your Honour?'

'I asked if you wish to cross-examine the doctor.'

'Thank you, I do.' He turns to a new page in his notebook, and places alongside it his copy of the witness's medical report, his marginal notes in red ink.

'Ms Oriolo told you that she'd had sexual intercourse about ten hours previously?'

'Correct.'

'You found independent, objective evidence of that?'

'Correct.'

'She also told you that she was three months pregnant.'

The magistrate looks sharply at the doctor.

'Correct.'

'And you found independent, objective evidence of that?'

'Yes.'

'You being a gynaecologist?'

'Having gynaecological expertise, yes.'

'So even if she had said nothing to you, you were able to establish as a matter of independently proven, objective fact, that she had had recent intercourse, and that she was already pregnant?'

'Correct.'

'You were unable, however, to establish by any examination you conducted that the recent intercourse she'd had was anything but consensual, were you?'

'Look, I already told the court—'

'No, please answer that question either yes or no. I'll repeat it: the simple, unvarnished and unqualified truth is that you were unable to establish by any examination you conducted that the recent intercourse she'd had was anything but consensual, were you?'

'That question can't be answered yes or no.'

The magistrate frowns at the witness. 'It certainly can be, Doctor, and I'll thank you to do so.'

Arabella turns back and says to Chris, 'He doesn't like her much, either.'

'Then the answer's no.' She is visibly displeased.

'And, Doctor, would it be correct to say that you've conducted physical examinations of scores of rape victims, or at least people who claimed they had been raped?'

'Probably.'

'In any of those scores of examinations, did you find what I shall call independent and objective evidence of non-consensual intercourse?'

'Most of them.'

'Please tell his Honour what signs you have seen, on previous occasions, that you consider to be consistent with rape.'

'Obviously, signs of violence. Bruising or tearing to the vaginal area, bruising to the upper body and face. Some have even been punched in the face. I've seen badly broken noses, teeth knocked out.'

'Nothing like that in Ms Oriolo's case, was there?'

'I found nothing, but she didn't complain of any violence.'

'The truth is, if you can put your obvious bias to one side for a moment, that what you saw on examination of this young woman was entirely consistent with normal, consensual sexual activity?'

'It wasn't inconsistent with it.'

'Oh, you can do better than that, can't you, Doctor? Bearing in mind the Expert Witness Code of Conduct that you signed, and its emphasis on objectivity, you can say, can't you, as an independent expert unmotivated by sexual politics or any other irrelevancy, that Ms Oriolo gave every appearance of having engaged in normal, happy sexual conduct?'

'How can I know if she was happy? I'll agree with normal, whatever that means.'

'Which will do me, thank you.'

The magistrate gives a snort of disapproval, but Harry has more to get. Arabella points to the medical report and whispers something to him. He nods. 'She told you, at the time you examined her, that she was already booked in for an abortion, didn't she?'

'The word "abortion" doesn't appear in my notes, so far as I can see,' Dr Gibson says, looking at the report in front of her.

'Disingenuousness doesn't really suit you, Doctor—'

'I reject that, Mr Curry. I won't allow insulting comments.' The magistrate steps in.

'My apologies, and to you, Doctor. Doctor, the word appears there in your handwriting "STOP", doesn't it?'

'Yes.'

'Will you tell this court what that acronym means?'

'Surgical termination of pregnancy.'

'An abortion?'

'Correct.'

'So, whatever you may have written, there can be no question that Ms Oriolo told you when you examined her that she was pregnant, three months, but that she was already booked in for an abortion at home in New Zealand?'

'Correct.'

'Have you spoken to her since you examined her?'

'Yes.'

'When was that?'

'Yesterday.'

'At your rooms?'

'Yes.'

'Did you tell Ms Novak about that meeting?'

'Why should I?'

'That's another no, is it?'

'It is.'

'Did Ms Oriolo have the baby?'

'No. She told me she had a termination, as planned.'

'Doctor, can the court assume that you did basic psychiatry in your undergraduate training?'

'Yes, the usual.'

'When you saw Ms Oriolo yesterday, did you think anything of her affect?' Harry knows the jargon.

'Well, yes, to some extent. A bit unusual, in all the circumstances. Not like other victims I've seen before they gave evidence.'

'Passing over your use of the word "victim", what was your opinion about it?'

'It was as if she didn't care about all this. It meant little or nothing to her. She didn't really care too much. She told me her father had bought her new clothes.'

'But she wasn't tearful, or afraid? Not apprehensive?'

'Not at all.'

'That's the cross-examination, your Honour. Thank you, Doctor.'

'Thank you, Mr Curry. Any re-examination, Ms Novak?'

'No. Can the doctor be excused, your Honour?'

Harry voices no objection, and Dr Gibson leaves the court, looking daggers at Arabella. *Why me?* she thinks. *Gender traitor?* Arabella's thoughts are interrupted by Harry and the prosecutor discussing the next day's arrangements with the magistrate. Harry forgoes the right to cross-examine Mr Domenico Oriolo, given that there is no possible basis for him to challenge his evidence that Bernadette complained to her father at the first opportunity that Baby (or 'some fat Indian' as she put it) had raped her. The agreement is, finally, that the complainant will be back in the witness box at ten o'clock, after which legal submissions will be in order. The court adjourns.

Arabella's out on the balcony of their room, having changed into the hotel bathrobe. She looks down from fifteen floors above street level at the late-afternoon joggers and cyclists. Is the whole population of the Gold Coast training for the world's biggest Iron Man event? she wonders. More directly below, she looks down on the hotel pool, in which a few swimmers can be seen.

After a moment's thought, Arabella surprises Harry by announcing that she wants to go for a swim. Five minutes later, they are both swimming serious laps. It's cool in the hotel pool, with the building's shadow falling across the water. She's in a very strange mood, Harry thinks, as if she's gleefully harbouring some secret. He can't escape the word 'smug' in trying to define her attitude. As if to reassert his place at the head of the team, Harry swims hard in a choppy, lifesaver style, executing fast tumble turns, leaving Arabella, who swims a very English sort of breaststroke, way back in his wake. The other hotel guests keep out of their way. This goes on for the best part of half an hour before Harry pulls himself over the lip of the pool and waves to a waiter.

Arabella climbs out of the pool, pulling her cap off. Not for the first time, he is struck almost speechless by how beautiful she is. But not so speechless that he can't order a light beer for each of them. They lie on the pool lounges until they've caught their breath, and then remain silent until their beers are finished. Harry has his in one go.

Arabella's smile is driving Harry mad. 'I will, eventually, be put out of my misery, won't I?'

'You're miserable, are you, Harry?'

'Your — I can only think of it as smugness — there's something I'm missing, isn't there?'

'Have I ever complained?'

'You know what I mean. The doctor's evidence. You think the explanation for her bizarre performance is there, don't you?'

'What I love about you, Harry Curry — actually this is just one of many things I love about you — is that the big strong man, the fearless advocate, the crusader, is actually one of the most unworldly people I have ever met.'

'My mother always said that worldliness was nothing to be coveted.'

'True. But a little street smartness doesn't always go astray in the criminal law, surely?'

'And what do your street smarts tell you that can't make its way into my thick skull?'

'Think about it, Harry: she's seventeen, living with her father, who is a very strict Catholic. No doubt virulently anti-gay, with a medieval attitude to pre-marital sex. You can assume he opposes contraception, and he's absolutely certain to regard abortion as murder. How is a kid in that position, barely out of school, ever going to be able to tell her father not only that she's sleeping with her boyfriend — and I'll bet old Domenico didn't even know there was a boyfriend — but also that she's pregnant by him? And it gets worse: she's committed to getting rid of the baby. She knows full well that that's murder as far as dear old Poppa's concerned. And we can thank the nasty doctor for making such diligent notes of the pregnancy and the planned termination, and for the news that the abortion was performed, must have been at least six months ago. Now, here she is — little Bernie, I mean — totally detached, just going through the motions of giving evidence of being violated. Admitting practically everything you put to her, as if it doesn't matter any more.'

'So ...'

'So Baby's served his purpose and is now surplus to requirements. Penny starting to drop now, is it, you naive old darling?'

It's already hot when they climb out of the taxi outside the courthouse. Harry puts the Globite down on the footpath and struggles into his jacket. On the one hand, there is a certain amount of triumphalism in his mind. They can, if he manages this right, have the charge dismissed. It could happen. Which would see justice done — Baby doesn't deserve to have to endure the ordeal of a full-scale criminal trial (stupid as he was in leaving the little kids alone, and even stupider as he was in thinking that this dopey girl had instantly fallen in lust with a pudgy 39-year-old), and much less does he deserve the destructive publicity that's certain to attend a rape trial, even if he's acquitted. But on the other hand, Harry has never taken any pleasure in discrediting foolish adolescents, let alone destroying them in the eyes of their nearest and dearest, and even more keenly so in sexual offence trials. He hates defending these cases. Harry knows that he's won plenty of them for guilty men, simply by the force of his personality — dominating and confusing victims to the point where they destroy their own credibility under relentless cross-examination. Often, late at night, he cringes when he thinks of that. But he has his duty, and he's going to have to do it.

Arabella, though, has a glint in her eye — she's looking forward to the denouement, heedless of the effect it may have on Bernadette. The family expected her to save Baby, and she outraged them by refusing to conduct the defence. It took a huge effort for her to get them to accept Harry as their defender, and now comes the crunch: Baby may go to trial and from there to prison and ignominy, in which case Arabella has failed the family, despite all her cleverness, her Cambridge degree and membership of the Inns of Court in London; or she, Harry, the family and Baby will be vindicated. Chris, who's aware of Arabella's make-or-break case theory, worries that it's all going to come apart. The harsh reality is that all rape cases heard in Southport go to trial. He's never heard of one that didn't. Local knowledge counts, he's thinking, as they shepherd Baby back into court.

The magistrate comes on the bench carrying an armful of legal monographs and law reports. Arabella can see that at least two of them are judgments of the High Court, and she taps Harry on the elbow, pointing at the books.

'When the facts are against you, resort to the law,' he says.

'Now,' says the magistrate, 'my understanding is that Ms Oriolo will resume in cross-examination, and she will be the last witness. Is that right?'

Counsel assure him that it is. He tells the prosecutor to re-call her witness. Dressed in exactly the same clothes as yesterday, she is resworn and asked her name for the record by Ms Novak, who then defers to Harry.

'Good morning, Ms Oriolo.'

'Good morning.'

'I hope I won't have to keep you long.'

'It's all right.'

'Is your father here today?'

'No, he has to go home to Auckland. My grandmother's sick.'

'Thank you. How is your relationship with him now?'

'Good.'

'Has it always been good?'

The prosecutor objects on the basis of relevance. Harry stands again and says to the magistrate, 'I give the court my undertaking that I shall make this evidence relevant. I don't wish to sacrifice a forensic advantage by making submissions at this time, and I ask your Honour to accept, in the usual way, the undertaking of counsel.'

'Ms Novak, I'm going to accept Mr Curry's undertaking unless you wish to say anything further.'

'No, your Honour.'

'Please continue, Mr Curry. I will, however, bear that issue in mind.'

'Do you remember the question, Ms Oriolo?'

'Yes. I haven't always got on well with my dad, no.'

'What was the problem?'

'After the divorce, he said he hated my mother and me. He said women take your money and betray you.'

'How long was it before you got on an even keel with him?'

'All the time Mum's court case was going on, it was terrible. He just wouldn't go to the court about the divorce because he says he doesn't believe in it. But after three or four years, he settled down, and it was okay when I was in my last year at school — when I was sixteen. I was living with him. My mother had moved to Southland.'

By this point, Bernadette appears perfectly relaxed. She seems to enjoy talking about the family dramas.

'You've told the court that your father is a very religious man. Are you also a strict Catholic?'

'No. I mean, I go to Mass with him, and that, but I'm not strict.'

'Have you ever discussed with him the Church's attitude to sexual matters?'

'He's discussed that stuff with me.'

'Where does he stand on homosexuality?'

'He says it's wrong.'

'Contraception?'

'Wrong.'

'Sex before marriage?'

'He doesn't like that. He says girls should wait.'

'Girls?'

'Yes.'

Harry speaks briefly to Arabella. 'Thank God Domenico's gone home. I don't think we could have got any of this.' He turns back to the witness. 'Ms Oriolo, what has your father told you, if anything, about his view of abortion?'

'He says it's murder.'

'You were pregnant when you came to Australia, to the Gold Coast, to celebrate your birthday, weren't you?'

'What's that got to do with it?'

The magistrate addresses her in a kind tone. 'Please answer the question. I promise you that Mr Curry won't be permitted to ask any question that isn't important to the case, and I'm ruling that this question is important.'

'All right, yes, I was.'

'You told Dr Gibson three months pregnant.'

'Yes.'

'Do you have your own doctor at home?'

'Yes.'

'Had that doctor counselled you about a termination of the pregnancy?'

'Yes, she said I could have one.'

'And she booked you in for the termination before you came to the Gold Coast?'

'Yes.'

'And can we take it that the procedure was carried out once you got home?'

'I had the abortion, yes.'

'You had not told your father, at the time he brought you here on the holiday, that you were pregnant, had you?'

'No.'

'You have never told him that you were pregnant at the time you came here, have you?'

'I don't have to answer that.'

'Yes, you do.'

'Well, I won't. It's none of your business.'

'Ms Oriolo, what time is your father's plane out of Australia?'

'Four o'clock this afternoon.'

'Will it be necessary for me to ask the prosecutor to have the police bring him here from the airport, so that I can ask him the same question?'

Bernadette looks at Harry with hatred. Then she turns to the magistrate, who says nothing. She pauses, and thinks. 'No, you don't have to bring him back. I've never told him that I was already pregnant, no.'

The magistrate, having waited for that matter to be resolved, intervenes. 'Mr Curry, it's almost eleven o'clock. I'm minded to take the short adjournment early, on the assumption that you have some further matters to put to this witness, but that you will not need a great deal of time, and that we can move to submissions before luncheon. Would that suit you?'

'Certainly, your Honour.'

'We'll resume at 11.25.'

'Why did he want to break early?' Arabella asks.

'Needs a drink,' Chris says, very softly.

'Local knowledge, Chris?'

'You got it.'

Thanking Chris for fetching the coffees, Arabella asks how much of a problem the beak has.

'Used to be very bad, but it's been much better lately. He got some help. Unfortunately, one of his kids has been charged with a drug offence — heroin — and he's not too good at the moment. That's why he likes to get as much done in the morning as he possibly can. He knows he's going to get into it over lunch. He's pretty well liked here, and the lawyers do as much as they can to help.'

Arabella asks Harry, 'Is there much of it? Alcoholic judicial officers?'

'More than you'd think. It's a horrible job.'

Chris adds, 'It's the pressure and the loneliness. People who are used to working in a team, whether they're solicitors or barristers, get appointed to the bench — any bench — and suddenly they have to cope on their own. No moral support, no collegiate atmosphere. It's often worst in the bush, where you're isolated in every sense.'

'Well, let's see if we can give him a hand, Chris, by getting this finished a.s.a.p.'

Harry notes that the magistrate is a little flushed when he returns to the bench and indicates that the defence should complete its cross-examination of the complainant.

'Thank you, your Honour. I hope they gave you a cup of tea, Ms Oriolo?'

'Yes, thanks.'

'Ms Oriolo, will you please listen carefully to what I'm going to put to you now. You don't have to comment until I come to the very end. Do you understand that?'

'Yes.'

'Thank you. This is what I put to you is the truth. I want you to tell me which assertions of fact I am now going to make that you would dispute: what you did to my client was, not to put too fine a point on it, a set-up. He didn't rape you. You hatched a plan that while you were in Australia, you were going to be raped. You were going to find someone to have sex with, and as soon as that had happened you were going to cry rape.'

He pauses. 'Do you understand what I'm putting to you at this point?'

'Yes, but why would I—'

'No, Ms Oriolo, I don't want your response yet. Please be so kind as to wait until I've put the complete scenario to you. You were going to have an abortion. You were committed to that, you had arranged it, before you came here on holiday. But you were afraid that when you did, you would forever lose the affection of your father. You were already alienated, through no fault of your own, from your mother. You knew that having an abortion would cast you in your father's eyes as a slut and a taker of human life. There are no greys with him, only black and white. But somehow

— whether through your own knowledge, or from some other source — you were prepared to stake everything on the hope that your father would make an exception in his attitude to abortion in a case where his own daughter, his only child, had been raped.'

Harry pauses again. 'Are you still following what I'm putting to you?'

'Yes.'

Harry looks at the magistrate, who is writing furiously. Harry waits for him to finish before resuming. 'So, you landed here, had dinner with your father, and told him something to the effect that you were tired and going to bed. You thought up some excuse, it doesn't matter what it was. Your father went to his room. But you changed into your sexy outfit and went to a pub or a club somewhere, where you had too much to drink. It's called Dutch courage. And then you stood in the queue outside that nightclub until some single man, or should I say some man on his own, came along. It didn't matter to you who it was, my — and I hope he'll forgive me for saying this — somewhat unprepossessing client, old enough to be your father, or anyone at all. Any man. And you threw yourself at him. I needn't go into the details, you've already admitted what you did, and the court knows that it was you, not he, who was making all the sexual advances. Advances that had only one purpose, and only one meaning. You even expressly agreed to have sex with him. He asked if you wanted to, and you told him that you did. You've admitted that.'

Harry takes another pause. The magistrate is no longer writing, but staring at the witness. Arabella looks at him.

'Are you still with me?'

'Yes.'

Harry looks at Bernadette. 'Okay. And, to exculpate yourself, all you can do is try to stick to this silly story that you blacked out. Which is a blatant fabrication. You engaged in predatory sexual foreplay, you agreed to have sex, you had sex — sex that you initiated and to which you admit you consented — you cried rape, and your father approved the termination of what he thought was a pregnancy resulting from a rape. You got him to abandon his principles by deceiving him. And you got what you wanted, never mind the consequences for my client.'

The courtroom has gone very quiet.

'Are you asking me a question now?'

'Yes, Ms Oriolo. I am asking whether there is any substantial part of the scenario I have put to you that you would wish to challenge.'

'You know what?' she says, picking up her big handbag from the floor of the witness box, putting it in front of her, opening it and placing a wad of tissues inside. 'I don't have to.'

'That's true, but you will be adopting it as correct.'

'I don't have to deny anything, and I don't have to put up with any more of this.'

She stands as if to leave the courtroom. The magistrate reacts angrily. 'Witness, sit down. I have not excused you. Please sit down.'

'What are you going to do?' she says, stepping down, swinging the handbag. 'Arrest me?' As she passes close by Arabella, one word is spoken. 'Bitch.' She walks out of the room without a backward look.

Harry looks at his junior counsel. 'You didn't tell me she knew you.'

'You'll keep, mister.'

After that, the magistrate adjourns the court for ten minutes in order for the parties to consider their respective positions.

The defence team doesn't leave the court during the adjournment. Baby's parents are permitted to join the discussion with Arabella and Chris at the Bar table, while Harry takes Ms Novak outside for a word about where they go from here.

Mrs Singh is uncomprehending. Arabella can't successfully explain to her that the disappearance of Ms Oriolo is an insuperable problem for the prosecutor, not for them. Baby, too, thinks she has unilaterally denied him his chance for a discharge. Neither can he be made to understand. Mr Singh is smiling broadly, so Arabella infers that he, at least, has some grasp of the situation. Chris doubts that this can be the end. He thinks Ms Novak's going to ask for a delay until tomorrow, so that she can bring Bernadette back. Arabella is confident that nothing like that is going to happen. When Harry returns from speaking to the prosecutor, he simply shakes Baby's hand.

It's nearer half an hour than ten minutes before the magistrate resumes the hearing.

'Ms Novak, what position does the Crown take, in view of Ms Oriolo's withdrawal?'

'I've spoken to the deputy chief prosecutor in Brisbane over the adjournment, your Honour. Our position must be, I'm afraid, that we will support the defence's application.'

'Over to you, Mr Curry.'

'As your Honour pleases. It's our application that you dismiss the charge and discharge my client. Your Honour will be satisfied that a jury is unlikely to convict on the evidence called before you.'

'Yes. Well, counsel, I don't know that I agree with either of you. But let me put your client out of his misery, Mr Curry. Please stand up, Mr Singh. In view of the absence of the prosecution's principal witness, without whom there can be no case against you, and the fact that you have been denied the opportunity to complete cross-examination, which would amount to a denial of procedural fairness, I exclude all her evidence from consideration. My ruling is that the prosecution has failed to establish even a *prima facie* case. There is no evidence in conflict with the interview you gave the police, which is prosecution evidence in this case — having been tendered by the Crown, not your counsel — to the effect that Ms Oriolo actually consented to having sex with you, and that you honestly and reasonably believed that you were having consensual sex. You are free to go whenever you please.

'Counsel, this case promised to present a somewhat novel situation, where I was going to have to consider several hundred years' precedents in higher courts dealing with analogous principles: whether consent is withdrawn because a woman falls asleep, or becomes unconscious, whether due to illness or intoxication or for some other reason — the whole concept of implied withdrawal of consent. I'd been reading it up overnight, but I have to say that I'm a long way from a final answer. Happily, I say from my selfish point of view, I'm not going to have to give that answer. As to the scenario that you put to Ms Oriolo just before she decided to leave us, Mr Curry, I just don't know. At first, it sounded pretty far-fetched, but — as things went on — I could see the force of it. I suppose we'll never know for sure.'

'Quite so, your Honour.'

'I thank all counsel for their assistance. The exhibits can be returned. The court's adjourned.'

There's the usual hugging and kissing on the footpath once they all make it down there. Arabella's the one congratulated by Baby's parents, which is fine with Harry. Chris shakes everyone's hand and takes his leave as soon as he can. Harry and Baby's father stand a little apart from the other three, talking quietly about cricket until Arabella comes over to them.

'Harry, we've been invited to the celebration in Woolgoolga tonight. I trust you like bananas cooked in every possible way?'

'There's nothing I like better, Bella.'

Baby's mother gets to the point. 'Mr Curry, what about the costs?'

'What about them, Mrs Singh?'

'Mr Worthington's bill will be more than $25,000.'

'I suppose it will. Some of that's for me and Arabella.' Which embarrasses Mrs Singh. 'On the other hand,' says Harry, 'you could think of it this way: had you not involved Arabella, and she's the one who came up with the strategy that won us the case, you would have lost. But much more cheaply.'

'There is that,' says Mr Singh.

Read on for a preview of the next collection of
Harry and Arabella stories from Stuart Littlemore

Harry Curry: The Murder Book
Avaliable 2012

No discount for mass murder

These are the facts. They're bad enough without embellishment ...

Adrian Flowers was born to a 15-year-old girl and brought up by his grandparents in a rundown house on a few dusty acres outside Shellharbour, a bit south of Wollongong. The house was crowded with not just his mother and grandparents, but also his three knuckle-dragging uncles, who brutalised the little boy even before he could walk.

Adrian, when he got to Shellharbour Primary, was further bullied and beaten. He was a soft target — lonely, inarticulate, weedy, uncared-for and with a girly name. His mother had long gone — good luck to her — and his idea of 'home' didn't imply any comfort or warmth or affection or belonging. It was just where he went when there wasn't anywhere else.

On his eighth birthday, a hot day in January, the little boy was driven a few kilometres, grudgingly, in the family's FJ Holden ute to Shellharbour village and its little beach, enclosed with a breakwater. While his grandparents drank shandies in the pub and watched horse races on TV, Adrian was left to fend for himself on the beach, clad in his singlet and underpants. Watching the children of the Macedonian steelworkers from Port Kembla splashing happily in the gentle swell, he walked in and kept walking — until the water was over his head. Adrian stood looking up at the sunlight dappling the surface for over a minute. A watching mother dragged him out and laid him face down on the wet sand to cough up the saltwater he'd breathed in. Adrian didn't mention it when his grandparents collected him an hour later.

The bullying he endured at primary school continued at Warilla High until the boy turned fourteen. Then a growth spurt took over his body and transformed him into the biggest boy in his class. The work his grandfather forced on him — digging the vegetable garden, cutting and carrying the firewood, cleaning and stacking second-hand bricks for resale — developed his arms and his chest and his sense of personal power. The Police Boys Club taught him to box. To the strapping and determined youth, boxing wasn't about self-defence. His priority was to learn to attack, pitilessly. After a couple of bouts in which Adrian dismayed his instructors with his savagery, he was asked not to come back to the club. He didn't mind. The Police Boys had served its purpose.

With chilling efficiency, Adrian systematically cornered and beat senseless every Warilla boy who had ever bullied him, sometimes taking on two at a time. Then it was his uncles' turn. The sixteen-year-old showed no mercy to the men, aged in their late twenties and early thirties, and forever after they regarded him with surly fear. He continued to sleep on the verandah of his grandparents' weatherboard house, to which he had been despatched as an infant, and never spoke more than he needed to. The household was afraid of him.

Unlikely as it may seem, there was one teacher who saw something in the young brute and went out of his way to encourage his biology studies. When Adrian confided that he wanted to train as a nurse, the teacher took him for an interview at the Wollongong Hospital, and helped him get a start there as a porter. After two years' hard graft on the wards and on the strength of a good reference from his supervisor, he was hired by the Ambulance Service as a trainee paramedic. His ambition was to learn to fly a helicopter and work in marine rescue. He'd been attracted by television coverage of rescues at sea of the crews of stricken Sydney to Hobart racers in a terrible storm. In the meantime, he was transferred to the Moruya Ambulance Station, further down the coast.

Three days before Christmas 1989, Adrian was woken in his flat above a real estate agency in the main street of Moruya by his clock radio, turning on in time for the 8am news. What he heard was that an hour earlier, two tourist coaches had collided on the Princes Highway near Bodalla and it was feared there had been 'significant loss of life'. He was off duty that day, but immediately dressed in his Ambulance Service uniform and, unshaven and unshowered, rode his motorbike the twenty kilometres south to the accident site. He was waved past the police barricades to be confronted by a ragged, jagged explosion of shattered glass and twisted metal — two big shiny aluminium-bodied buses fused into one. Steam and smoke and weeping filled the air as oil and diesel leaked onto the road from beneath the buses' engines. The crash was ringed with ambulances, police vehicles and fire engines. On the fringes, the residents of nearby houses, still in their dressing gowns, were gawping and chattering and getting in the way, except for a practical few who were shuttling back and forth with mugs of tea for the rescue workers and the walking wounded. Ambulances were leaving with their sirens on low growl, ferrying the injured to Batemans Bay Hospital. The dead were placed in a respectful line on the grass verge outside the closest house's fence, where blue and white agapanthus flowers were nodding incongruously.

Adrian parked his bike and strode to the ambulance officer with the most pips on his epaulettes. 'You can go in and get people out of the blue bus,' he was directed. 'Most of them are dead.'

It was hard to get into the bus. The access door was useless, jammed shut with a body wedged behind it. The driver, Adrian thought, glimpsing a uniform soaked in blood. He used a domestic ladder that had been placed on the opposite side of the bus to climb through one of the windows, broken glass snagging at his trousers and the skin of his thighs. Firemen, police and other ambulance officers were already in the bus, trying to help the living. Someone was crying softly, an old man, perhaps. On the back seat lay three girls in bloodstained summer frocks. They all looked to be about fourteen, but it was impossible to tell as they had been neatly decapitated by a dislodged window. Adrian sighed and averted his eyes, looking over their heads at a bright blue summer morning sky. The girls' dresses were around their waists, exposing their underwear. Without really thinking, he pulled down each dress to cover them to the knees. Then he carried the first girl to the smashed-out window and called to a fireman to take the body from him. She seemed so light.

Adrian remained at the scene for three hours, lifting and carrying, until the last of the injured had been taken to hospital, and the bodies of the fifteen who died at the scene had been photographed, covered with shiny blue plastic tarpaulins, and attended to by the Bodalla clergyman who had been there almost from the start. Adrian had a quick word with the incident commander, climbed back on his bike, and rode to Moruya Heads, where he took off his clothes and walked into the surf. He stayed in the water, rubbing wet sand into his face and hands, until he stopped crying. Then he went home and got back into bed. About six months later, he injured his back lifting a patient out of a car wreck and was invalided out of the ambulance service. He never forgave them for that.

Ten years later, two psychiatrists disagreed about the significance of Adrian's experience at the Bodalla bus crash. One refused to support a diagnosis of post-traumatic stress disorder. Neither thought it explained Adrian's sociopathy. What they agreed upon was that his personality disorder could be traced to his childhood at Shellharbour.

For Adrian, his dreams of a career smashed beyond repair, fell among thieves, and worse. He found a job serving summonses for solicitors and insurance companies, who rightly assumed that his fearsome bulk and habitual scowl would ensure that those served with the unwelcome documents would at least not put up a fight. He drank in the back bars of south-western Sydney pubs with like-minded people, and crooked policemen. He was violent, and was paid for it. He received and resold stolen goods. He funded and took part in robberies. He invested in a brothel. He financed drug dealing. He did some really bad things that no one knew about. Over ten years, he murdered five people.

Five years after the last of the killings, on a mild October morning, Adrian Flowers was on a drug run from Adelaide to Sydney. The boot of his Commodore was crammed with orange garbage bags full of cannabis and two smaller clear plastic bags of methyl amphetamine powder. On the Sturt Highway about three kilometres east of Mildura, a police breath test unit was still being set up when an over-eager probationer jumped the gun and waved Adrian to pull over. The sergeant in charge, who was in no hurry, was about to countermand the direction, but decided to let the process take place.

The hand-held breath analyser was pointed through the open window of the Commodore, and Adrian was ordered to count to five. Negative. Standing back to wave the car away, the probationer noticed that one of the back tyres was almost flat. 'Hang on, mate,' he called, 'you're going to have to change that. You've got a spare, haven't you?'

And that's how it all fell apart. By the time David Surrey, solicitor, was able to clear his desk and pick up a flight to Mildura, Adrian was halfway through a six-hour video-recorded interview with detectives that initially covered the drug ring he was running with, but then progressed to involve a confession to all five of his killings. The police were incredulous, as Harry Curry would be when Surrey provided him with the police brief, instructing the barrister to plead his client guilty to the lot. It turned out that all the homicide detectives had ever had on Adrian Flowers were some insufficient suspicions about two of the deaths.

And those are the facts.